# LARRY's NYC

N / W / E / S

GRANTS TOMB

MANHATTAN

CENTRAL PARK

BOX OFFICE

TIMES SQUARE

SAINT PATRICK'S

CAMBODIAN CHILDREN'S FUND

GREENWICH VILLAGE

RITA'S

JACK'S

FINANCIAL DISTRICT

STAR S

BATTERY PARK

BROOKLYN BRIDGE

CADMAN PLAZA

BR

BLOOMING GROVE

UNICORN DIN

BORASCH'S

STATEN ISLAND
(BAYVIEW MANOR)

HARLEM

OLD LADY
W/BAD LUCK

# BRONX

DOLPHIN
CREDIT
UNION

WAY
OVER ---▷
YONDER

# QUEENS

INE'S

# ROOKLYN

ER

ALSO BY JACOB M. APPEL

*The Man Who Wouldn't Stand Up*

# THE
# BIOLOGY
# OF
# LUCK

## JACOB M. APPEL

To Teresa
A wonderful host.
Enjoy!

ELEPHANT
ROCK
BOOKS

Thanks to the Generous Support of the Leo and Rose Burrello Literary Endowment.

This novel is a work of fiction. Names, characters, places and incidents are either the product of the author's imagination or are used fictitiously, and any resemblance to actual persons, living or dead, events, or locales is entirely coincidental.

For information about permission to reproduce sections from this book, contact Permissions at elephantrockbooks@gmail.com. Elephant Rock Books are distributed by Small Press United, a division of Independent Publishers Group.

ISBN: 978-0-9753746-8-9

Library of Congress: 2013937248

Printed in the United States of America

Book Design by Amanda Schwarz,
Fisheye Graphic Svcs, Chicago

First Edition
10 9 8 7 6 5 4 3 2 1

Elephant Rock Books
Ashford, Connecticut

*To Rosalie, obviously*

# THE BIOLOGY OF LUCK

## JACOB M. APPEL

We are driven by something as simple and as obvious as the desire to be happy, and, if that fails, by the belief that we once have been.

—André Aciman


The sublime, ephemeral and transcendental are natural interpretations of the trite, melodramatic and clichéd when uttered by someone with whom you wish to have sex.

—Kristen Brennan

# PART I

## THE FACE OF MORNING

# HARLEM

Harlem sleeps late. The rest of the city has already accelerated to full throttle. Along Canal Street, the storefront gratings have been up for hours as the pungent odors of smoked mackerel, fresh shellfish, and cured meats slowly smother the background aroma of the metropolis, that faint blend of diesel fuel and decaying produce and bodily fluids to which urban noses have developed an immunity. The subways have yielded their stench of urine to the bustle of the early morning commute; Wall Street has papered over all memories of yesterday's perspiration; in Park Avenue's door-manned buildings and Madison Avenue's upscale galleries, where the previous night's frenzies still trail a scent of alcohol and vomit and lust, upscale matrons fortify themselves against the day with sprays of rose water and lilac perfume. Only Harlem ignores the call to battle, dozes comfortably in the fumes of its own refuse. It is as though a sanitizing cloud has erupted from the depths of the Port Authority Bus Terminal and Grand Central Station, rousing the downtown citizenry to industry, to sobriety, to spit-and-polish, and that this cloud—like just about everything else in New York City—will not cross 125th Street until all of the well-off white people are provided for.

Larry Bloom strides up Broadway with his *New York Times* tucked under one arm and a pack of Marlboro menthols bulging from his shirt pocket. He is an unattractive man, although not disfigured or crippled or mutilated in such a way as to provoke pity or indulgence, but just plain enough to feel a certain solidarity with the dark-skinned inhabitants of the vast swath of city where the trains still run along elevated tracks. Being unattractive is much like being black, Larry thinks: one makes you a second-class citizen in the world of business, the other a peon in the realm of romance. The only difference is that there hasn't been a civil rights movement for the nondescript and homely people of the world, the short, bald, broad-faced Jewish-looking men who stumble into their thirties unloved and unscrewed. Not that it would matter.

One glance up Frederick Douglas Boulevard, the nation's great emporium of check-cashing establishments and notaries public and beeper retailers, says more about the state of America's melting pot than all the great platitudes about affirmative action and interracial healing will ever reveal. You can change your standards of beauty, much as you can change the complexion of poverty, lighten the skin to cream and trill the *r*s, but in the end somebody has to be hideous and somebody has to be indigent. It's what they call inevitability. It's the one thing Larry would like to share with the Dutch tourists he will soon lead on their Big Apple crash course, the secret behind Broadway and Lady Liberty, but nobody wants to see grown men scavenging for recyclables and automotive parts through the belly of the afternoon. Especially not while on vacation.

The homeless veteran who panhandles at the McDonald's drive-through throws Larry a cursory glance and decides he isn't worth the effort. And he's right. Not that on a tour guide's salary Larry has that much to give. The homeless vet is neither homeless nor a veteran, after all, just a scruffy opportunist whose wife drops him off from a tawny late-model Cadillac sedan every morning. He is a staple of the neighborhood, a legendary character like the emaciated dwarf who feigns hunger pangs in front of the Columbia University gates and the three blind men who sing golden oldies on the express train for pocket change. All black. All ugly. The comedy of it is that they will probably all earn *New York Times* obituaries someday, eulogies to their model poverty, while the real victims, who work the night shift at Kentucky Fried Chicken, or sew hem linings for three dollars an hour, or deliver guided tours atop double-decker buses for tips, will pass away unnoticed. Only today, Larry will cross into the kingdom of the chosen. He feels this as strongly as he feels the hot steam from an exposed manhole slashing his face. Today, an otherwise balmy and thoroughly nondescript day in June, Larry Bloom will discover both love and fortune.

He enters the post office at 125th Street and Frederick Douglas Boulevard. It is nine o'clock. A fortuity of urban planning has assigned Larry's niche of Morningside Heights to the central Harlem postal zone, has lured him beyond the perimeter of gentrification to seek his fortune. The post office itself is part neoclassical monolith, part Turkish bazaar. Despite the rusting lockers and frosted glass windows that line the dimly lit lobby, one senses the subtle pulse of a hidden commerce beating against the marble floors and swaying the cast-iron chandeliers, a brisk trade in good cheer and shared resignation, as well as every illicit substance one could desire. A makeup-caked woman in a tight leather skirt argues with the white clerk at the passport counter. She has a child in tow. It appears that the woman is not the child's mother, an admission she is heatedly trying to retract, and Larry suppresses the urge to step forward as the child's father.

At her right, two portly women have wedged themselves between the cordon and the package retrieval window. They are wearing colorful hats, dressed for church although it is a Wednesday. A sign posted *inside* the window—one cannot be too careful—reads, "Pick up parcels between 9:30 a.m. and 11:00 a.m." The heavier of the women, arms akimbo, rakes Larry with her eyes. Her fishlike mouth hangs open to reveal a gold-capped tooth. He fears she is reading his thoughts, his pity for the makeup-caked woman who will someday, soon enough, wait for packages in church-wear, but maybe she is just deciding whether he will attempt to usurp her place in line, for she purses her lips to emit a soft-pitched hum and smiles approvingly.

Some people might speak to the portly women, small talk, chitchat, but Larry is not one of those people. He wishes he were.

He ought to have responded to the woman's smile with a greeting, an inane observation about the impending heat or the inconvenience of the package window hours. But he didn't and it is too late. Any words now would sound forced, even threatening. It is that barrier, so much like the barrier that has kept him from expressing himself to Starshine, that keeps Larry a prisoner of his own inhibitions. Yet tonight, he is determined to speak to Starshine. To offer his love. He will present himself not as Larry Bloom, nondescript tour guide, but as Larry Bloom, published author. How can a woman, even an attractive, self-assured woman, turn down the advances of a man who has spent two years immortalizing her in manuscript form? Not only immortalizing her, for that matter, but immortalizing the very day of her life which will culminate in his offer of devotion. In his gut, he knows the answer, senses that he has scoured the floors of his apartment in vain, but there remains hope that Starshine Hart is also trapped behind a barrier and it is this hope that must buoy him through the day.

"I thought you said nine o'clock," declares one of the portly women. "I could have sworn you said nine o'clock."

"That's what they told me," answers the other. "I phoned them up and that's what they told me."

The women are not speaking to each other, not really, but rather to the crowd of postal customers who suffer with them on an ever-expanding line; they let their words ricochet across the lobby like grapeshot, so that their comrades-in-waiting will hear their indignation. They may also hope to shame a third heavyset black woman, younger with bad skin, who stands perfecting the art of idleness behind the drop-off window. When Larry offers her a questioning look, she glares through him. He averts his gaze to the floor, focuses his attention on an object beside the express mail bins that looks like a child's sneaker, and he cannot help thinking of the recent terrorist attacks, of the watches and wallets and key chains strewn for blocks around the remnants of the Twin Towers. Larry would like to lecture this woman on the dangers of bureaucracy—he momentarily envisions himself a modern-day Rosa Parks, standing up for the rights of postal customers everywhere—but his one semester stint lecturing at Jefferson Community College has taught him that this woman has likely never heard of Rosa Parks. Besides, he is nonconfrontational by nature. Does half an hour really matter? He does not need to be at Grant's Tomb until 10:15.

"Nine o'clock," the first woman announces again. Her dental plates rattle when she speaks and Larry is embarrassed for her. "I know what I was told."

The clerk ignores them. The minute hand on the wall clock winds its way past 9:30, 9:40, 9:45. Sweat builds on Larry's palms. He wipes them on his jeans, sniffs the faint traces of tobacco on his fingers. Impatience is getting the better of him. He has ordered a hold on his own mail, putting off the arrival of Stroop & Stone's answer until the morning of his date with Starshine, but he suddenly fears that he will receive a large envelope and all hope will be lost. Rejection is a possibility. All of the other major agencies have turned down his manuscript. *The Biology of Luck* is not for them. And yet Stroop & Stone responded so warmly to his query, promised him a reply to the manuscript within two weeks. It has been four. Larry scans the counter on the other side of the package window, but there are many large manila envelopes, so he has no way of knowing what to expect. Finally, one of the uniformed squadron milling around behind the bulletproof glass notices the time.

"It's nine forty-five," declares the heavier woman. She steps toward the drop-off window and points at her watch. "The sign says nine-thirty. 'Pick up parcels between nine-thirty and eleven.' Well, it's a quarter to ten."

The acne-scarred clerk nods. Then she pulls down the security glass of the drop-off window, steps into the next cubicle, and slides open the security glass of the package window. This is the quintessential Harlem moment, the city that the Dutch tourists with their gospel brunches and Apollo Theater outings will never see. The portly women appear unfazed. Maybe they are used to cutting corners at their own jobs, taking two-hour lunch breaks at the Department of Motor Vehicles or remaking hotel beds with soiled linens. Who knows? Larry certainly doesn't blame them. He walks quickly to the revolving doors and steps into the early morning heat.

He ducks into an alcove opposite the loading docks, hiding behind a row of identical postal vehicles so he can enjoy a cigarette without countless strangers begging him for a smoke. One entire wall of the loading dock is plastered with flyers warning "If you see something, say something." From his vantage point, Larry can see just enough of 125th Street not to want to look any further. He savors the refreshing tingle of menthol against the back of his throat.

Harlem is awake now. Not truly sanitized, not yet poisoned by the sterile cloud, but rubbing its eyes to midmorning and deciding that industry and sobriety, if not desirable, are unavoidable. The air is thick with exhaust fumes, but also the gentle aroma of frying plantains. At some distance, on a park bench across from the housing projects, two elderly men sit shirtless. Their chests sag into their guts; they are motionless. Larry cannot even tell whether they are awake. Are they happy? It is an absurd question, as absurd as wondering if the portly women with the church hats are happy, if they know enough themselves to wonder whether or not they are happy, if they know enough *not* to wonder whether or not they are happy, but it often seems that only the answers to absurd questions really matter. What makes some postal workers cut corners while others take out their supervisors with sawed-off shotguns? Why does one man's happiness depend upon the availability of a park bench and another on the size of an envelope? What makes a man write a novel for a woman and then hold his mail until the day of their date? These are the questions Larry asks himself in moments of lucidity, but he understands that even these brief episodes of clarity are an illusion. There are no answers, just park benches and packages.

The portly women step onto the sidewalk, each carrying a cardboard box against her bosom. Larry grinds his cigarette butt into the asphalt and walks rapidly to the package retrieval window.

He offers his driver's license. The clerk runs her index finger along a series of cubbyholes and produces a stack of envelopes. Small, white envelopes. Larry flips through them rapidly at the counter: telephone bills, water bills, credit card bills. Each letter is a lost opportunity. His stomach tightens. What if they haven't answered him at all? What if his manuscript is waiting on some desk, in some cubbyhole, at the bottom of a sea of paperwork? Yet here it is, the magic letter, the distinctive quill of Stroop & Stone's letterhead emblazoned on the envelope.

The envelope is thin, crisp. Larry runs his fingers along its seams, admires the heft of the bond paper. Then he folds the envelope in two and stuffs it into his breast pocket behind his cigarettes. He will wait until after his date to open it. It will either serve as consolation or as icing on his cake. A third possibility exists, of course, the possibility that Larry's perfectly constructed New York City day will collapse into rubble like the grandeur that was Rome, but for a moment, it is a beautiful Harlem morning scented with maple blossoms and exotic fruit, and he is happy, happy in the way he knows he can be if he wills away the inevitable and succors himself with the remotest of hopes. That is the purpose of his book. That is the subject of his book. That is the reason that the city rises from its slumber.

THE BIOLOGY OF LUCK

# CHAPTER

## BY LARRY BLOOM

The rooster crows her awake again and her first instinct, fed by the
semidarkness of her bedroom, is to go into the courtyard and silence
the beast with a kitchen knife. Starshine will do nothing of the sort,
of course. She does not eat meat or poultry. The sight of blood turns
her stomach. On an ordinary morning, when the bedsheets stink
of alcohol and aftershave and sex, she finds a certain amusement
in the bird's mournful song—it reminds her of a bugler hallowing
the end of a great battle—but today she rises alone to her private
reflections and the onset of her period and the uneasy sensation that
she would rather be someplace else. Anywhere else. Her anger at the
poor creature melts into a general frustration with the world. It is
enough to know what the Dominican Jesus freak on the first floor
intends to do with the rooster, to know that Brooklyn at the dawn of
the twenty-first century, in goddam Greenpoint of all places, people
are still worshipping icons and raising chickens for the stew pot, to
make one wish for imminent holocaust or nuclear winter. Or at least
another half hour of sleep.

She sits up in bed. The remains of the overnight breeze flutter
the thin baize curtains, sending a shiver down her spine. The cool draft
in the otherwise still room is sublime, almost romantic. It reminds her
of the windswept beaches along the Maine coast where she passed a
distant summer with her former lover, a bicycle messenger killed in
the line of duty. Starshine remembers the afterglow. She'd sit on the

deck of their borrowed cabin, naked under her parka, listening to the herring gulls while the boy tossed cigarettes over the railing into the breaking surf. She vividly recalls watching the waves extinguish the tobacco embers. She does not remember the sex. It amazes her that after so many lovers, virgins and aspiring Casanovas and even one guy who had ruler markings tattooed along the upper ridge of his penis, she can't conjure up any specific moment of arousal or intimacy. Maybe they are all the same. Like cab rides. Like funerals. Maybe, when you get right down to it, intercourse is the great Marxist equalizer.

Her anger has evaporated. It's not like her to be angry—even these days when she feels she's being pulled at from all directions, when it seems like every man in her life wants to plant a proprietary flag on her like some newly discovered continent—and all it takes is the sound of the teakettle purring on the gas range to restore her sense of equanimity. God bless Eucalyptus. The girl is nuts, but she is the ideal roommate. Starshine shuts the window, pulls her heavy purple bathrobe over her tattered sleeping T-shirt, and tiptoes bleary eyed into the kitchen.

Starshine's roommate is seated at the counter, diligently shaping a contraband ivory horn with a cauterized sail needle. The girl makes scrimshaw for the black market. The countertop bears six months of jackknife scars and lampblack stains. Her sometime boyfriend works for an international sheet metal dealership and smuggles the horns through customs. It's a strange arrangement, sex for tusks, but although poaching strikes Starshine as morally repugnant when she thinks about it, she'd decided not to think about it. She has come to view her roommate's hobby as an exotic form of needlepoint.

"Good morning, darling," says Eucalyptus. "You alone?"

"But not lonely."

Eucalyptus grins. "You've been saving that line up, haven't you?"

Starshine pours the hot water into two earthenware mugs, slides one across the table and sinks into a wicker chair. The morning *Times* is already neatly folded at her place setting, unmussed, only the large gaps where Eucalyptus has clipped celebrity obituaries revealing that it has been devoured from cover to cover. Starshine's roommate boasts a morbid streak. She is trying to learn history through death notices.

"Any important bigwigs kick it?" Starshine asks.

"Not really. There was another former President of General Motors, though. That's the second this month. It kind of makes you wonder . . . ."

"Conspiracy?"

"He was ninety-eight years old."

"I see."

"And diabetic."

"Poor fellow."

Eucalyptus shrugs. "Win some, lose some. Say, why no man *du jour?*"

"I'm taking a vow of celibacy."

"Bullshit."

"Then practicing for the convent."

"Double bullshit."

"I think I'm in over my head."

Eucalyptus carefully places her ongoing masterpiece, a miniature schooner, into her lacquered workbox. She breathes into her glasses and wipes them on her blouse, then replaces them and smiles knowingly at Starshine. "It's easier to start sleeping with a guy than to stop, isn't it?"

"Damn straight," Starshine agrees. "So who wants to stop?" But she has to stop, and she knows it. Starshine raises three fingers in a Girl Scout pledge, although she has never been a Girl Scout—could never belong to any organization so rigidly structured. "I'm placing a moratorium on men. At least new men."

Two men are already planning their lives around her and juggling them is anxiety enough. How in God's name could I handle a third? she thinks. Yet the truth of the matter is that she's still lonely, that nine years as the swan haven't made up for twenty as an ugly duckling, and that if she can't conceive of a future without either of her principal lovers, she can't imagine a future *with* either of them. Maybe that's why she has brought home three other men in the past month.

The casual flings mean nothing: Her two principal suitors mean a lot. Probably too much.

Colby Parker has the sharp-featured good looks and lanky body of the British upper class and the charm to match, although he is generations removed from his aristocratic Saxon roots. His father, the illustrious Garfield Lloyd Parker, is a third-generation lawn chair magnate who presides over family dinners like the Mighty Oz but plays fast-and-loose with his hands when greeting a prospective daughter-in-law. Colby solves every problem with a box of chocolate truffles or a dozen long-stemmed red roses. When she threatened to break things off, he sent twenty-four *dozen*. Two hundred eighty-eight goddamned blossoms! They arrived every hour, on the hour, in batches of twelve, like some mechanical toy gone berserk. Eucalyptus dried them and suspended them from the ceiling. Starshine hates the flowers—hates the money behind the flowers, the emotional blackmail behind the flowers, the painstakingly choreographed future that awaits her on the Parkers' suburban Chappaqua spread—but she loves Colby in spite of it all. How can a girl resist a guy who says "thank you" after screwing?

Jack Bascomb has nothing, except a line of coarse black hair running down his chest to his navel, but she loves him too. He's fifty-four years old and looks it. Beer gut, graying beard, the works. And then there's the matter of personal hygiene. Even three decades on the lam can't excuse shit-stained briefs and day-long morning breath. But Jack Bascomb believes in something, believed in it enough to join the Weather Underground and blow up recruiting stations, and still believes in it enough to turn down the government's offers of leniency. And Starshine believes in what Jack Bascomb believes in. Sometimes. Enough to be twenty-nine years old and refuse any job that require her to wear shoes. Enough to chain herself to the sprinkler head at the local community garden to ward off the city's bulldozers. Not enough to emigrate to Amsterdam with a cancer-riddled, over-the-hill revolutionary determined to live off freelance carpentry in the *Buitenveldert*. There lies the problem.

Starshine walks over to the kitchen window and breathes in the damp, verdant air of the courtyard, absorbs the trumpet of taxi horns and the banter of mating starlings and the awkward indifference of several pigeons resting on the fire escape. She hoists herself onto the wide sill, a ledge of wood splinters and chipping paint, perching herself inside the frame and letting her bare legs dangle over the edge. The window apron wheezes under her weight. Her back adjusts to the cool morning air while her arms and face remain warm and snug inside. The sensation is that of a self-induced fever. It is vaguely pleasurable.

One of the privileges of rising at the crack of dawn, Starshine reflects, is that it offers her license to do absolutely nothing. She has earned a brief respite from obligation and responsibility, a momentary lull before she puts on her adult face and steps through the looking glass into another day. There are things she must do, phone calls to return, necessities to purchase. There is the infuriating business of her appointment at the credit union, where she must haggle or plead for the forty-five dollars which have mysteriously vanished from her account, then the gourmet fruit basket she will purchase with the proceeds, then the exhausting visit to the Staten Island nursing home where her great aunt will nuzzle the fruit against her withered cheeks. There is nothing more depressing than bringing bosc pears and artificially sweetened figs to a blind woman who speaks through a tracheotomy. But all of that is later. It is half past six in the morning and Starshine can't even run down to the grocery to pick up a box of cornflakes, at least not until seven when the beefy Pakistani proprietress replaces her son behind the counter and she no longer has to fear another marriage proposal. All she can do for the moment is sit, bake, freeze, shiver, be. It is all so simple.

"So what's on tap for today?" asks Eucalyptus.

"The usual," answers Starshine. "Breakfast with Colby, lunch at Jack's. And lots and lots of canvassing."

"So much for the convent."

"Oh, and dinner with Larry Bloom."

"That should be a blast."

Although Eucalyptus has not actually met Larry, she has seen him at the helm of his tour bus and formed her judgments. Starshine knows that her own descriptions and anecdotes haven't helped his cause. This makes her feel marginally guilty, but only marginally so, because the jury is still out on her dinner companion. He's a bit too pliable, a bit too attached to her for comfort. He's given her too many of the cheap key-chains and coffee mugs and refrigerator magnets he receives gratis from tourist traps. Theirs is one of those New York friendships, struck up over a mutual interest in the history of landfills (years before when Starshine, for several months, developed a fascination with the changing contours of the Manhattan shoreline), that might easily fade away into acquaintanceship and unease. Only it hasn't faded, somehow, maybe because Larry's the one man in whom she has no romantic interest. He has become her sounding board, her authority on the coupling habits of the male subspecies. And tonight, of all nights, she is feeling like she needs any insight she can get.

But Starshine is a pushover, not an idiot. She prides herself on the distinction. She realizes that Larry has his own hopes, his own muted expectations. Someone famous and dead once said that "all exercises have objects" and there's a reason this guy endures her tales of romance and confusion. He's addicted to them like a housewife hooked on daytime soaps. But that's his business, not hers. It doesn't make her a bad person, does it? She'd fix him up, if she could, but she doesn't know the sort of women who date the Larry Blooms over the world, and she imagines he must have other opportunities. Some woman—but decidedly not Starshine Hart—will see his inner beauty. And yet sometimes, against her visceral instincts, she wonders what it would be like to bestow herself on the hapless guy (bestow is a funny word, somehow the only one that seems appropriate to the circumstances), to purge her life of Jack Bascomb and Colby Parker and all the rest and to bestow complete happiness on someone who might bask for the rest of his life in the glow of his own gratitude. Like Scarlett O'Hara's first marriage in *Gone with the Wind*. How much would it really matter? It's all nonsense, of course. Shit, stuff, and nonsense. Somebody else's pipe dream.

"You know," says Starshine, "if we were famous, life would be much easier."

"Uh-huh," Eucalyptus replies indifferently. "If we were famous, we'd still end up dead."

"Well, if I were famous, honey, you'd run down to the corner store and pick up a box of cereal for me."

"Yep," agrees Eucalyptus, holding a jeweler's glass in front of her ivory schooner to admire her handiwork. "But you're not."

"Not yet."

Soon enough, though, thinks Starshine. Eventually. Maybe. She's not even thirty. There's plenty of time left for fame and fortune. She'll be brave in the interim. She'll weather the Don Juan of Karachi and purchase her own breakfast. But first, she'll paint her toenails. Green. Bright, bright green.

# MORNINGSIDE

No noteworthy disaster has ever occurred in Morningside Heights. Guarded at either end by those two distinctive barbicans of the establishment, Riverside Church and the Cathedral of Saint John the Divine, shielded from harm's way by the no-man's land that is Morningside Park, and rent stabilization, and the twenty-four-hour security service of Columbia University, the sleepy Westside suburb north of 110th Street offers an oasis of public buildings and wide concourses where budding scholars stroll oblivious to their surroundings and elderly Chinese couples shake the ginkgo trees to collect nuts for roasting. The community boasts its own share of minor catastrophes, four-alarm blazes, limousines driven through storefront plate glass, widows beaten and strangled in prewar apartments, but if one excludes second-tier Beat poet Lucien Carr's stabbing of a male admirer in Riverside Park, an event more farcical than tragic, the area surrounding Grant's Tomb has avoided the Triangle Shirtwaist Fires and General Slocum explosions and Crown Heights race riots which keep the tabloids on the newsstands and remind surviving New Yorkers of their perennial good fortune. Larry Bloom can attest to this tranquility. He is a resident. He is also an uncredentialed expert. His incomplete dissertation on the subject, "The Fire Last Time: Public Disaster and Private Response in New York City, 1869–1914," yellows in a footlocker beside his nightstand. Perhaps that is why he welcomes the spectacle on Riverside Drive with tempered amusement, the cynical relief of one who has been waiting from the get-go for lightning to strike.

There is a police cordon composed of blue wooden sawhorses and cops in riot gear. It bisects the granite plaza in front of the mausoleum, separating harmony from discord, suggesting that both are sides of a commemorative coin minted specifically for the occasion. On one side of the barricade, all is order. The Dutch contingent has paid good money to mingle with minor dignitaries, to sip champagne on the steps of the Grant family vault, to admire the size of the caskets, the plenitude of the buffet offerings, the intricate weave of the tricolor bunting. They cluster beneath the banner touting the Dutch-American Heritage Bruncheon, ruddy-cheeked and bespectacled in the spirit of a Van Dyke portrait, deeply concerned that the term *bruncheon* is not to be found in their pocket dictionaries, absorbing the surrounding uproar as a matter of course. Japanese tourists might view the scene as a photo-op, Israelis as fodder for political harangue, but the Dutch are too sanguine, too constrained, for such antics. Funny Americans, they think. Cowboy President, McPuritan culture. An odious word pops into Larry's thoughts, a word he associates with nineteenth-century novels and whalebone corsets and his ever-practical father, Mort, warning him not to place his feet on the coffee table that his parents "plan to die with": Bourgeoisie.

Beyond the cordon lies chaos. Ordered, orchestrated chaos, the worst variety of confusion, the Old Left's vision of its own Armageddon. The crowd sports gold chains, denim jackets, military fatigues, full feather headdresses, Mao pajamas, tie-dyes, vintage coonskin caps, even a conspicuous wimple. There are gourd rattles, cane flutes, chirimias. Also banjos, kitchen pots, bullhorns. Also a topless woman whipping a wooden cigar store Indian with a leather strap. Sharp young men in freshly pressed suits navigate the throng, the crimson "inverted-A" badges of the Organized Anarchist League conspicuous on their lapels. They make notations on clipboards, calculating the size of the protest, or its longevity, or possibly its karmic energy. They distribute water bottles, folded pamphlets. They compete with the purveyors of pocket-sized New Testaments, little red books, gardenia wreaths, with the men vending snow cones and glow-in-the-dark yo-yos and oracular crystals. But all is not mayhem. When you've given up sniffing for the starch on the organizers' collars, resigned yourself to the vapors of incense, braced for the impending sting of burning sulfur and smoldering tires, you notice the glass beads. Even madness has its unifying elements, the glimmer of turquoise and orange, the omnipresent necklaces and bracelets and waist chains, the placards reading, "No Pete Stuyvesant, No Bedford-Stuyvesant, No More," and "Take Back Your Trinkets and Sail Home," all of which reassure you that the heavenly puppeteer may be palsied but that he still holds the drawstrings. It is all harmless. It is a high-stakes Mardi Gras and nothing more. But then, if you are Larry, you notice the other distinctive blemish that bales the crowd toward collective action: A disquieting absence of beauty.

The moment has the makings of a noteworthy disaster.

Larry scans the tableau behind the cordon for a familiar face. He'd like to push his way through the blockade like a plainclothes detective on a crime show, to stiffen his back, undaunted by the harsh Irish physiognomies of New York's finest, challenging them to deny him access to his rightful place among the upstanding burghers at the banquet tables, thriving on their frustration when his identity is affirmed, but he knows he is better off seeking corroboration at the outset. He does not need to wait long. P. J. Snipe, the tour supervisor, nods in Larry's direction and escorts him into the sanctuary of the privileged.

"This is a goddamn nightmare," says Snipe. "I feel like I'm at a Dylan concert."

Snipe isn't fooling anyone. Larry is confident his boss hasn't ever listened to a Dylan song, much less attended a rock show. He is the sort of over-the-hill minor-sport athlete, in this case archery, who one can't imagine at any variety of cultural event, who would sleep his way just as easily through a chamber quartet or an outdoor bluegrass festival or a stadium concert of Hogtie and the Pentecostal Five, all the while managing to look smug with his eyes shut. He is also the sort of over-confident micromanager who thrives on disruptions such as this one. They hired him over Larry's head, impressed by his fifth-tier law degree, probably also by his gold wedding band and toned biceps, although the cretin failed the Mississippi state bar three times and wears the ring to attract unpossessive women. Snipe is a sham. A robust, clean-cut sham. But Snipe makes no pretense of being anything but a sham, hangs it out there on his sleeve until you're surprised to discover that you've known him three years and he still hasn't sold you an annuity or an Arizona condo, until you realize that—in spite of your initial determination and better judgment—he's endeared his way into your life.

"Do you realize what a nightmare this is, Bloom? The Dutch consul is set to show up in twenty minutes and he's expecting brotherly love, and bagels and lox, and that New York shit. Not a Christ-forsaking freak show! Do you know what this is, Bloom? I'll tell you what this is. This is dog piss."

"But what exactly *is* it?"

Snipe has steered them into a shaded alcove behind the guard tower. His conversation voice carries over the staccato of the wooden spoons on brass, but Larry needs to shout to make himself heard.

"How the hell should I know?" demands Snipe. "Something about Native American Indian Liberation Day. We apparently scheduled our event for the same day as their event—and they took it as a slight. And now this!"

"They could have at least warned us."

"They did. They sent a petition with three thousand names. I double-checked with Fed Ex. Some moron lost the letter."

Larry holds his tongue. He'd like to speculate on the identity of the moron, suggest that the idiot be instantly terminated, but the last thing he needs is to get himself fired for impertinence on the day of his date with Starshine. All he wants to do is get through this ordeal of a day, hour by hour, minute by minute. Tomorrow, he will have an agent and a live-in lover, a raison d'être, a justification for phoning Snipe and proffering his resignation. Or for not phoning Snipe, for letting Empire Tours float over the horizon of his life like so much driftwood. There will be no more questions about his long-term plans, no more jokes at Christmas parties about colleagues decapitated by traffic lights. Larry Bloom will never again stand in solitude on the platform of a red tour bus describing Captain Kidd's role in the financing of Trinity Church and wondering whether the full-breasted temptation in the third row is old enough to ask out. So why doesn't he ram his fist into Snipe's mandible? Or even dare make a joke at his expense? Larry's eyes have locked onto his supervisor's chiseled chin, his angular jaw, the florid patches of flesh where a razor has chafed too close. He imagines they would make an easy target, if he truly wished to deck Snipe, but he wouldn't even know the mechanics of the swing. Hitting just isn't his medium.

Snipe rubs his jaw, stamping approval on his shave. Then he cups his palm and punches it methodically with his fist. "You want some coffee, Bloom?"

"Why not?"

"That's the one thing we seem to have enough of this morning. And it's fresh. They sent up seventy-five gallons. Who is going to drink seventy-five gallons of coffee? If Juan Valdez at the caterer's spent a little less time brewing coffee and a little more time baking bagels, we might fatten these Dutch fellows up some. They sure could use it. . . . Try this. . . ."

Snipe hands Larry a Styrofoam cup filled with coffee and a poppy-seed bagel.

"Dog piss," says Snipe.

Larry nearly breaks his teeth on the first bite. "A bit on the hard side."

"It's granite. It's marble. It's a goddamned marble statuette of a bagel, that's what it is. We've been trying to unload the extras on the freak show, but it seems they also have standards. Even the cops won't take them. By the way, Bloom, you have a car, don't you?"

Larry nods. Snipe knows he has a car. The bastard has borrowed it twice. Both times he claimed he had a funeral to go to in South

Jersey, which might have been the case, but Larry has a hunch that Snipe's overnight trips are more likely to end in a birth than a burial. The second time, Snipe brought Larry the program from the service, a two-page foldout bearing the Twenty-third Psalm and a requiem to his godmother, but that only added to Larry's suspicions. Who brings back a program from an interment as though it were a playbill or a National Park brochure? But Larry spent a full Saturday morning fine-toothing the backseat of his Plymouth, searching for so much as a Virginia Slims filter or a stray blond hair, an entirely futile endeavor, and the episode left him twice as convinced that if his boss is lying to him, he'll never be able to prove it. For all he knows, Snipe is banging the director of a funeral parlor.

"That's right," says Snipe. "I remember now. A 1970-something white Plymouth. I wasn't sure if you still owned it."

"I still own it."

"Well, here's the thing, Bloom. I was kind of hoping I could borrow it."

"I see."

"Tonight, that is."

"Let me guess. A death in the family."

Larry stuns himself with his own audacity. After years of humoring his boss, he has suddenly hinted—not too subtly—that he thinks the man would kill off his own relatives, in a manner of speaking, if it suited his pecker. Then a worse idea strikes him: What if *this time* somebody has actually died?

Snipe grins and crushes the bottom out of his empty Styrofoam cup. He does not appear insulted. "So you heard already. Word travels fast in the world of tourism. Anyway, here's the deal: I have this girl I'm seeing, just hooking up with really, and her grandmother passed away last night."

"I'm sorry," says Larry.

"Don't be. The old lady was a cow. She had it coming. But that's neither here nor there. The thing is, the woman lived up in Riverdale, and she owned this vintage sewing machine, or maybe it's a sewing cabinet, but the bottom line is that Jessie has had her eye on it for a long time, and it looks like it's going to end up going to some cousin unless we take matters into our own hands. Pronto, I mean. So I told her that a buddy of mine with a car might have an hour or so to move the contraption before they seal the place and probate kicks in . . . and everybody starts suing the pants off each other. It's one fucked-up family."

"Tonight?"

"It'll just take an hour or two. Jessie is also up in the Bronx. Co-op City. I'll owe you one . . ."

Larry reaches for his cigarettes, checking himself just in time. Empire Tours is a smoke-free employer. "How about tomorrow night?" he asks tentatively.

"It has to be tonight. Even that's a stroke of luck. The cousin skidded off the road on the drive down from Albany, so she's not coming back until the morning . . . ."

"I have plans tonight," says Larry. "I kind of have a date."

"Not a problem. The whole shebang will take an hour, tops. Bring me a receipt and you can even charge your dinner bill to the company, okay?"

The arrival of the Dutch consul prevents Larry from protesting any further. Two white stretch limousines inch their way to the curbside and a phalanx of chauffeurs and liverymen, decked out in the ceremonial red-and-gold regalia of the Netherlands' mission, maneuver themselves into two long files to create an imperial catwalk. They carry neither swords nor guns, but hold their right arms behind their backs, bent awkwardly at the elbows, so that they resemble an army of overdressed dance instructors about to lead a team lesson in the minuet. Between their ranks pass two security attachés, then a gaunt, long-faced official carrying a portmanteau, and finally the consul on the arm of a significantly younger woman. The damning contrast between the rotund, mustached diplomat and his svelte companion leaves one to speculate whether she is the wife or the daughter. Or possibly an escort provided by the Dutch state for festive occasions.

The cortege crosses onto the plaza. The approaching consul

walks slowly, leaning on his companion's arm for support; the pair reminds Larry of a Salvador Dalí print depicting a miniature debutante dragging a teapot. A brass band strikes up the anthem of the House of Orange, reinvigorating the demonstrators beyond the cordon, who reply with a salute of jeers and cacophonous banging. Snipe slaps Larry between the shoulder blades. He steps forward to confer with one of the couples waiting to greet the consul, an American couple, unquestionably, presumably among the Hudson Valley philanthropists who have sponsored the event.

Larry glares at his boss, his anger mounting. He knows Snipe too well for his own good. The prick doesn't believe him—doesn't believe that he has a date. But Larry doesn't have time to give his boss the silent tongue-lashing he deserves. He is suddenly surrounded by silence. Brass and tympani bleed to an awkward halt; the howling fades to a murmur. For a moment, Larry thinks that the weather has shifted, that the heavens have opened. He looks up into the clear, distant sky. His eyes are sorting through the swirling tree-scape when the first bagel pegs him square on the forehead.

All around Larry, the self-satisfied Dutch burghers are taking cover. They're scrambling on hands and knees to find shelter beneath the banquet tables, jostling for space behind the plastic recycling dumpsters. While the police have been shielding the visitors from the canaille beyond the cordon, a second group of protestors has climbed atop the rotunda of the tomb. They've concealed themselves between the dome and the parapet, smuggling up surplus food from the unguarded caterer's tent, stockpiling projectiles for their culinary onslaught and biding their time. The arrival of the Dutch consul has sparked them to combat—he looks official enough, after all, although most likely the protesters have no clue who he is—and they've begun pelting the defenseless revelers below with preserved eel, canned sardines, and nuggets of Edam cheese. Larry crouches under a folding chair and watches as the privileged few (the consul, the gaunt dignitary, several self-selected American philanthropists) seek the refuse of the limousines and speed down Riverside Drive while the remainder of the targeted audience is left to fend for itself. And then he sees Snipe, standing tall at the center of the pavilion like a general on horseback, steadily directing the Dutch tourists onto the awaiting busses.

The riot police have their shields up. They are engaged in a tidal struggle with a mob. The overhead barrage has come to a halt, but the assault continues from the ground as kitchen utensils and pocket-sized New Testaments replace the depleted edible ammunition. Larry decides to make a break for it. He double checks his pockets to make sure that he has not lost his cigarettes or his treasured letter, then charges through the storm to the nearest of the chartered coaches. There is a line waiting to board. He stands between the Dutch tourists and the mob, allowing those near the front of the line to take the brunt of the attack while he regains his bearing. The "shelling" soon abates. The police have resisted the first advance of the forces of disorder and it appears unlikely that the glass-bead brigade will regroup. Most of the demonstrators have already retreated from the scene of battle. Here and there, a long-haired white kid wages a losing war against a cop's baton, but boarding the bus, Larry senses that the revolution has been suspended indefinitely.

Larry examines the innocent victims of the massacre, the beset Dutch tourists who have seated themselves in the coach like a model kindergarten class and now await further instructions. They seem largely unperturbed. A few are nursing their clothing with handkerchiefs, but the vast majority peer through the tinted glass for a view of the action. Many are even smiling. Larry glances out the window and watches in amazement. Three holdouts—two black teenagers and a bearded white man in what looks like a zoot suit—have mounted one final charge against the cordon. They are using the cigar store Indian as a battering ram. One of the teens is bleeding from the head and neck. On the steps of the mausoleum, near the caterer's tent, Snipe shouts at a diminutive, copper-skinned man in a baker's apron. Larry turns away in disgust. He blows into his microphone, opens the company guidebook, and reads the first words of the scripted tour.

"Good morning and welcome to New York City."

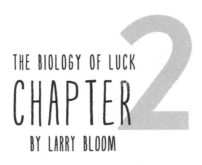

THE BIOLOGY OF LUCK

# CHAPTER 2

BY LARRY BLOOM

It is a morning of promise and bustle.

Starshine coasts through commuter traffic, pedaling only when necessary, leaving the downhills to the forces of natures. A fine moisture clings to the air: it limns her honey-colored hair and wilts the bandanna around her neck; it gilds the handlebars of her Higgins with a patina of cold droplets. The bleary-eyed creature in a tattered T-shirt has blossomed into a beautiful woman on a bicycle. She knows what she is about.

Heads turn as she weaves her way south through Williamsburg. There are the approving smiles of the elderly Italian men playing chess outside their social clubs, the ambivalent leers of caftaned Hasids returning from their morning prayers. Packs of junior high playboys shower her in catcalls. Papaya vendors whistle under their breaths. From the open windows of striped Dodge Darts and glaring purple Chevelles float offers of easy sex, of unparalleled sex, of midnight trysts and moonlight weddings and even cold, hard cash. Compliment and insult fuse to the obscene rhythms of longing and lust. In Starshine's wake, ancient women adjust their lipstick in pocket mirrors, young mothers grope for the arms of their male companions, the middle-class white kids who panhandle in herds simulate lovemaking on the street corners. All pay tribute to life's sole universal truth: A beautiful girl on a bicycle is communal property.

Colby, oblivious to this spectacle, will be waiting for her in the coffee shop across Atlantic Avenue from the Unicorn Diner. He'll be perched on one of the platform chairs that face the street, hiding behind his *Wall Street Journal*, sipping the dregs of his second cup of coffee. A potted cactus wrapped in a paper cone will be braced between his pinstriped thighs; his fingers will toy nervously with the ribbons. This is Colby's little white secret. He'll squander a full hour of a glorious spring morning willing the minute hand of his pocket watch toward eight o'clock in the mistaken illusion that when he enters the Unicorn Diner ten minutes late, droplets of perspiration frowning across his brow, his arrival will convey just the appropriate degree of devil-may-mare spontaneity. The image leaves Starshine grinning.

She has seen through Colby since their first breakfast date. She blew out a tire on her bicycle and showed up flustered and out-of-breath at eight-thirty; her lover materialized, unconvincingly apologetic, at a quarter to nine. Starshine wonders how far to push this game, contemplates feigning oversleep and arriving in the vicinity of noon, but deep down she derives a perverse enjoyment from Colby's persistence, from his unflagging effort to undermine his own identity, because there is a certain charm to his ongoing quest to become the man he thinks she desires. In effect, to become more like her. Sometimes, Starshine asks herself how this crusade reflects upon her own identity, whether he pacifies some post-Freudian tapeworm at the core of her being, but she is less troubled than amused by the possibility. What she knows, for certain, is that she has no business disabusing Colby of his aspirations or exposing his trifling deception. The contrived spontaneity is his crutch, his delusion. It fosters his well-being. It does her no harm. In the context of the painstakingly layered card palace of doubletalk and mutually satisfying half truths and outright lies that are the greater part of all human interactions, especially romantic relationships, she recognizes that her omissions are far more destructive than Colby's. Most of the time. There are also some days—and she fears today is one of them—when she'd like to shake him by the lapels.

The city falls away from Starshine, the dilapidated warehouses, the moribund waterfront, row houses, roof gardens, East Williamsburg,

Fort Greene, the enclaves of bohemian chic beyond the Navy Yard. She traverses Cadman Plaza at Tillary Street, cuts south at the intersection of Henry and Montague. Brooklyn Heights unfolds before her, the nation's first great suburb, an enduring testament to the futility of escape. The neighborhood embodies Colby Parker's enlightened view of déclassé. To him, this is downscale. Gritty. But to Starshine, the foundling, the orphan of a failed oboist and a lounge crooner, cutting corners on three hundred dollars a week, this world of gourmet patisseries and bridal shops is as alien as the Brooklyn Heights of Truman Capote or even Walt Whitman. Sometimes Starshine imagines she would prefer that lost Brooklyn to this one, that she is the corporeal incarnation of a Whitman poem. She is relieved that she remembered to wear cargo pants. Unshaved legs are a no-go in yuppiedom.

Starshine removes her bicycle lock from around her waist, loops the chain twice beneath the basket, and secures her Higgins to a lamppost, then saunters up Atlantic Avenue and through the heavy glass doors of the Unicorn. The twenty-four-hour breakfast nook is its own small universe of paper placemats, table jukeboxes, pseudo-nautical décor. Kodachrome desserts rotate in glass cases; lobsters struggle for elbowroom in the undersized tank. She waits for Colby in the lobby, as she always does, between the pay telephone and the cigarette machine. The stiff-backed Greek maître d' examines her with suspicion. His eyes accuse her of shoplifting acclimatized air, of planning to dine and flee. Precisely ten minutes pass before Colby arrives with the paper cone in one hand and a long-stemmed red rose in the other. He offers her both. Starshine swallows her displeasure.

"I couldn't resist," says Colby. "It was the last one in the bucket and it had your name written all over it. You're not mad, are you?"

"It's fine, just fine," lies Starshine. "It must have been suffering there, all alone. Poor, poor flower. But this is the last time, Colby. Got it?"

"I swear."

It won't be the last time, of course, only a prelude to a momentary respite, but Starshine is powerless to resist a gift unless she determines to spurn the giver. And she is not prepared to do that. Not yet. Early on, she made the mistake of telling Colby that she hated flowers, that as far as she was concerned a cactus was as romantic as a rose, but the poor lightweight took the warning too much to heart and now her apartment rivals the hot house at the botanical gardens. Colby Parker cannot be anything other than Colby Parker. He is indefatigable.

The maître d' leads them to a corner table. Starshine notices that they are the youngest couple in the room, if they are indeed a couple, that they are surrounded on all sides by clusters of gaggling women in their sixties and ancient, bow-tied men lapping oatmeal in solitude. The men all share the same hangdog look; the women exude hunger and desire. Maybe Colby has chosen the Unicorn for a reason, Starshine muses, maybe he is subliminally exposing her to wedlock's cruel alternatives. But her lover is not that clever. Nor would the plan work. One look at the elderly couples eating in silence along the far wall, reflected and rereflected infinitely by the mirrors at either end of the row of booths, reminds Starshine of the Matrushka dolls which Eucalyptus collects in the knickknack cabinet beside her bed: Yes, marriage is like a series of opposing reflections, inverse images getting ever smaller like nesting dolls, each one of you trying to squeeze yourself smaller to fit inside the hopes of the other, until one of you cracks or stops existing. Starshine would prefer to die a spinster.

"So have you thought things over?" asks Colby.

"Not *that* again."

"I'm not putting pressure on you. I'm only asking."

"Can we talk about something else?"

"Like what?"

"Like anything. Like the poetry of Walt Whitman."

"What about the poetry of Walt Whitman?"

"Nothing in particular," says Starshine. "Never mind."

Colby reaches into his breast pocket and produces two longs slips of heavy paper. "So I took the liberty of getting us plane tickets," he says tentatively. "Tuscany in August. No pressure, just something to think about."

"I can't go," says Starshine. "It's very sweet of you, but I just can't. Maybe eventually. Maybe after the summer when things settle down."

These proposals are the most trying part of Colby's game, Starshine finds, the surreal aspect of their regularly scheduled Wednesday breakfasts. He hopes to plan her into monogamy, clutter her life with so many obligations and commitments that she'll wake up one morning in Chappaqua with one child in a bassinet and a second on the way. It is love approached with the outlook of a biochemist or an economics professor, of a man who approaches her ambivalence as a problem to be solved. How long will she be able to resist? It isn't only about the money, of course, about his multimillion dollar inheritance and her lapsed health insurance. If that were the case, it would all be too easy. But the fact of the matter is that she loves Colby Parker, maybe she's even in love with Colby Parker, and the prospect of Wednesdays without French toast and marriage proposals and prickly pear cacti would shatter her heart. If only there were no breaking point. If only their arrangement—or rather, their multiple arrangements, for Colby knows that she gets her toes wet now and then, but he knows absolutely nothing about Jack—could continue indefinitely.

"You shouldn't have spent the money ahead of time like that," she says. "It makes me uncomfortable."

"It wasn't that much money," he answers, crestfallen. "Besides, what else am I supposed to do with it? You can't take it with you, right?"

"There are other things to do with it," she snaps. "Think about it."

"Jesus," says Colby. "I was trying to be nice. I'm sure any other woman in the world would be flattered—overjoyed—to take a trip to Tuscany with me. In fact, if you don't want to go, if you're so dead-set against it, I'll send that couple over there. They look like they could use a vacation."

Colby waves the tickets in the air, signaling for the waiter. Starshine reaches for his arm, tugs at his sleeve from across the tabletop. Her water glass totters on the edge of the Formica and then shatters in the aisle. The couple along the far wall glance toward them and quickly returns to their own purgatory. "Goddamnit," cries Colby, stooping to dry the corner of his penny loafer with a napkin, the thought of sending their fellow diners to Europe now far from his thoughts.

They order, eat. Colby carries the conversation, avoiding all references to Italy and marriage, trying to earn back his lost ground. Starshine picks at the condiments around her whitefish salad, shreds the lettuce into infinitesimal strands. She can picture Colby at this father's office later that afternoon, making the most of his sinecure, memorizing Walt Whitman's "Brooklyn Bridge" to impress her. She can also picture him laid out in a crypt at Woodlawn, surrounded by gold bars and photographs of Starshine Hart, like some modern-day Egyptian pharaoh determined to take it all with him. This last bit strikes her as uproariously entertaining. She is rippling with laughter by the time their dishes are cleared, and Colby, thinking that hindsight has transformed their spat into a comic memory, leaves an exorbitant tip. They both exit the Unicorn in good cheer.

"I'll call you during the afternoon," says Colby.

"I'm going out to Staten Island to visit Aunt Agatha. We'll talk tomorrow."

"And we're on for Friday night?"

"Last time I checked."

"Then Friday night it is," he says. "Send my best to your aunt."

Colby is a favorite of Aunt Agatha's, although the pair have only met once. The old woman frequently reminds her niece that there is no crime in loving a wealthy man—a man who can take care of you in your old age, with private attendants, so you don't get railroaded off to a nursing home. And Colby, of course, believes that Agatha's opinion might sway Starshine's, as though marriage were a matter of familial consensus—which, of course, it is not.

"No problem," answers Starshine. On the tip of her tongue are the words, Why don't you take *her* to Italy, but she doesn't want to provoke a fight.

"And for what it's worth, I'm sorry."

Colby waves his arm to signify all those transgressions for which an apology might be in order. Starshine pecks him on the cheek and turns quickly on her heels, refusing to hear whatever words he is calling after her. She is in bright spirits again, and her morning has no room for apologies or regrets. Her lover will spend the rest of his day replaying their breakfast, supplying extra dialogue and second-guessing their parting, but she will not. She will return home, look up the address of the credit union's central office, deposit her cactus on the window ledge, and place her flower in water. No, she won't even do that. Starshine pins the red rose under the windshield wiper of a random parked car and smiles at her handiwork. It all seems so easy.

# NEW AMSTERDAM

They expect to see Dutch New York, the city of Diedrich Knickerbocher and Peter Minuit, but they are sure to be disappointed. Their imperial seat has been swept away by time and progress, its yellow-brick mansions razed by fire, its tidy cow paths bloated to great boulevards. The shimmering monoliths of Big Coal and Big Oil and Gargantuan Capital have swallowed the foundations of the Fort Amsterdam settlement, its vistas, its contours, even its very soil, burying the vestiges in the bottomlands of steel-framed canyons. Landfill scooped from Midtown's hills has honed the waterfront to perfect symmetry. All that remains from forty years of Dutch rule are a handful of incongruous place names: Wall Street, where a frontier fence once stood; Bridge Street, to mark the shoals of a thwarted creek; Bowery; Old Slip; Gouverneur Lane; the unlikely Bowling Green at the mouth of Broadway. These Dutch emissaries have come a long way to discover that they should have vacationed in Pretoria or Jakarta or Paramaribo, that they really don't matter in Gotham, that they never really mattered. That New York can get along fine without them.

Larry primes his audience with atmosphere, background, trivia. He blends history and legend, hot yarn and cold fact, pulling every last trick from his tour guide's magic sleeve, serving up a smorgasbord of myths supplied by his employer and distortions culled from memory and outright lies fabricated for the occasion. He wants to impress the dimpled teenage godsend reclining in the fifth row; her momentary pleasure is the breadth and depth of his constituency. As Big Louise pummels the accelerator into the floorboards, plummeting the coach down Riverside Drive with the full force of her ample weight, Larry sermonizes on the age of the harbor, on its span, on its bridges, Verrazano and Hudson, Colonel Roebling and Robert Moses, before detouring into an anecdote about wampum-dealer Frederick Phillipse's love for an Indian princess. The Dutch tourists listen with polite deference. Big Louise grits her teeth as she tears through potholes and amber stoplights. The girl in row five fidgets, stifles a yawn with her hand, and leans forward in her seat to meet Larry's stare. He speaks faster, describing the moonlit night of the couple's final meeting, painting a pastoral, even romantic, portrait of seventeenth-century New Amsterdam. There are mighty patrons, noble Wappingers, spiteful Portuguese slavers. He is making it up as he goes. The bus picks up speed, lurching, its skeleton rattling; Big Louise jolts over manholes, cuts off taxis, moaning and cursing under her breath; the Dutch girl smiles, bathes Larry with a flush of attention, maybe even a spark of interest, her long hair shimmering in a panel of light. This is his moment. But suddenly, with all the advance warning of a boiler explosion, long after Larry's charges have abandoned courtesy for a view of the downtown skyline or the Jersey coast, precisely at the moment of climax, of passion, of bloodshed, when it has become clear to him that his anecdote is not an anecdote at all, but a hackneyed rip-off of Alfred Noyes's "The Highwayman," the coach rasps to a halt at the foot of Battery Place, drowning Larry's fable in the wail of burning brake lines. The Dutch tourists blink themselves alive. Big Louise slides open both sets of the double doors. Larry's teenage beauty slings her backpack over her shoulder, whispers briefly in her mother's ear, and sashays her way down the aisle, exiting the rear of the bus. Larry rolls his eyes at Big Louise, to say here we go again, to say wish me luck, and he steps into his workday of asphalt and heat.

There are already other tour groups on the plaza: hordes of Germans and Italians, Koreans posing for snapshots, day-trippers on double-decker cruisers, a battalion of heartland senior citizens basking in all their porcine glory. The Germans carry Baedeker's guides and canteens. The midwesterners lug beach chairs and ice chests. Each group eyes the others with muted scorn. They are all part and parcel of the same game, victim to the universal folly which convinces travelers everywhere that they blend, that they can pass themselves off as locals, should the exigency arise, while others cannot. Larry waits for his own team of upscale refugees to stow their personal effects and disembark. He waves at another tour guide, a pudgy-faced old-timer whose name he no longer remembers; the veteran nods in his direction. They exchange the knowing, jaded looks of the enlightened. Unlike the sun-visored midwesterners or the happy-go-lucky Dutch, they know the somber truth: This is business, not pleasure. It is immigration in reverse, the start of the day's tribute to Lady Liberty and Ellis Island, a routine which will repeat itself with different faces until the end of time. There is no escape.

One of the Dutch tourists steps forward and pats Larry too intimately on the shoulder. He is a stately, older gentleman with thin-rimmed spectacles and an unconvincing hair weave. His wife, also taller than Larry, holds her lips perpetually pursed as though about to spit out a cherry pit. They share the look of academics, of know-it-alls, the sort of people who view you as a burdensome accoutrement to their own self-guided tour.

"Willem van Huizen," the man says in the Queen's English, extending his hand. "I wanted to take the liberty of complimenting you on your handling of this morning's— how shall we call it?— Episode? We Netherlanders aren't accustomed to civil disturbance. At least not in modern times. I dare say that some of my countrymen may have taken a scare. But not me and Klara. We have lived in New York before. Diamonds are my trade, but I consider myself something of an amateur historian of the American colonies. Isn't that right, Klara?"

"He certainly does," agrees his wife. Her words are earnest, not ironic.

"I'm writing a book on the trans-Atlantic trade. From an economic perspective, naturally. My focus is on currency, bullion, precious stones. I always say one ought to stick to one's area of expertise. Mercifully, colonial gems and jewelry are a relatively untapped field. Did you know that the trinkets with which my countrymen purchased your lovely island were worth slightly more than sixty guilders? That's the equivalent of five florins or twenty ducats. In present day terms, that's one month's rent on a studio apartment in this city. Inflation adjusted, of course."

"Of course."

Larry looks around for an opportunity to desert his newfound friend. If only the stragglers would disembark more rapidly, he could excuse himself to begin the tour. He has no use for armchair scholars and dilettante pedagogues, aggressive glad-handers writing books and citing minutiae to impress their wives, especially those who spruce up their names with ersatz *vans* and *vons*. Does the blockhead really think he's fooling anyone into believing he's an aristocrat? Van Huizen! It sounds like one of those puffed-up surnames adopted by second-tier Nazis, like Von Papen or Von Ribbentrop. But Van Huizen, the diamond dealer? That's the beginning of an off-color joke, a potshot at self-hating Jews. Van Huizen the diamond dealer and Von Goldberg the deacon walk into a basilica. . . . Larry hasn't been to a synagogue in nearly a decade, but he can see his own heritage, maybe his own worst instincts regarding that heritage, reflected in his companion's disguise. He knows Van Huizen's type. He knows the man will profess a deeply personal interest in Grace Church. He knows—and here lies the dolt's one redeeming quality—that he will offer a generous tip. Gentrified European Jews are the backbone of historical tourism. They are a dime a dozen.

Van Huizen's next move confirms Larry's suspicions.

"*Blowm*," he says, reading Larry's nametag in the Dutch style, merging the o's to elevate him to the stature of Roosevelt and Van Loo. "Is that a Netherlander name?"

"Bloom," answers Larry. "German."

"I see," van Huizen says apologetically—and maybe with a hint of pity. "I thought you might be related to Pastor Bloem of the Reformed Church. He's an old friend of our family."

"No doubt."

Van Huizen steps closer, his face florid with conspiracy.

"I was just telling Klara how much I enjoyed your talk on Frederick Phillipse. A seminal figure, unquestionably. Wall Street's first lion, a forerunner of Astor and Morgan. And you did him such justice. For the most part. I don't want to overstep my bounds, *Meneer Blowm*, but isn't it possible you erred in the quantity of wampum he paid to the Wappinger chieftain for his daughter's hand? You said fifteen tons, but I recall reading fifty tons. This *is* my particular field of expertise, you understand."

"Fifty tons it is. It's not the first time I've made that mistake."

Larry catches sight of his teenage inspiration. She seems older in the daylight, eighteen, maybe even twenty. Her breasts push against the front of her tank top. Larry wonders for a moment whether he will have the courage to speak to her, if she will accede to his advances, if there is the remotest possibility that she might cast off the shackles of her dour-faced parents and meet him for a nightcap, for an early evening stroll, but then he recalls Starshine, his dinner engagement, and the matter of Snipe's girlfriend, also the pageant of other young women, equally innocent and alluring, whom he has had the forbearance not to pester. His future rests with Starshine; hope endures in those quarters. It is a universally established truth that teenage girls don't appreciate come-ons from down-at-the-heel tour guides. Larry taps the letter in his breast pocket. He excuses himself, too brusquely, from the Dutch couple and launches into his show.

Larry walks backwards. He steers his burghers around Hardenbergh's Whitehall Building, points out the black smoke billowing from the Standard Oil headquarters, pays tribute to the Downtown Athletic Club and the ornate friezes of the custom house. He preps his pupils for Castle Clinton, waxes rich on its previous incarnations as an aquarium and concert venue. The Dutch nod appreciatively at the names P. T. Barnum, Jenny Lind, Fiorello La Guardia. They have absolutely no idea what he is talking about. Larry has given up trying to impress the girl, and now he is free to talk over the crowd, through them, to address his wisdom to the whole expanse of lower Manhattan, to the stalagmitic towers of granite and glass, letting his words reverberate through the bowels of world capitalism and reach for the distant peaks of the Times Tower and the Empire State Building. His words are the mantra of a hollow culture, an incantation to form over substance. His lips must keep moving, his larynx quivering until it burns, but the content of his discourse is as trifling, as thoroughly irrelevant, as are the conversion figures in Van Huizen's book. Larry can say absolutely anything he desires. Anything at all.

They pass through the heavy wooden doors of Castle Clinton. The rounded walls of the fortress stand eight feet thick, solid stone, equipped with twenty-eight cannons, none ever fired except in target practice, and Larry shares all of this, striving to do his duty, relating in painstaking detail the firing of the first salute, Evacuation Day, November 25, 1811, but the Dutch prefer to stroll the gangways and battlements at their own leisurely pace and to poke their noses into the barrels of the guns. A handful of loyalists, including both Van Huizens and the parents of the teenage beauty, cling to Larry as he leads them through the fort and onto the exterior boardwalk. A pair of twin boys in matching shorts, not affiliated with Larry's tour, toss pieces of Styrofoam packaging from the fortress into the surf; these synthetic fragments float for a moment, and then the sea swallows them ferociously.

The girl scales the parapet and balances herself, arms outstretched, like an aspiring ballerina. Her pale skin stands out against the deep, opulent blue of the harbor. She is a fitting masthead for this island nation, for the undisputed capital of glamour. But she is too young, much too young. Larry turns his back on the girl and acknowledges several park rangers, crisp young men, more polish than spit, and he wonders if they share his unhealthy thoughts. No matter. All will go home empty handed. It is enough to know that girls like this exist, to survive hand-to-mouth on the distant promise that such a beauty might someday be his, may fall into his lap, that he may share a stalled elevator with such a radiant creature or rescue her off a window ledge or win her heart with an epic novel, to keep Larry going, to keep his lips moving, to buttress him against the Willem van Huizens of the world.

"Is it true," asks Van Huizen "that the channel used to freeze over frequently? It is my understanding that O'Callaghan and Hastings, who in my opinion are the two most trustworthy chroniclers of the city, differ on the subject. My own inclination is that Hastings has the better half of the argument, but I'd appreciate your thoughts. . . ." Van Huizen tucks his hands into his pockets, his chest cocked forward, every joint of his soft body announcing that he doesn't give a damn for Larry's thoughts.

Even by the standards of men like Van Huizen, this strikes Larry as a particularly pompous question. Larry knows little of the long-dead Edmund Baily O'Callaghan and Hugh Hastings beyond their names and has no reason to believe them particularly gifted historians; he does know that the harbor has only frozen once in recorded times, during the winter of 1779–1780, and he begins to recount that frigid episode. Halfway through his answer, Larry hears the splash.

His first vision of the calamity is on the faces of the crowd. Eyes widen, mouths drop. All at once there is a frenzied charge toward the parapet, led by the girl's mother, accompanied by wild gesticulations and shouting in a foreign tongue. Shock rapidly diffuses into panic, even terror, before stabilizing itself on the bedrock of helplessness. The girl is flailing, sputtering, sinking. The water lashes against the concrete flood break, churning up clouds of spray. The crowd is hollering, pointing, pleading. The girl's mother pummels the father's chest, blaming him for the ultimate disaster, although it has not yet transpired, her mournful wail suggests that the girl's death is already a fait accompli. Larry's universe slows to freeze-frame. This is the opportunity he has been waiting for all of his adult life, one of those rare instances of heroic potential. He takes in the drowning girl, also a pair of tugboats guiding a barge through the bay. The water churns cold and turbulent. Larry slowly, methodically, unbuttons his shirt; his actions are as precise and meticulous as those of a watch smith dismantling a mechanical timepiece. He vaults himself onto the parapet. He looks over his shoulder, capturing the ambivalence of the spectators, the hope, the apprehension, the mother's distorted features, Van Huizen's bemused grimace, the unadulterated befuddlement of a stout woman in a beige shawl. Larry steps forward, braces himself. And then, as the girl's head nears the point of submersion, her bare arms slackening, the tension easing from her face, in recognition, maybe in resignation, she resurfaces on the shoulders of a park ranger armed with a life ring. The ordeal is over.

Larry has no place in the bathos that follows. He is not a hero, not even a player, only a bare-chested tour guide standing on a parapet, holding a button-down shirt—a man self-conscious of his concave chest and sun-starved skin. The park ranger receives the applause, the grateful maternal hug, the generous-if-gauche gratuity from the armchair historian. They lay the girl out on a cushioned tarp, drawing her hair away from her slightly bloated face. She sputters water, smiles. Soon sirens announce the arrival of professionals, paramedics, strapping men equipped with a gurney and gauze. They do not offer Larry medical attention; they do not even inquire after his health. Their only concern is loading the teenager onto an ambulance, shepherding her parents in after her, transporting the VIP trio out of the war zone at a high rate of speed. The Dutch tourists disperse. They replay the incident in hushed voices, queuing for tickets to the Ellis Island ferry, still determined to make the most of their morning. No irreparable damage has been done. Nobody has died. If their numbers have been marginally reduced, it is their responsibility, their moral duty, like alpine hikers or characters in a murder mystery, to compensate for the loss. They are up for the occasion.

Larry is the only genuine victim of the episode. His moment of glory has degenerated into self-consciousness, his teenage beauty lassoed from his clutches like a rodeo steer. His book will fail. His date will fail. It is all carved in stone. Men like Larry Bloom don't win the love of women like Starshine Hart. Men like Larry Bloom don't publish epic novels to literary acclaim. When you get right down to it—and Larry doesn't think he can go much lower at the moment—men like Larry Bloom don't do much of anything.

One by one, his fingers refasten the buttons of his shirt.

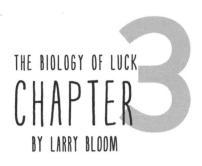

# THE BIOLOGY OF LUCK
# CHAPTER 3
## BY LARRY BLOOM

Word on the street: Bone, the one-armed super, can get you anything.

He sits in the forenoon sun, eyes closed but not sleeping, absorbing his beauty rays with a silver reflector, so that if his aluminum lawn chair weren't planted on the Fillmore Avenue sidewalk, if his Hawaiian shirt weren't clipped at the top with a bolo tie, if the shades resting in his tight-cropped hair didn't boast a bridge of custom-made gold leaf, in short, if he were not Bone, but just another olive-skinned cripple at the curbside, you might make the gross mistake of feeling sorry for him. He seems so harmless, so overtly innocuous. It is difficult to imagine, at first glance, that this emaciated creature is the kingpin, the Alpha and the Omega, the man who has connected the sorts of people who know each other. But it would take only one blink of a lizard's eye, one snap of Bone's calloused fingers, to supply you with anything, absolutely anything, contraband and coveted. Bone is the Wells Fargo wagon of the nascent millennium. He can get you high, he can get you screwed, he can get you shot. He can arm your band of mercenaries with Kalashnikovs and M-16 rifles, load them onto state-of-the-art personnel transports and deposit them within hours in the mudflats off the Guatemalan coast or Havana harbor. He can wipe clean your record as a pedophile, get you elected to the legislature, have your political opponents' families dismembered with machetes. If you have the money, if you have the need, if your personal welfare depends upon securing a year's supply of napalm or nude photographs of the Queen of England or fucking identical twins simultaneously, if your fetish is panda fur or celebrities' tampons, if your talisman is World Series rings or severed human tongues, if you crave early Christian relics or your employer's wife or a particular print at the Metropolitan Museum of Art, Bone can make it happen. That, at least, is the word on the street.

To the tenants of number 72, the enigma of Bone offers a perennial motif for gossip and idle speculation. Rumor holds him to be the illegitimate son of the Lucchese family don, also a disinherited heir to the Walker cosmetics fortune, even the scion of a long line of distinguished Yemeni rabbis. He speaks English with a French accent; his French stops and starts with the glottal punctuation of a German. Nobody knows his origins, his history, the source of his thick roll of bills or the cause of his disfiguring wound, whether he really fought beside Che in Bolivia or against Che in the Sierra Madre or helped the CIA destabilize Iran in 1955. Nobody even knows if Bone is his first name or his surname or possibly a cognominal homage to his lack of flesh. All that is certain is that the one-armed super will move your automobile to the ebb and flow of alternate-side parking for a modest fee, and that your daily existence will prove much more pleasant if he likes you. Unless, of course, he likes you more than you like him, which is why Starshine takes pains to avoid his presence.

She chains her bike down the block and attempts to sneak past Bone at a brisk pace. The Dominican Jesus freak and his pregnant sister-in-law are lounging on the stoop, sharing segments of a diced mango, jabbering away in Spanish. The Jesus freak's name is actually Jesus. Jesus Echegaray. He works the Transit Authority night shift. She has given up saying hello to him. Sharshine's key is already in the lock when she can sense the super's gaze upon her, only one eye raised like a pirate, its intensity stronger than the shock of a taser.

"Three-J," Bone calls out.

The turnover is too rapid for the super to learn his tenants' names, even if they catch the fancy of Mr. Little Bone, so he relies upon apartment numbers. To Starshine, the bark of "3-J" is never good news. She stops dead in her tracks.

Bone levers himself out of his chair and approaches her slowly, measuring each step as though it were a precious spice. His gait heralds his power, his placidity. Bone has all of the time in the world.

"Bedsprings," he says.

"Excuse me?"

"Bedsprings," he repeats. "At night, you make this noise with the bedsprings. The neighbors complain."

Bone raises and lowers his hand, palm down, in an effort to mime the compression of bedsprings. His lips form a thin, dark gash. It is impossible to decipher his intentions: Is this a come-on? A warning? Starshine is fairly confident that it is not a joke. The one-armed super is decidedly above humor.

"I'm sorry," stammers Starshine. "I'll be more careful."

"You'll be more careful," agrees Bone. "The neighbors complain."

Starshine is too uncomfortable with the subject, with the super, to pursue the matter further. But it makes her blood boil. Here these people are operating an illegal poultry farm outside her windows, papering the second floor landing with posters of their so-called savior and the Virgin Mary, discarding their cigarette butts and fast-food wrapping on the stoop, not to mention overpopulating the world with excess children, cramping them all together in a railroad flat with at least two pit bulls and God knows how many flea-infested cats and a deranged brother-in-law who proselytizes door-to-door, and they have the nerve to complain that she has an occasional houseguest. It really is too much to stomach.

"I'll take care of it," Starshine promises. "I didn't realize they could hear us."

"Good," says Bone. "We go up and see."

Arguing would serve no purpose. Bone has done this before, has invited himself into her apartment on one pretext or another, although none as compromising as this one, but the visits are short in duration, more like inspections than social calls, so Starshine has learned to acquiesce to the course of least resistance. After the super's first visit, an examination of the bathroom grouting in response to a flood on the second floor, Starshine made the mistake of complaining to the management company. A midlevel agent humored her for twenty minutes. Her hot water supply vanished mysteriously for three consecutive days. Although she could substantiate nothing—afterward she couldn't even document the loss of hot water—Starshine learned her lesson. She is an at-will sojourner in the kingdom of Bone.

The super leads her into the dimly lit vestibule.

"You pick up your mail," he says. "I wait."

"What?"

"You did not pick up your mail yesterday. I wait while you pick it up."

Bone folds his arm under the pit of his stump. Starshine, tears of frustration pooling behind her eyes, fumbles for her mailbox key. She feels violated, torn to shreds. It couldn't be any worse if Bone mounted her forcibly to test the decibel level of the bedsprings. How can the asshole possibly know whether or not she has collected yesterday's mail? But he does, damn it. She hastily retrieves her allotment of correspondence, mostly bills and late notices, and stuffs the assortment of official-looking envelopes into the waistband of her pants. She will not humiliate herself any further by examining them in his presence.

They ascend the narrow staircase in tandem, navigating a graveyard of children's toys, the overhead bulb dancing on its wire, projecting their silhouettes against the warped plaster, consecrating the doll torsos and tanker trucks abandoned to the stairwells. The reaffirming strains of Edith Piaf's brassy voice float from Starshine's apartment. She knocks to give Eucalyptus fair warning. Her roommate replies with the rustle of clothes, the sticky patter of bare wet feet on hardwood. The door opens, first a crack, then all the way. Eucalyptus, her long black hair hidden under a lavender bath towel, stands at the threshold.

"He needs to examine the beds," explains Starshine. "The loonies downstairs complained."

"You mean he needs to examine *your* bed, darling," says Eucalyptus.

Bone follows Starshine into the apartment, peeking through each doorway as though on a realtor's tour. He pauses momentarily at the entrance to Eucalyptus's room, taking in the wall collage of celebrity obits and the cabinet of tchotchkes and the harpoon mounted over the rosewood bureau, then passes through the common room and, like a rodent drawn by a pheromone, sniffs the musty air before targeting Starshine's bed. Starshine does not follow him. Bone won't take anything, she knows, nor does she own anything worthy of pocketing, and she would like to have as little to do with this intrusion as possible. She retreats to the comfort of her wicker chair and sorts through the previous day's mail.

"Visa bill, jury summons, a friendly letter from our Community Board," she enumerates. "Here you go, honey. Personal correspondence from the Internal Revenue Service. For Eucalyptus Caroll. Shall I open it?"

"Go for it."

Eucalyptus is burnishing a fresh chunk of ivory with glass wool. Starshine tears open the envelope.

"Ode to joy! You're being audited. Do not pass go, do not collect two hundred dollars."

"You've got to be kidding."

"Read it and weep."

Starshine slides the letter down the tabletop and continues sorting. All of it—the bills, the overdue library notices, the increasingly threatening letters from the Selective Service Bureau erroneously reminding her that she is a male between the ages of eighteen and twenty-six and must register for the draft—will go down the trash chute. It isn't worth the hassle. She refuses to waste her precious waking moments arguing with vengeful computers. She's doing the best she can. What else can they expect? If her seventy-eight-dollar credit card payment is so damn important to them, they can send somebody over in person to discuss it. That would be civilized, decent. And she'd even brew coffee for their representative.

"Do we know a Peter Smythe?"

"No sale."

"Well, we've both been invited to his wedding."

"Are we going?"

"It's in Halifax, Nova Scotia."

"Guess not."

"Discard pile?"

"Isn't that always the way, darling?"

Eucalyptus crumples her audit notice into a ball and tosses it in the direction of the wastepaper basket. From the bedroom comes the high-pitched rhythm of Bone playing Sherlock Holmes. The beat grows faster, more frenzied, almost ecstatic, suggesting that the super is at his worst, warning Starshine that she will have to wash her sheets, but more unsettling because it exposes her to an outsider's perception of her own passion. Can she really be *that* loud? Has she developed an auditory immunity? It only makes sense that one's other senses are dulled in the heat of the moment, that the bedspring chorus, not to mention the symphony of mewing and moaning and expletives, must be pure torture to the sex-starved lunatic downstairs. But we all have our crosses to bear, don't we? At least Jesus Echegaray doesn't have a one-armed pervert doing something unimaginable on his bedspread.

A personal letter catches Starshine's attention. There is no stamp, no return address. The envelope is frayed, indicating that is has been squeezed through the narrow aperture in her postal box. Her curiosity has been piqued. She slides her finger gently under the flap. The stationer's card is written in a tight, distinctively female hand, garnished by a bouquet of printed roses.

"Take a look at this," says Starshine. "Any guesses?"

The message reads:

Dearest Starshine:

Please tell me you love me as I love you.

I can wait no longer.

You know who

Eucalyptus scans the note and groans. "That could be half of New York. But if I had to put my money somewhere, I'd go with that friend Larry of yours. He sounds like the type."

"Larry?" Starshine answers, forcing a laugh. "You overestimate him, honey. He'd never had the courage to do something like this. He's one of the puppy dogs. One of the wait-and-seers."

"You may be right, darling. Then again, you may be wrong. What's that they say about advice? It's what you ask for when you need somebody to confirm your opinion."

"It's a woman," says Starshine. "You can tell by the handwriting."

"Maybe his mother wrote it for him."

They share a laugh. There was a time when Starshine would have been alarmed by such a note, fresh off the bus from San Francisco with her post-teenage angst regarding stalkers and sex predators and all the deviants of the night who prey on young women in the big city, but life experience has taught her that the vast majority of men are stupid and harmless. Especially the sorts of men who leave notes in women's mailboxes, the types who can't distinguish love from lust, the ones who really believe she can solve their problems like some druggist's cure-all. The dangerous ones are the guys who don't give a damn, the ones who don't worry where their next fuck is coming from because they know they'll get it somehow, the ones who would batter the living shit out of the Larry Blooms of the world for a pair of sneakers. But why did Eucalyptus plant the idea in her head? Starshine attempts to conjure up Larry's handwriting, to feminize it, but her memory draws a blank. She never would have suspected Larry. He would have been the last human being on earth to cross her mind, but now that her thoughts have been rutted into a particular path, she can't imagine it being anybody else. Poor, poor fool. She'll have to say something at dinner.

Bone reemerges. His trousers are buttoned, his forehead free of sweat. Maybe she won't have to wash her sheets after all.

"Water bed," he says.

"What?"

"You get a water bed," he announced. "No more problems with bedsprings. No more neighbors complain."

"I'll take care of it," says Starshine. "I didn't realize it was that loud."

"I can get you a water bed. I'll bring it by tomorrow."

*A water bed?* She recalls that she once had a lover with a water bed, an ambulance driver, and every time they screwed she felt she'd been cast as Wendy in some obscene version of Peter Pan. Water beds leak. Water beds ooze. Water beds sway like pirate ships. Starshine needs an old-fashioned bed, a bed that bounces like a trampoline, that contracts and expands, that makes music like an accordion, like a set of bagpipes, a bed that isn't going to puncture at precisely the wrong moment and leave her high and dry. Water beds are for orthopedic patients, for undersexed tour guides. She's a four-poster kind of girl. But all of this would be lost on the one-armed super, determined as he is to take control of her sleeping arrangements, already having let himself out without so much as a good-bye, and now happily ensconced in his aluminum chair, so what the hell is she supposed to do? She'll deal with it later. Tomorrow. Tomorrow is far, far away.

"I'm going to fight it out with the bankers," she says. "Wish me luck."

"You don't need luck. You need a tight-fitting skirt."

She will not wear a tight-fitting skirt, of course—she does not even own one. But tight-fitting, acid-washed jeans seem a reasonable tactic to disarm a credit officer. After she changes, she admires herself in the bathroom mirror. If she were a banker, she thinks, she'd give herself the keys to the vault.

Starshine looks up the address of her credit union in the phone directory. She pulls the apartment door shut behind her, takes a deep breath and kicks a dolmen of multicolored toy blocks down the stairs. They ricochet into the abyss. Good riddance to bad rubbish! She won't have misguided children constructing makeshift altars, at least not on her landing, because then they grow up into the sorts of men who make their landlords equip the neighbors with water beds. It is all part of the same pandemic, the original sin behind her impending fight with the credit union and her aunt's deterioration and all the men who keep picking and poking at her. The cycle must be broken. Starshine mounts her Higgins and coasts toward Long Island City; she has already passed the towers of the Queensboro Bridge and eclipsed Roosevelt Island when she realizes that she's left her financial dossier on the kitchen table.

No matter, she thinks. These things happen.

They'll deal. It is their problem, not hers.

# MAIDEN LANE

There is no more fitting place to meet Ziggy Borasch than at the deluxe McDonalds.

The upscale burger joint stands at the intersection of Broadway and Maiden Lane, a sentinel at the northern tier of the Financial District, catering to the divergent needs of Wall Street's harried financiers and the enclave of working-class immigrants who have commandeered the tenements south of City Hall. A tuxedo-clad doorman welcomes customers into a stately glass-and-wood dining hall where the lighting is incandescent, the plants aren't synthetic, and the background music rolls off the keys of a baby-grand piano. Even the cutlery, no longer silver on account of the security risk, is made of stainless steel. In a world of fast food, which so often is neither, the snappy counter staff serves up double cappuccinos and gourmet pastries imported from an East Side bakery. It is hard to believe that, excepting the napoleons and éclairs, this ambience operates in the service of an orthodox Golden Arches menu, Big Macs and Happy Meals and assembly-line hash browns, that the napkins and ketchup packets are still tightly rationed, dispensed only upon request by aproned Latino women earning seven dollars and fifteen cents an hour, but there are limits to the corporate board's benevolence, even in New York City, even at their international headquarters, which is why Larry thinks of the Maiden Lane McDonalds as so much whitewash on the Aunt Polly's fence that is American capitalism. The luxury is an illusion, the restaurant a modern-day Theresienstadt. And yet the food does seem to taste better, the beef more tender, the sausages leaner, as though it is the vinyl booths and rough wallpaper, not something inherent to the freeze-dried cattle loins, which account for the numbing uniformity of the standard franchise fare. Our senses, after all, are slaves to expectation. The king's broth curdles in the mendicant's cup, while beggars' scraps become pheasant and venison on the platters of royalty. It is true of food. It is also true of people. Yet somehow, among all the chameleons and pretenders who vie for Larry's veneration, it is most true of Ziggy Borasch.

To many, particularly the entrenched stewards of the academy, Borasch is a crackpot. He has steered his ship of independent scholarship so far from the narrow, demarcated channels of ordered intellectual liberty that no rescue party dares tow him back to shore. He is a renegade, a buccaneer. His first published book—an historical novel in which an aging Harvard history professor exposes the American Civil War as an elaborate hoax—will surely be his last. Now pushing fifty, unmarried, untenured, surviving on the modest legacy of an entrepreneurial grandfather, which enables him to rent an efficiency apartment in the Park Slope section of Brooklyn and to stock his hard-cover library, but not much more, Borasch devotes his days to two equally elusive, some might even say quixotic, pursuits: He is writing a multi-volume treatise on the nature and implications of coincidence, and he is struggling, so far without success, to produce the Great American Sentence. When Larry spies his mentor in the nook behind the piano, Borasch has already finished his meal of chocolate chip cookies and Coke and is scribbling in a cloth-bound notebook, one of several strewn over the tabletop, his distended blue veins bulging at the temples. Borasch's long gray hair is tied back in a ponytail. His hands shake with a Parkinsonian tremor. Flesh pockets like canvas sacks sag under his glassy eyes. An interstate roadhouse might color him a derelict; Maiden Lane casts him as an eccentric, a sage.

Larry orders a combination breakfast and slides into the seat across from Borasch. The pianist, all hands and teeth, croons the

Everly Brothers' *Bye Bye, Love*. He arches his back as he plays. His voice is somber, but undistinguished. Borasch, still scribbling, holds up his hand to keep his guest at bay. Several minutes pass before he has recorded his full train of thought.

"Sorry about that," he finally says. "I thought I had something."

"Any progress?"

"None whatsoever. Except that I've discarded another possibility. Who said that genius is the dross of the process of elimination?"

"Sounds like Edison."

"That's the problem. I've read too many books of quotable quotations. Everything these days is starting to sound like Edison. Tell me the truth, man, you don't think I'm nuts, do you? I had a conversation with my sister-in-law last night and she made me out to be certifiably stark-raving bonkers. It kind of shook me up."

"Don't you always say there's a fine line between genius and madness?" Larry answers, choosing his words carefully. "What about Nietzsche? And Immanuel Kant? Most great thinkers go unappreciated in their own lifetimes. Are you a bit idiosyncratic? Certainly. But crazy? Don't let it get to you. What in God's name does your sister-in-law know about genius?"

"The half-wit holds a MacArthur fellowship," says Borasch. "But I take your point. I like to think of myself as functionally insane, you know, but sometimes I get to thinking that maybe she has it right, that maybe everybody else has it right, and I really am mad as a hatter. Can you reassure me one more time? You don't really think I'm nuts?"

"Not at all."

Larry's gaze wanders over the rows of indecipherable squiggles in Borasch's open notebook and he wonders precisely what he should think about the state of his guru's mental health. He's spent so many years reassuring his former colleague since the strike-shortened semester when they shared an office as adjuncts at Jefferson Community College, in the dark age when Larry still believed that flair at the lectern might lead to conquest in the bedroom and Borasch laundered his clothing regularly, that it's difficult to cast off the cloak of the loyal disciple and form an objective opinion. Larry knows Borasch's search for the Great American Sentence is pointless, an intellectual cul-de-sac. It is the final refuge of an obsessive-compulsive perfectionist who has abandoned one too many Great American Novels and Great American Short Stories. The fate of the treatise on coincidence is less certain. Larry attempted to read several early chapters, mostly pages of logic symbols and Greek letters scrawled in longhand, and the material proved to be as dense, as thoroughly abstruse, as *Principia Mathematica* or *Finnegan's Wake,* maybe more so, so while there is no saying that Ziggy Borasch isn't a latter-day Bertrand Russell, deep down Larry suspects that *Fate, Fluke & Happenstance* is more style than substance.

Borasch examines Larry with his appraiser's eyes, seemingly searching for his own sanity in his companion's reassuring smile. But even Borasch must know that he doesn't have whatever it takes to write a revolutionary book; his only hope is to maintain the illusion that his meditations will alter the course of Western Civilization, for his own ego, for the expectations of others, until it no longer matters. Is that insanity? Quite possibly. And yet Larry would probably act no differently under like circumstances. Ziggy Borasch has done Larry so many good turns over the years, touting his abilities to an acquaintance at Empire Tours, referring him to his former agent at Stroop & Stone, that Larry feels obliged to perpetuate his mentor's delusions, to revere the man into his dotage. We all have our hours of need; some just last longer than others.

An unlikely couple occupies the table opposite: The man, although suffocating under a three-piece suit like an armored knight, is archetypically handsome. He boasts defined cheekbones and high temples, a sharp nose and a cleft chin, his strong but studious features converging on some mid-century standard of beauty. His is Anglo-Saxon perfection, Cary Grant and Gregory Peck and Henry Fonda rolled into one. The woman, no less stunning, flaunts a decidedly less-refined appeal. Her leather skirt cuts off at mid-thigh and the color of her aureoles is visible through her sheer cotton top. The two are bickering in hushed tones. The woman's eyes are red and swollen. Larry suppresses the urge to lash out at them, to tell them how spoiled they are, to remind them of all they have to be thankful for. He'd give anything to kill his morning break with a girl like that. Anything. But his lot is to play court jester to Ziggy Borasch. It is all so fucking unfair.

Borasch reaches for Larry's cup and takes a sip of his coffee. His hands tremble in seismic jolts. "I can't drink this glue with milk," he says, scowling. "Anyway, do you want to hear my latest failure?"

"Go ahead."

Borasch flips through the pages of his notebook. The piano melds the final chords of *Build Me Up, Buttercup* into *Hey Jude.*

"'Some people peel like an apple, down to a solid core,'" reads Borasch, "while others peel like an onion, losing layer upon layer until nothing remains.' Passable, don't you think? There's something distinctively American in that. I feel like I'm getting closer and closer by day."

"I like it," Larry agrees. "It has potential. On another subject, we had a minor calamity this morning at Grant's Tomb. A food fight, if you can believe it."

"I can believe anything. Or almost anything. The only thing that I have trouble believing, man, is the pandemic ignorance of humanity. It never ceases to amaze me. Try this on for size. I was at the movies yesterday, maybe the day before, and on the way out this absolute cretin is raving to his girlfriend about how the license plate of the get-away car in the flick is the same as his childhood phone number. The first two letters even match the old exchange code. 'What a coincidence!' he keeps saying. 'What a coincidence!' And all the time he's grinning like he just hit the mother lode. Like he's won the lottery or the Cold War. So I walk up to him, as calm as I can manage, to set him straight. I politely remind him of all the other movies he's seen in his lifetime, hundreds, thousands for all I know, in which the license plate *didn't* match anything at all. And then I point out all the numbers that *this* license plate didn't match his social security number, his mother's birthday, his own goddammed license plate. And you do know what the guy does? Right there in the middle of the Movieplex? He spits on my shoe."

Larry stretches to glance surreptitiously at his watch. He still has an hour before the Dutch contingent returns from their trip to Liberty Island, but he isn't in the mood for one of Borasch's tirades. He'd like to talk about Stroop & Stone, about Starshine, about the drowning girl, but he knows that Borasch's own agenda, as always, will take precedence. Larry is preparing to excuse himself when he catches sight of the handsome man struggling with his date. The woman, for some reason or another, has taken hold of the man's wallet and he is squeezing her wrist, bending her slender arm back at the elbow, in an attempt to break the grip. The woman's eyes have contracted into narrow slits. Her words are drowned out by Borasch's soap-boxing, by the speciously optimistic chorus of *Leaving on a Jet Plane* playing in the background, but Larry understands, without hearing, that she is pleading against her inevitable extinction. Maybe she is a girlfriend; more likely she is a mistress, an expendable part of uber-WASP's harem, his flock of willing females that at least partially explains Larry's own romantic difficulties. Distributed equally, there are enough pretty women to go around. But who wants to share the wealth? Would Larry, if the tables were turned? He watches the woman's arm slowly folding against itself, willpower fighting against tendon, love battling bone, knowing that in this case biology has pre-determined the outcome. Intervention would prove futile. Some situations invite rescue, a girl drowning in the bay, a naked waif on a window ledge, the victim offering herself to the highest bidder, but other traumas are personal affairs, cataclysms restricted to a private membership, and Larry recognizes that this is one of the latter. His intrusion might temporarily salvage their relationship, offer them the respite of an outside threat. It will gain him nothing.

Borasch is reading aloud from one of his notebooks, his tongue tripping over his own penmanship. The pianist is flourishing his way through pop hits and Golden Oldies, tunes to make you forget your diet and your purse strings, music telling you that you were young once, that you are happy, that there is no real danger in a McFlurry and a packaged apple pie. Or, if you are alone, reminding you of the teenage love that has passed you by. Serenading you to tears. The woman's grasp breaks without warning and the man's wallet falls to the floor in the aisle, skidding to within inches of Larry's left foot, sealing the couple's fate. The man retrieves it. He counts his bills, slams a portion of his accumulated capital on the tabletop, the ultimate souvenir of vengeance and spite, then storms out of the restaurant before his companion can shred the offering. He is gone. She is crying. There is no longer any need for display, for dignity, so she counts the money and stuffs it into her handbag. Then she sits in solitude, stirring her lost lover's coffee with a wooden swizzle stick, joining Larry Bloom in the world of the forsaken. But her stay is transitory. His may be permanent. He is down to his last, best hope.

The music rivets him suddenly. Unexpectedly.

"Listen!" shouts Larry.

Borasch peers over his notebook in irritation and alarm.

"Do you hear that music, Borasch? Do you know what that means?"

"What's gotten into you, man?"

"Nothing," Larry apologizes. "I'm sorry. I didn't mean to interrupt."

Borasch, placated, returns to his monotonous drone, but his audience is off the radar screen. Larry's ears are elsewhere. His fingers tap to the music. Hope does somersaults in his soul. And all around him, like a messianic reveille in the land of the dead, cascades the glorious, triumphant sound of the pianist covering Strawberry Alarm Clock, crooning the most exquisite phrase in the repertoire of Western song. "Good Morning, Starshine."

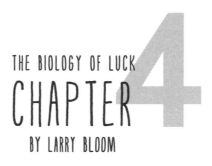

THE BIOLOGY OF LUCK

# CHAPTER 4

BY LARRY BLOOM

Starshine leans against her Higgins in front of the Dolphin Credit Union and scans the street for inspiration, for anyone or anything capable of driving a distressed damsel to tears, but the languid warehouses and wheezing factories of Long Island City offer little to provoke emotion. Yet emotion—and specifically, sorrow—is what the occasion demands.

She has been around the block enough times to understand the rules of the game: the practiced comptrollers of the credit union are too unfeeling, too meticulous, to confront without the benefit of a young girl's desperation. Either she overcomes her good cheer and strides through the revolving doors as a spool of nerves, fit to unravel at the least provocation, so helpless and hopeless that even the hardest of hearts will melt at her first sob, or her presence must inevitably arouse another instinct, that natural urge of street-corner loan sharks, and then her mission is doomed. Why in God's name hadn't she opened an account at a real bank like Aunt Agatha had advised? What made her think that a rag-tag army of graying swamp rats and over-the-hill tree-spikers could handle money responsibly? And yet the environmental credit union had seemed like such a good idea when she signed up, a safe, progressive alternative to the corporate megabanks with their monthly fees and minimum balances. It was the choice between saving endangered sea mammals every time she wrote a check or earning a free toaster oven if she ever took out a mortgage. How was she to know that this five-and-dime Politburo would abscond with her fruit basket fund?

Starshine sifts through her childhood, searching for tears. Her thoughts pan across past distress and anguish, first loves and last rites, delving for the enchanted moment that will send her over the brink. There are the dead: Her father at the steering wheel of the family Chevrolet, idling in the parking lot of the local strip mall, unloading a handgun into the depths of his throat; her mother, ten years younger than Lou Gehrig, gradually petrified to stone; her Uncle Luther, tight-lipped and bitter in an open casket; the bike messenger, Jim Bratton, hazel eyes plastered with shock; a dog, a brindled Boston terrier, laid to rest among her aunt's forsythias. There are the soon-to-be dead: Aunt Agatha, rasping through a slit in her larynx; the cancer, metastasized, gnawing at Jack Bascomb's liver and nodes; Colby Parker's father, so quick with his hands, laboring toward his third heart attack. And then there are the inevitably dying: Bone, the one-armed super, mangled beneath a water bed on the second-story stairwell; her boss at the Children's Fund, Marsha Riley, finally strangled by one of her countless foster grandsons; even Eucalyptus, dear Eucalyptus, asphyxiating on a fine carving of elephant tusk. Starshine flips through a scrapbook of grief and lament, assembling the mourners, chanting the requiem, casting the soil, but her eyes remain dry. All that misery, all that suffering has been wasted. Sorrow heeds no beck and call.

Yet without tears, Starshine knows the prospect of procuring her forty-five dollars is hopeless. Beloved Aunt Agatha will pass away without her apricots and tangerines. She abhors this thought, almost preferring her own demise to what must unavoidably be a strained, draining hour beside the confused elderly woman, while dreams of sugar-plums dance in the poor soul's addled head. It is all so unjust! So cruel! Dammit, she'd rather be dead herself!

That's all it takes. Her own funeral rises before her like a prophetic vision. She sees her corpse at repose on purple velvet; white lilies envelop the casket; gardenias and forget-me-nots wreath her hair. Eucalyptus, her eyes swollen, folds Starshine's waxen hands around a miniature engraving of a trident-armed mermaid. Aunt Agatha, draped in black, sobs hoarsely through the perforation in her throat. Jack Bascomb and Colby Parker wrangle for the prerogative of first mourner and then embrace each other with the clemency of grief. They're all there, Bone, Marsha Riley, Larry Bloom, the Jesus freak counting his rosaries, the faces of her life paying tribute, their own lives shattered like so much cheap glassware. Even the Bishop of the Society for Secular Harmony, His Mystic Eminence, takes time out from his studies to eulogize her as an empyreal beacon on a sea of otherworldly darkness. The scene is so bleak, so alluring. The floodgates spring open and Starshine, fortified with the calamity of her own death and the facade of unparalleled woe, mounts the steps of the credit union in the highest of spirits.

The interior furnishings of the Dolphin Credit Union, despite the best intentions of the decorator, do not instill confidence: no more so in those customers seduced by ideology than in the smaller number attracted by geographic proximity or bargain rates. The spacious, sterile marble lobby might pass as a discount wing at the Museum of Natural History. Glass display cases and dioramas line the exterior walls, exhibiting badger skeletons and arrow heads, elucidating the hibernation cycles of birch mice and the courtship rituals of crayfish. A tin folding table, finished to resemble teak, offers customers propaganda from Greenpeace and the Committee to Save Long Island Sound, as well as a smattering of interloping flyers from Planned Parenthood of Queens and ACT-UP New York and the eight-page broadsheet of the local Communist cell. The banner above the reception desk announces: "Invest in a Sea Fund and Make a Dolphin Your Interest." But Starshine does not have a Sea Fund. She does not even have a pension plan. All she possesses—by her own reckoning—is a measly $420 tucked away in a checking account, three hundred of which are earmarked for next month's rent and another forty-five for Aunt Agatha's fruit basket, so she passes under the green-and-white standard feeling like a fourth-class citizen in the world of third-rate finance. "Living for Today" and "Saving for Retirement" are mutually incompatible objectives. She has embraced the former. The stubby, thickset young agent who escorts her to his windowless office has clearly chosen the latter.

Her credit representative's name, according to a white-on-black plastic placard, is Hannibal Tuck. His office is really nothing more than a sparsely furnished freestanding cubicle located toward the rear of the lobby. While Starshine waits for the computer to process her name, she examines the personal effects that offer a peephole into Tuck's outside life: a gold wedding band; a framed photograph of two toddlers on the lap of a mousy young woman; a second, smaller photograph, tucked into the first, of the mousy young woman beside Tuck; a college badminton trophy; and a nautilus shell paperweight with an analog clock and a barometer embedded in its jade base. Although Hannibal Tuck will never lead elephants over mountain passes, probably never take any risk greater than waiting on the platform at Massapequa Station, he will surely never confront defeat. Not on the racquetball courts, not in the bedroom, and not in front of his computer screen. Of all the bankers on the face of the planet, Wall Street financiers and small-town Rotarians, cigar-smoking stuffed-shirts and flashy S and L swindlers, Warburgs and George Baileys, Starshine has landed upon the lender least likely to remit her forty-five dollars without the appropriate paperwork. He is a man who doesn't speak any of her languages.

"Now what can I do for you this morning, Miss Hart? Can I interest you in one of our special offers on a Sea Fund? For every thousand dollars you invest, Dolphin Credit is able to contribute ten dollars to deserving environmental causes. "

"It's about my account balance. There seems to be a mistake. "

"Well, we'll have to straighten matters out, Miss Hart," says Tuck. "Now what seems to be the problem?"

The agent leans forward in his swivel chair, clasping his hands together on his desk blotter, scrutinizing Starshine with patronizing indulgence. A dark stain discolors the cuff of his jacket sleeve, a vestige of his morning's coffee or the brand of an early corned beef lunch, and Starshine focuses all of her attention on this minute imperfection, Hannibal Tuck's tragic flaw, in the fleeting hope that it will prove fatal. She takes a deep, heavy breath and plunges headlong into the depths of panic.

"I'm supposed to buy a gourmet fruit basket for my dying aunt, Mr. Tuck," she says. "She's bedridden at a nursing home in Staten Island and she's blind as a bat and one of the only joys left to her is to be able to press fresh fruit against her cheeks. My problem is that a nice fruit basket, even a modest one, is going to run me forty-five dollars, minimum, and I've been keeping track of my spending so I'd have enough to buy one, but now it seems that there's been some sort of terrible mistake, and my account balance doesn't match the amount I thought I had in the account, and I need the rest of my money to pay next month's rent, so without that forty-five dollars, I'm going to have to choose between my aunt's dying wishes and having a roof over my head, and, oh God, I feel like I'm about to start crying. I'm so sorry. I'm really not at all like this."

"There, there, Miss Hart," Tuck answers. "I'm sure we can get to the bottom of this. Can I see your checkbook and your most recent statement?"

Starshine buries her face in her hands, sobs briefly, and composes herself. "That's the worst part of it, Mr. Tuck. I don't have them. I've looked everywhere for them and I can't imagine what happened to them unless my boyfriend took then with him when he walked out on me. I'm usually very responsible, and this is *so* embarrassing, and I really don't know what I'm going to do. Is there any way you can check if there's been some sort of computer glitch or something?"

Tuck swivels to the computer monitor. "I've pulled up your file. According to our records, Miss Hart, you have a balance of $475.19. You're telling me that you believe that forty-five dollars have been inadvertently deducted from your account, is that right?"

Starshine nods and helps herself to a Kleenex. She is suddenly thankful that she left her financial dossier at home because her statement balance matches the one from the screwy computer and the entries in her checkbook are so cryptic and haphazard that even she often has a difficult time deciphering them. Her records would only serve to impugn her credibility. The best opportunity lies in feigning hysteria and hoping that even as staunch a bureaucrat as Hannibal Tuck will let this one slide. Just this once. After all, the credit union must control millions of dollars in assets and she's asking for only a piddling forty-five. They'll forgo forty-five dollars to retain a loyal customer, won't they? It's good business sense.

"I'm sorry, Miss Hart," says Tuck, "But without your records, I'm not sure there's anything that I can do for you. And quite honestly, even if you did have your statement and your checkbook, I doubt it would make a difference. Our records are highly accurate. I can tell you which of your checks have cleared, if that will help. "

"You don't understand, Mr. Tuck. I need that forty-five dollars or I can't buy my aunt a fruit basket. I can't fulfill the dying wish of the woman who raised me. I know this isn't your fault—you seem like such a kind man and I'm sure someone will catch the mistake in a few days—but what am I supposed to do in the meantime? Can't you credit my account now, and when the error turns up, we'll be even?"

"I can't do that, Miss Hart," says the agent. "As much as I'd like to. I'm sure you understand. I'll be happy to print you out your balance sheet for you. It's a small amount of money. If there is a mistake, and although it is highly unlikely, I am not ruling out the possibility, I'm confident we'll clear it up soon enough. That's the best we can offer. "

Now Starshine's tears are genuine. Years of experience have taught her that any man, no matter how callous, no matter how straitlaced, will capitulate to her unremitting whimpers. She's wept her way out of traffic tickets, into rock concerts, through dozens of cab fares. Once she even sobbed a two-hundred-dollar dental bill in half. Men *always* grant carte blanche to doe eyes and bursts of anxiety. Always. So what's gone wrong? Has she grown too old to play the helpless female? Have desperate women hoodwinked Tuck one too many times before? Do the reasons really matter? Starshine makes an effort to collect herself. The moan of a distant siren resonates through the lobby, magnifying the otherwise antiseptic silence of the credit union, warning Starshine that she ought to make a graceful exit. Her eyes plead with Turk, imploring, beseeching, but it is no use. His loyalties lie with the mousy girl in the photograph. With the two toddlers dressed in matching red frocks. It strikes Starshine suddenly, for a split second, that Hannibal Tuck is truly an upstanding individual, a divine human being, maybe the only man she has ever met who is so devoted to his homely wife and tedious job that even her tears will not move him, that he will never yield to temptation, but then she thinks of Aunt Agatha, of the old woman's disappointment, of her scorn, and Starshine wants the mousy creature's head on a platter. She is bawling again. Why is life so goddamn complicated?

Tuck is about to speak, probably to suggest that her visit is winding down, that she'd best sing her swan song and depart, when an equally stubby, thickset young man, distinguishable from Tuck only by his thick-rimmed glasses and a pronounced mole on his upper lip, pokes his head into the office. "Sorry to disturb you while you're with a customer, Tuck, but you really have to see what's going on across the street. It's a once in a lifetime. "

"Please, Bill," her representative answers—but his doppelganger has already vanished.

Tuck apologizes profusely and excuses himself. Starshine trails him through the lobby, suddenly alive with dozens of Tuck-like men and even a few Tuck-like women, garnished with brooches and frosted highlights, all emerging from hidden doorways and freestanding cubicles like marmots surfacing from a burrow. Beyond the panoramic windows of the credit union, she sees the collage of emergency vehicles and official uniforms, the synthetic navy of police officers, the all-weather yellow of the fire department, the pristine white of the medical service. She hurries through the revolving doors. On the other side, the sirens have gone suddenly mute and, in their wake, an ominous silence has descended upon the street—the haunting stillness of shipwrecks and combat lulls—as though the eye of a category-five hurricane had momentarily settled above the decaying infrastructure of

Long Island City. Starshine follows the heads of the crowd, inspecting the upper stories of an adjacent building, the boarded-up windows, the potted geraniums on curtained sills, the vertical banner advertising discount meats, before the curiosity suddenly registers, the once-in-a-lifetime, the spectacle to end all spectacles, the image that embodies every man's wildest fantasies and every woman's deepest terror. It is the gender gap, the glass ceiling, the war between the sexes. It is human sexuality and the impenetrable divide laid bare. It is a stunning young woman performing a public striptease.

The girl is perched on the fifth story ledge of a residential building, already topless, her pallid skin cutting a sharp contrast with the exposed red brick. Two of New York's bravest have scaled a nearby fire escape, but dare not advance any further. Their all-weather suits are no match for the half-naked waif as she removes her purple skirt and waves it at the crowd like a matador taunting a bull. One of the firefighters extends his hand through the rusted bars of the fire escape, and from the sidewalk it is impossible to tell whether he is reaching for the girl or the garment. Starshine backs into the granite pilasters of the credit union, wincing with each step in the girl's macabre dance, longing for the ordeal to conclude, for the girl to inch back to safety. That is the only possible finale, she promises herself. There is no other way. For Starshine loves the girl on the ledge, viscerally, impulsively, feels more for this nameless stranger than she will ever feel for Jack Bascomb or Colby Parker or even for her cherished Aunt Agatha. It is the devotion of a starling sheltering her brood, a lioness defending her cubs. Starshine loves the girl for all the reasons people love one another, for her beauty, for her vulnerability, for her own desire to protect that which is beautiful and vulnerable, but primarily because she sees herself mirrored in another human being, a girl not too much closer to the edge than she is, everyday, a girl who could easily be her. The men on the street see only an individual tragedy, private pain exposed as public psychosis. They sympathize. They pity. But they do not understand. Only the women, the stunning young girls and the faded beauties who have not yet forgotten the pressures of being a stunning young girl, can fully comprehend the stress, the urgency, the unwanted advances, the persistent picking and pulling, the sheer madness of it all, that magnets every potential Helen toward the parapets of Troy, and that sometimes, on desperate days like today, drives women like Starshine Hart to run stark naked into the open streets. It is the path of least resistance.

The girl on the ledge has broken free of the madness. She advances inch by inch, her bare toes resting on the lip of death, and lets the skirt fall lifeless into the crowd. Then she raises one leg, her weight shifting forward, her entire frame tottering like a diver aborting a plunge, before she slips back onto the ledge, maybe intentionally, maybe inadvertently, where she folds her arms across her bare chest and shivers violently. Her fans murmur in relief, in disappointment. While the men in yellow escort the quaking girl though an open window and into her prison of prosaic madness, the spectators filter back to their berths and cubicles, giddy, soothed, yet alive with the disquiet of unfulfilled promise. The ordeal is now an anecdote to share with their mousy young wives, their colleagues on sick leave, the like-minded couples with whom they share tables at college reunions. It is an artifact, a negotiable commodity, to be bartered for tales of subway gunmen and celebrity sightings and hearsay about the latest scandal at Gracie Mansion. It is something to discuss while eyeing the centerpieces at weddings. It is another New York story and nothing more.

"Miss Hart!"

Starshine has unlocked her bicycle and walked it as far as the corner when Tuck, jostling his way through the throng, finally overtakes her. He plants his stocky form on the sidewalk in front of her, at a safe distance, his eyes downcast, and shoves his hand uncomfortably into his pocket. Starshine fears that she has committed some unpardonable transgression, that she has accidentally walked off with the banker's cufflinks or umbrella. He is a dangerous man, this Tuck. He will push her further toward the edge. But no! Is it possible? Super-agent Tuck, the curate of red tape, has reached into his wallet and forced three twenty dollar bills into Starshine's hand. His own money, not the credit union's. He stands at the intersection for another moment, waiting, expecting, the Don't Walk sign flashing above his head, then he mutters her name one more time, the words "Miss Hart" stumbling over his tongue, and he steps past her into the crowd. The entire exchange takes less than fifteen seconds.

Starshine counts her sixty dollars and grins. She has not yet lost her magic.

# THE BATTERY

Larry bids farewell to Ziggy Borasch and ambles along Broadway at the height of good cheer. He flirts with the eight Athenian maidens perched above the vaulted doors of the Bank of Tokyo, stares down the gargoyles guarding the approach to the Trinity Building, lets himself drift into the current of pedestrian traffic. The streets are a sea of herringbone suits and Harris tweeds, cordovan shoes and double-pleated slacks. Bicycle messengers navigate the throng, whistling, cursing, risking life and limb, speeding their enigmatic missives and secured parcels from the Stock Exchange to the Reserve Bank. Droves of office boys and secretaries on summer hours picnic on the Trinity churchyard, laughing, bantering, discarding plastic forks and aluminum tins before Alexander Hamilton's faded headstone. Red-eyed analysts swagger in the resplendence of their pinstripes. Everywhere surges the exhilaration of late morning, the scramble, the blitz, the frenetic maelstrom of unfilled orders and unfilled promises, the hailing of taxis, the quoting of prices, the leveraging of empires and the placement of lunch reservations and the determined trampling of the morning's ticker-tape that precedes the great tsunami, noon, when for a fleeting instant the city takes stock of itself, cataloging what has been accomplished and what may still be accomplished. Possibility is ubiquitous. Although Larry has walked down this very stretch of Broadway every Wednesday for three years, past the Smithsonian annex and onto the bowling green, this morning he feels he is experiencing mankind for the first time, living the pulse, sensing the throb, taking in the sublime grandeur of the city's beat. The pianist's forecast of "Good morning, Starshine," echoes in his ears.

Battery Park resonates with lust as the sun approaches its zenith. A primal impulse takes hold of the young couples strolling the gravel walkways, the newlyweds who have paused to admire DiModica's bronze bull, the truant teens laid out on the cool grass. Maybe because all flesh tantalizes in the early summer, in the right light, or most likely because, at this time of year, there is more flesh exposed, midriffs, cleavage, inner thighs, the park is suddenly transformed into a dynamo of panting and groping. This desire is not the tender affection of evening, the wistful intimacy of the twilight's last gleam. It is raw, concupiscent hunger. It devours decorum, banishes shame and flouts the loftiest ambitions of the penal code—and still thrives, unappeased. It is also an unwitting slap in the face to those deprived, those shackled by time and refinement, those deficient in the desire, in the performance, those too old, those too far away, those bereft, those who for one reason or another, clinical frigidity or clerical vow, but most often lack of opportunity, do not have a playmate to fondle among strangers. It is the hollow one feels in one's gut, like the aftermath of a submarine colliding with a depth charge, when one spies a handsome, carefree young man with his palms cupping the breasts of a stunning teenage beauty, shamelessly groping her on a picnic blanket only yards from the pedestrian walkways, and knowing that one will never again have a chance to be him. It is the reason that, on an ordinary June morning, Larry avoids the park.

Today is different. Striding across the shaded lawns at an invigorating pace, ignoring the Hope Garden and the Verrazano Monument and even the pubescent sweethearts dry-humping behind the Korean War Memorial, Larry stops at the base of the Walt Whitman statue to offer his gratitude. How many cold winter mornings has he stood on these very flagstones, the park moribund and barren, staring through the miasma of his known breath, invoking inspiration from the Bard of Brooklyn? How many evenings has he passed before the word processor in his study, eyes numb, forearms aching, spirit bankrupt, thinking of Whitman laying bricks in the torrid summer heat to bankroll his first edition of *Leaves of Grass*? Larry recognizes that he has embraced the wrong idol. Whitman had his devils, yes, but as different from Larry's own as the scorch of fire from the burn of ice. Whitman had beauty, presence, grace; his agony lay elsewhere. Melville is Larry's proper graven image. Nearsighted, homely, infirm Melville, the patron saint of the underappreciated, scribbling away at his custom house desk through indigence, through ignominy, through the premature loss of his sons, denied both acclaim in life and eulogy in death. Larry knows that his altar should be Melville's birthplace on State Street. And yet somehow he feels no kinship, no solidarity, with the Shakespeare of the Sea. Maybe Whitman is his star because Starshine is his subject, because she embodies all the spirit and splendor and sensual abandon that the Herman Melvilles and Larry Blooms of the world can only hope to experience vicariously. For Starshine is a Whitman poem, a blooming lilac, the body electric. Gazing up into the hero's larger-than-life tribute, the maestro's marble features beaming perpetually over a polished beard, Larry wonders if he has done justice to both master and model. He is certain he has. Other men expend their vitality in the act of living; he has consigned his ardor to the printed page.

Larry realizes that he is no longer alone in his contemplation. A young woman has joined him on the flagstone concourse before the Whitman statue. She is tall, pale, flat chested. Her hair has the texture of cord. Although her features are delicate, if a bit too narrow, her sober expression and awkward bearing undermine nature's limited gifts. Even her attire—a dull floral-print dress—strives toward the unattractive. Larry notices the woman is sizing him up, deciding whether he passes muster, participating in the same ritual of abortive courtship, the scoping out of total strangers in public places, women riding subway cars and waiting in airport terminals and filling out informed consent forms at the dentist's office, a pantomime of mating that always ends in the same place, absolutely nowhere, when he notices the final defect that solidifies his intentions: under one arm, on this glorious summer morning, the woman is carrying a folded umbrella. He does not know why, of all things, the umbrella is decisive. But it is. His fellow Whitman admirer is not for him. She has been pigeonholed among the unattractive, banished beyond the pale. Larry retreats to the far edge of the concourse, careful to keep his eyes on the statue, hoping that his companion will judge him similarly and depart. There are no bedfellows, no kindred spirits, among the ugly.

The woman holds her ground. Although his gaze is focused on the statue, he senses that she is staring at him. He catches her approaching in his peripheral vision and notes that her manner exudes all the joie de vivre of a pallbearer hauling a casket. She stands beside him for a full twenty seconds before speaking.

"Do you enjoy Whitman?" she asks.

"Me?"

"I don't care for him myself. All that bunk about daffodils and the scent of wheat and celestial orbs rising and whatnot. I never understood it. That's not part of my shtick. I need something meaty, something epic. I'd trade ten Whitmans for one Tennyson any day. But I'm only saying that, you know. I'm not actually sure if I mean it. It's all part of my persona. Tennyson seems to dovetail with the umbrella. "

Larry has inched backwards during the course of the woman's onslaught, struggling to expand the personal space between them, but she has inched forward simultaneously. He has no facility with strangers, and they must sense this, for they ordinarily pass him by. He often wishes it were otherwise. But now, confronted with this peculiar young woman who values poets like trading cards and off-handedly subverts her own opinions, he longs to return to the evil that he knows. What can this aggressive creature think he has to offer her? What has he done to solicit her attentions? Is it possible that, fortified with a book deal and Starshine's potential love, he is emitting some previously untapped pheromone, some pent-up aphrodisiac, which will magnet lonely eccentrics in civic plazas. In the future, he will have to be more careful.

"I'm scaring you off, aren't I?" asks the woman. "It's this over-the-top, in your face thing. But don't worry. I'm really not like this at all. I'm quite reserved, almost pathologically shy. This is my way of overcompensating. "

"Okay," says Larry.

"By the way, we haven't been properly introduced. I'm Rita Blatt. The reporter from the *Downtown Rag*. Please say they told you I was coming. "

"I'm confused."

"I knew this was going to happen," Rita says. "I just knew it. The right fist never knows who the left hook is punching, if you know what I mean. I'm a reporter for the *Downtown Rag*, the city's only free weekly dedicated entirely to the offbeat—I'm sure you've picked up a copy in a pizza shop or something and thrown it away—and I'm supposed to be doing a story on a group of Dutch tourists coming back to New York to discover the city's roots. They should have warned you. Whatever. Anyway, I was going to meet you at Castle Clinton, but one of the park rangers said I had at least an hour's wait before you returned from the Statue of Liberty, so I thought I'd kill some time in the park and, what do you know, I end up running into the very person I'm looking for. Small city, isn't it?"

"Let me get this straight. You're a reporter doing a piece on my tourists?"

"You're catching on, Larry Bloom. And you look just like your company photo, although I probably wouldn't have had the courage to speak to you if not for your name tag. I have an eye for detail, you know. Of course, if I really had an eye for detail, I'd be a foreign correspondent with the *New York Times* instead of a thirty-four-year-old stringer with a paper nobody reads, but that's neither here nor there. "

"Did Snipe sign off on this?"

"That name sounds right. But don't depend upon it. I'm dreadful with names. I did a feature last month on some tycoon philanthropist who set up a guns-for-furniture exchange. For every weapon you brought in, his company gave you a free patio set. The whole thing was preposterous, but it looked like it was going to work. These kids would come in with assault rifles and leave with chaise lounges. Nobody bothered to find out what a bunch of ghetto youth were doing with garden chairs. It turns out they were selling them on the West Side Highway. But the point is that the millionaire's name was Garfield Lloyd Parker and I accidentally called him Parker Lloyd Garfield throughout the article. Protestant names work like that, I suppose. But the old stuffed-shirt went through the roof! So I'm not really sure who I spoke to, but the important thing is that we found each other and I'm coming on your tour."

"I'll have to phone the office."

"As you wish. I was supposed to meet you up at Grant's Tomb, but I got tied up. Between you and me, I had a huge row with my boyfriend. I'm still somewhat riled up. You can tell, can't you?"

"I never would have guessed."

"I didn't miss anything, did I? Wasn't it just some sort of catered breakfast?"

"You didn't miss a thing."

"That's a relief," says Rita. "My first major assignment ever as a reporter was to cover the Tyson-Spinks boxing match. Do you remember it? The ninety-one-second knockout. Well, I got stuck in traffic and showed up just in time to cover the mass exodus of fans. I'm unlucky, that way. A regular Calamity Jane. So I'm relieved I didn't miss anything this morning. "

"Nothing important," says Larry. "Now if you'll excuse me, I'm on break. I'll meet you at the ticket kiosk in about twenty minutes. "

Larry turns on his heels and walks briskly in the direction of the old IR Control House. It amazes him that life never offers completely smooth sailing, even for one day, that just when the morning seems as flawless as the mountain sky, a sinister cloud manages to creep its way over the horizon. And, what makes life even more mysterious, what truly probes the depth and complexity of the psyche, is that on an overcast day that one cloud would pass entirely unnoticed. But he will not let Rita Blatt darken his afternoon. He will not even phone the office. There are too many other pleasures to absorb, the feathery feel of verdant spring air, the overhead sun sparkling off the opaque glass of skyscrapers, the promise of Starshine's caress only hours away. Larry settles onto a vacant park bench on the shaded side of the footpath and smiles at an elderly woman feeding bread crusts to the pigeons. She wears too much lipstick and her hair is hidden under a lime-green kerchief, but somehow, at the end of this magic morning, even she is beautiful. Even the image of Rita Blatt henpecking her boyfriend is beautiful. It is this sensation, this moment of omnipresent promise, that Larry has striven to capture in his prose.

He often asks himself why writers write, other writers, good-looking established luminaries who no longer have anything to prove, anything to gain, but sitting in Battery Park on a fair summer's day, he fully understands their motivation. They long to capture the ephemeral bliss of the fleeting moment, the sun's rays twinkling on the freshly cut grass. They yearn to trap the tapering gleam in an old woman's eyes, to preserve her faded beauty like a rose petal pressed under a book, to give future generations a particular midday stroll, a purple butterfly, a young mother pushing a perambulator beneath a blushing red maple. Larry reflects upon all of the dogged, driven men and women throughout the city, throughout time, composing in longhand, running quill over parchment, blotting ink, upon their obsession, upon their self-doubt, upon Whitman crossing the Brooklyn ferry, upon Melville harpooning in his musty rooming house, upon Ziggy Borasch struggling for one perfect sentence, upon Anne Frank in her garret and Gramsci in his cell, upon the blind Joyce and the blind Homer and Heller Keller before her desktop Remington, all mulish, all muddling, all fighting the dark phantoms of boredom and fatigue and isolation. And for what? An old woman, a butterfly, a flock of craven pigeons? Not that. Of course, not that. Not even for a girl named Starshine. They dream of something grander, something immutable, something to transcend their own hunger and want and sacrifice. They dream of immortality.

Larry senses that he will soon be among the immortals, that his name and Starshine's will forever be imprinted in the collective conscience of Western Civilization, vividly, indelibly, their names intertwined like so many lovers of yore. He reaches into his breast pocket for a cigarette, determined to prolong his reverie, to keep the Dutch waiting if necessary, when he recoils at the realization that somewhere, maybe on the plaza before the Whitman statue, maybe while placating Ziggy Borasch, most likely bare chested on the parapet, but possibly anywhere, absolutely anywhere in a city of nine thousand thoroughfares and eight million people, his everlasting glory has met an untimely death. Somewhere, anywhere, he has lost his letter from Stroop & Stone.

THE BIOLOGY OF LUCK

# CHAPTER 5

BY LARRY BLOOM

Floral shops are the last havens of masculinity.

The act of raising flowers, of trellising roses, of laying out begonia beds and watering window-box petunias, also the art of arrangement, of melting paraffin into silver vases, edging nosegays with paper frills, weaving wreaths and chaplets, fashioning corsages and sprays, transforming isolated clippings into breathtaking mosaics—all of these endeavors bespeak the feminine. But for the brief interval when Mother Nature's magical blossoms lie constrained in tepid water, packed together like refugees behind a merchant's counter, each flower bears the frown of subservience, the imprimatur of commerce, which defines it as a serf to the patrimony.

Starstine knows that truth about floral shops:  that they are more virile than smoke-filled conference rooms, more exclusive than the floors of the stock exchange, more macho than conventions of Hells Angels at interstate truck stops. They are American's answer to Victorian drawing rooms. For the purchase of cut flowers anticipates candlelit dinners, hospital stays, theatrical productions, memorial services, promotion banquets, share holders' meetings, honeymoons, hearses, hours in seedy motel rooms, days in probate court, the full retinue and regalia of things men orchestrate, men pay for, men rely upon, the things men crave when they send women anonymous love notes, as though each time a man buys a woman a bouquet, he experiences a minor orgasm. No glass ceiling, in Starshine's view, is as impregnable, as the rolling doors of the floral display cabinet. Maybe that is why she has grown to dread flowers.

She has been inside Blooming Grove on two prior occasions. Once, at the behest of her aunt, to purchase white lilies for her uncle's grave site; the other time, to plead with the Armenian proprietor to cease dispatching a dozen long-stemmed red roses every hour, on the hour. Both visits traumatized her. The lilies proved to be as scarce as the roses were abundant. If the florist seemed perturbed that a bouquet of mixed spring flowers, irises and daffodils, wouldn't substitute for the lilies, the prospect that anyone might turn down virgin roses at $62.50 a dozen, especially when they came in crystal vases nuzzled by asparagus ferns and hypericum clippings, turned out to be beyond his comprehension. He seemed to think that the clockwork delivery was part of some familial dispute, maybe even a legal matter. Her request yielded to his entrepreneurial instincts, to the fear that he might open himself up to breach of contract litigation. But if Starshine can take on the Dolphin Credit Union, she heartens herself, if she can establish her footing in the arena of high finance, then she can stand up to this Armenian peddler and buy her fruit basket. At least, she hopes she can.

The proprietor allows her little time to adjust to the steamy, pollen-rich air of the shop. He is stocky, bearded, his broad forearms jutting from rolled shirtsleeves, a pencil stub balanced above his ear. He is on the far side of forty, the near side of seventy; his craggy, sun-dried skin defies further precision. The man could easily pass as an extra from *Zorba the Greek*. Starshine is his only customer at midmorning. He saunters forward, wiping his palms on his chlorophyll-stained apron and then rubbing them together like an overzealous butcher at some dubious abattoir, sizing up his patron's limitations and possibly her market potential. Starshine steps backward at his advance.

"How can I help you this morning, my dear young lady?" he asks, his voice rising as he speaks like the call to some exotic house of worship. "It is a long time we haven't seen you."

"I need a gourmet fruit basket," Starshine explains. "To bring to a nursing home."

"A basket for a nursing home," repeats the florist. "Baskets we have. Many, many baskets. I do hope your loved one is not too ill. "

"Not *too* ill," retorts Starshine. "All I need is a fruit basket. I'm in a hurry. "

She glances at the wall clock to emphasize her time constraints. She does happen to be in a hurry. She is due at the Children's Fund at noon, but her primary fear is that she will become the sole repository for the florist's pent-up longings and stymied ambitions. Men have the noxious habit of unburdening themselves to her, exposing their secrets and frustrations and anxieties with the zeal of a colporteur unloading religious tracts, confiding their gambling debt and the injustice of their child support payments and the final moment of their dying parents. The men who do this are often middle aged, often small-time clerks, often the sort of self-styled undiscovered geniuses who, under different circumstances, might dabble with necromancy or National Socialism. They are lonely souls who have no one to talk to, men for whom a brief intimate conversation with an intoxicating young woman is their only available substitute for casual sex. Starshine genuinely feels sorry for these men, for the widowed token clerk at the Nassau Avenue station, for the pockmarked dairy-counter attendant at the Safeway, for the Armenian florist, but not sorry enough to indulge them. That way lies madness and stalking.

The proprietor lifts a segment of the countertop and instructs her to follow. They pass through a narrow corridor, lined with potted African violets and bags of fertilizer, emerging into a stale, cedar-paneled chamber which does double service as both work chamber and stockroom. A carpenter's bench runs along the far wall; metal trays and plant stands clutter the entryway, also block the emergency exit; desiccated spider plants and wandering Jews hang from the exposed rafters. The unfinished floor is littered with wood chips and an array of empty clay pots. The room stands as a testament to the green thumb's Jekyll and Hyde existence, the grisly underbelly of sacrifice which makes possible the grandeur out front.

"So we need a sixty-five-dollar gourmet basket," says the Armenian.

"Forty-five," objects Starshine. "Forty-five is my upper limit."

Her host flashes her an almost hostile grin; she can see the points of his canines.

"I must have misheard you, my dear young lady," he says. "But forty-five, sixty-five, no matter. I'm sure your loved one will appreciate the thought as much as the deed."

It is questionable whether Aunt Agatha will be in any condition to appreciate either. The woman is eighty-one years old, permanently bedridden, marginally cognizant of the outside world. Her sole source of pleasure, other than the feel of fruit, is to sneak an illicit cigarette and puff herself to a head rush through her tracheotomy. A twenty-five-dollar minibasket might meet her needs. But Agatha Hart does have her moments of lucidity, those spells when the old battle-ax is liable to grill the nurse's aides on the precise dimensions of Starshine's offering, and Aunt Agatha, her surrogate mother through all those years of adolescent turbulence, is the only family Starshine has left. She's worth forty-five dollars. If Starshine had the money, if she could raise the money, Aunt Agatha would be worth sixty-five dollars, sixty-five thousand dollars. Starshine entertains the thought of marrying Colby Parker and expending his entire fortune on guavas and grapefruits, sending dear Agatha into eternity with the entire national citrus crop, but her aunt would be much happier with a forty-five-dollar basket and the continued independence of her niece. And so, for that matter, would Starshine.

The Armenian settles onto a wooden crate and examines the tags on various gourmet baskets. His shirt slides up when he bends forward, exposing a back of dark brown moles and tufts of gray hair. Starshine stares down into his bald spot. She is conscious that he is a larger man than she had first thought, that he has planted his body between her and the corridor. This is a neurotic concern, she knows.

The proprietor is harmless. A charlatan, yes. Possibly even a letch. But not a rapist. She tries to focus her attention on fruit.

"A nursing home, you said. Forty-five dollars. "

"That's right."

"You can't include wine for forty-five dollars. Are you sure you couldn't stretch to sixty?"

"My aunt doesn't drink."

"Your aunt doesn't drink," echoes the proprietor. "Myself, I take a glass of retsina every morning. It stills the nerves. How about figs and dates? Does your aunt have a sweet tooth?"

"I was hoping for something with fresh fruit. My aunt isn't actually going to eat the fruit, she's just going to feel it. "

The proprietor nods knowingly. "All is now clear, my dear young lady," he says. "Fruit to feel. Nectarines, apricots, carambola. For fifty-five, I can throw in a pineapple. "

"Perfect," says Starshine. "But no pineapple."

"As you wish, but it's a lucky pineapple."

"A lucky pineapple?" Starshine hears herself asking.

"That's right. Strong genetic stock. Most of your pineapples these days come out of Thailand or the Philippines, but this is an Hawaiian pineapple. Among the luckiest fruit in the world. Maybe your aunt will appreciate it. "

"No, thank you."

Starshine searches for a path around the Armenian, but there is no easy escape. She does not wish to be rude. She does not want to flee without her purchase. He has swiveled to face her, the cellophane-wrapped basket resting on his wide lap, his hands braced against the edge of the crate as though he might pounce. This is monologue stance: Starshine has endured it before. Although she doesn't know the content, at least the specific content, she anticipates the form. It will be long. It will be pointless. It will be painful.

"So few young men and women these days appreciate the significance, the truly earth-shattering significance, of genetics," declares the Armenian. "At least, not the genetics of fortune. They're worried about curing this disease, about that disease, about birth defects, about AIDS, but nobody takes any interest in the biology of fortune. Did you know, my dear young lady, that good luck is an inherited characteristic?"

Starshine shakes her head. She scans the carpenter's bench for scissors, garden shears, any instrument with which she can defend herself if the Armenian's verbal assault deteriorates into attempted foreplay. This has also happened before. One minute, she was suffering through a discourse on the panacean qualities of the Nagami kumquat, and the next thing she knew, the Chinese grocer has his hand between her thighs.

"Your ignorance does not surprise me, my dear young lady," continues the Armenian. "You are not offended by my use of the word *ignorance*, are you?" My words are limited. I was born in a different country. In another world. My name is Kalhhazian. John Kalkhazian. And I may call you . . .?"

"Starshine."

There are no potential weapons on the carpenter's bench, only a paper cutter.

"A pretty name, Starshine. Well, Starshine, it saddens me profoundly that so few Americans, especially younger Americans, appreciate the gravity of genetics. I will venture that you don't even know your own genes, that you've never explored the fate in your own gene pool. "

Starshine shakes her head again. She wishes she knew how to deal with these situations. She wishes she were Eucalyptus. That she were Jack Bascomb. That she were a man.

"I happen to carry a matching set of good luck genes. The odds against a pair are one in one hundred, maybe one in one thousand. This in itself seems like a testament to my good fortune, doesn't it?"

"I'm sure."

"Lady luck smiles on me. I've survived a jet crash, a bout of malaria. My wife and daughters died in the crash, but I walked away without a scratch. I just stepped out onto the tarmac in Ankara. Even the paramedics said it was a miracle. I started going to church to thank Saint Gregory. But then I had some tests done, official medical tests, and I found out about my chromosomes. I can show you the proof."

The proprietor reaches into the folds of his apron and shoves three faded, time-scarred pages into Starshine's hands. They are written in Armenian. She feigns interest, examines them closely, and returns them to her captor.

"They're not in English, of course," he explains, "so unfortunately you can't read them. But you do understand their significance, I hope. My genes are as lucky as those of an Hawaiian pineapple. I will live to be one hundred fifteen and die peacefully in my sleep. It is all part of the genetic blueprint. "

The Armenian rises suddenly, pushing himself forward off the bench, and Starshine cringes in advance of the blows—but they do not come. Instead he stuffs his paperwork back into his apron and hands her the fruit basket. "Are you sure I can't interest you in a pineapple, my dear young lady? They're very lucky fruit. "

"Okay," Starshine agrees readily. "I'll take it."

Her entire body relaxes. He isn't a predator after all, just a benign crank. He looks so pathetically harmless with his dress shirt half-tucked. Now she regrets suspecting him, feels awful about his dead wife and daughters. Of course, she'll buy his pineapple. It is the least she can do. She is afraid she may burst into tears. She follows the forlorn man back into the empty display room and scrounges in her pockets for the last of Hannibal Tuck's offering. She is running low on cash, but this is nothing new. Poverty is old hat to Starshine. Money was meant to be spent.

"Thank you for listening to me, my dear Starshine," says the Armenian. "You brought me much joy this morning. So few young people have time to listen. Especially to an old man like me. I hope your pineapple will bring you and your aunt much great luck. "

"I hope so too."

"Promise me you will come back again."

"Scout's honor," lies Starshine. "I promise."

She has already decided that she will *never* return again. To do so would be indiscreet, even cruel. The old man needs a confidante, probably a lover, but there are some things she knows she will never have it in her to give. Maybe, she finds herself musing, without any conviction, the Armenian's good luck gene is some sort of late-onset phenomena that will bring him fame and fortune in his golden years. Maybe he'll become the Grandma Moses of the flower industry. She wouldn't begrudge him the prosperity. If she were an over-the-hill Armenian florist trapped in a life of isolation and routine, she'd also probably subscribe to pseudo-scientific theories, and believe in the genetic luck of pineapples, and lecture pretty young women. But she isn't.

She is Starshine. She is in her prime. She is a spring beauty carrying a fruit basket through the heart of Greenpoint. The day still spreads out before her like an endless starscape, like a Whitman poem, its possibilities infinite, an entire city holding its breath in anticipation. Her crises melt under the noonday sun. She balances the fruit basket on her head and she feels like Carmen Miranda. Like a celebrity. Like the sort of woman for whom ships are launched, for whom kingdoms are imperiled, for whom epic literature is composed.

And she is.

# PART II

## THE BELLY OF THE AFTERNOON

# MUNICIPAL PLAZA

Although Gotham takes pride in never sleeping, thrives on a reputation as the arbiter of "making it," and secretly considers itself the only world-class city west of Paris, in one respect the hemisphere's unofficial capital lags behind even the average elementary school: New York City does not have a lost and found. This omission reflects a conscious decision on the part of the municipal power brokers, their concession to the unforgiving doctrine of logistical impossibility, an admission that some municipal services were created more equal than others. It is marvel enough, they argue, in a city of eight million residents, in five boroughs claiming more Jews than Jerusalem, more Italians than Venice, more Puerto Ricans than San Juan, that the trash is collected twice weekly and the traffic signals function and the offtrack betting parlors are inspected on a semiregular basis. A lost and found would be the boondoggle of a quixote. Where are the resources, the political capital, the constituent groundswell to support such a superfluous frill? It is true that, on rare occasions, having misplaced a silver tie-clip or a gold-plated cigar case, a reform-minded iconoclast on the city council will lobby zealously for the establishment of such a repository, but his fervor will last only until the next election season, when he will either abandon his cause célèbre for the higher ground of school vouchers and random drug testing, or he will awake one November morning to find himself the newly appointed vice chancellor of some outer borough community college. As a result, there will never be a meeting ground for the countless tokens and keepsakes mislaid each day on the streets of the metropolis, a place where shopping bags may socialize with children's shoes, and plastic key chains can hobnob among fraternity pins, for ever since the Dutch patent-holder dropped the first calfskin glove on the cobblestones of the East River jetty, it has been determined that the city's bereft shall be left to their own devices, compelled to rely on the kindness of strangers, while their portable property seeks shelter in the pouches of knaves or sacrifices itself for the good of the commonweal and donates its heft to the landfill. South Street and Battery Park City have been built upon the ashes of misplaced correspondence. Larry's magic letter will not be recovered.

He performs the requisite inquiries nevertheless, calling the Maiden Lane McDonalds from a pay telephone, leaving his name with the porcine deputy at the Castle Clinton information kiosk. He emphasizes the importance of the lost letter, while stressing its purely sentimental value, strenuously insinuating that the missing envelope contains neither food stamps nor cash. It would be no skin off his nose if Stroop & Stone's decision became public knowledge, of course, if his fate were even broadcast on the nightly news, but he understands that once the seal on the envelope has been broken, the bearer will most certainly destroy the incriminating evidence of his treasure hunt. Such is human nature. The letter will be returned either unopened or not at all. And not at all, the catchphrase of Larry's floundering existence, seems to be the writing on the wall. He could always phone the agency and relate his misfortune. He could tell them that he was mugged, even kidnapped by bandits. Or own up to his own incompetence. They certainly wouldn't cancel their offer on the basis of a one-time mishap; it wasn't as though he'd lost the manuscript. Accidents happen. Yet the names Stroop & Stone are as imposing to Larry as those of Scylla and Charybdis to the most cowardly of mariners. He recollects the white parlor in his parents' suburban home, a salon of Duncan-Phyfe chairs and Wedgewood china from which he'd been banished for the perpetuity of his childhood, so that the stately Duncan-Phyfes and delicate Wedgewoods acquired personal attributes, anthropomorphized into lords and ladies of a forbidden kingdom; similarly, the prospect of confronting the implacable Stroop and the impenetrable Stone sends seismic waves through his abdomen. He will have to write to the agency and request a second reply. He dares not brave a phone call. And that means that when he tenders his affections to Starshine this evening, in the upscale Greenwich Village bistro where he has had a table booked since late April, he will have to present himself as Larry Bloom tour guide, the author of an unpublished manuscript, one of thousands of wishful scribblers in a city of aspiring literati. She will laugh rather than swoon.

The return of the Dutch tourists forces Larry from his self-pity. They descend the gangway of the Ellis Island ferry like so many newly arrived immigrants, renewed, prepared to banish all memories of past misfortune and to explore the gold-paved streets of the welcoming metropolis. They have gorged themselves on knishes and cotton candy; they have purchased T-shirts and tote bags. Many of the older couples have bonded over sepia photographs of peasant families and have pooled their outrage at the immodest group showers in the delousing stations, so they are now able to exchange snapshots of their nieces and nephews in the recklessness of timeworn friendship. Van Huizen, a coffee-table book tucked under one arm, is resolutely talking the ear off a wizened specimen sporting an inverted collar. The priest cups his hand around his ear as though riveted by his companion's knowledge. Only when the pair advances down the boardwalk to the information kiosk, the historian rambling, the cleric smiling in complete serenity, does Larry surmise the truth: Van Huizen' disciple has turned off his hearing aid. The Dutchman has found the ideal audience. That is a minor blessing, Larry thinks. The last thing he needs on such a bleak afternoon is a blue-streaker poking at his buttonholes. He is waiting for the last of the stragglers to congregate in a half circle when Rita Blatt prods him in the ribs with the point of her umbrella. Larry suddenly wishes he too were hard of hearing.

"I have a couple of questions I've been meaning to ask you," she ventures. "I figure I better grill you now, or I'm liable to forget.

You know how it is. I once interviewed this woman who compulsively adopts foster grandchildren, more than a hundred at one time or another, and I got so caught up in her photo albums that I didn't inquire whether she had any children of her own. I had to write around the matter and it left a glaring hole at the heart of my story. So, if you don't mind, can you tell me the most interesting thing that's ever happened to you on the touring circuit?"

"Oh Lord," answers Larry. "I have no idea. It's pretty much your run-of-the-mill, nine-to-five job until you get fired or decapitated by a traffic light. Will you let me think about it?"

"Think, think, think. Take as much time as you need. I'll lob you another one while you're combing that old gray matter. A more personal question. You won't mind, will you? Some people get all huffy when you start asking about their private lives. They don't understand that it's nothing personal, that I'm just doing my job as a reporter as best I can. But like I was saying . . . Have you ever developed a—what shall I call it—a romantic attachment to one of your customers? Some pretty young girl from some exotic land?"

"Never," says Larry. "That would be against company policy."

"That is too bad," says Rita, still smiling. "It would have made such good copy. But the day is still young. One never knows what will happen on the streets of the Big Old Apple. That's the amazing thing about New York, isn't it? Of course you already know that. Why else would you have become a tour leader?"

"It pays the bills," Larry answers curtly. "And some things never happen."

He turns from Rita to his charges and addresses them in the slow, stentorian, pseudo-conversational tone that is the dialect of his trade. He strives to walk the tightrope between the official and the officious, imparting information without intimating ignorance, to convince his hardy Dutch burghers that he is knowledgeable, witty, hardworking, that he is a replica of themselves, albeit on a minor scale, and that is therefore worthy of a generous gratuity. It is all artifice, stratagem. He meets their expectations halfway. Lurking deep within their consciences, of course, beneath their benevolent transfixion, is the knowledge that their leader cannot be what he appears, that he must harbor his own longings and sordid fantasies, yet—in the way that grammar school pupils hold their teachers upon the loftiest pedestals of purity and compassion, even after they develop doubts—the Dutch burghers steadfastly refuse to be disappointed. Larry's thoughts can drift through self-pity and self-hatred, even toward suicide, as long as his legs carry them past city hall and over the Brooklyn Bridge. It is an arrangement of mutual convenience.

The mercury has risen into the eighties by midday and as the tour group puts distance between itself and the waterfront, Larry leading backward like some crab chieftain at the helm of a crustacean pilgrimage, ties are loosened and sleeves are rolled up. Even these decorous Dutch burghers, immune to the forces of lust that prey upon the lesser souls in the park, cannot withstand the unrelenting prowess of heat. Perspiration trumps decorum; comfort conquers convention. Larry loosens his collar in front of the gates of Saint Paul's Church during his discussion of the Great Fire of 1776, incorporating the move into his description of the rising flames, as he has done so many time before, simulating the illusion that he is acting on his guests' behalf and not his own. Then he leads his charges up lower Broadway, past the ornate vertical thrust of the Woolworth Building, onto the manicured green at the foot of city hall. There is no longer a teenage temptress to inspire his lectures, to enkindle his passions, so he toes the straight and narrow path of the official guidebook: His Dutch will hear that city hall was constructed at the outermost fringe of development in 1811; that the northern side of the structure was finished with common brownstone, rather than marble, because no self-respecting New Yorker was ever expected to stroll beyond Chambers Street. They will *not* learn that Mayor Jimmy Walker built the twin marble staircases inside for two underage sisters he met at a speakeasy. Larry's pockets are empty; sweat glues his shirt to his shoulder blades. He senses the indifference in his voice, his hackneyed anecdotes that boast all the verve of chewed string, but does it really matter? The words of Whitman and Melville may live long after their bridges and wharves have crumbled, but his own utterances will soon lie buried like those of some muted Milton in a country churchyard. He is neither a poet nor a lover, but only a paid hack. As much of a sham as Snipe or Van Huizen. Maybe even more so. They possess the power of self-delusion. He doesn't even have that poultice. Who in God's name does he think he's going to fool?

Larry crosses Park Row, ambles up Spruce Street and makes an offhanded reference to the welded-copper monument on the facade of Pace University's main building. It is Henri Nachemia's masterpiece, the sculptor's lustrous tribute to *The Brotherhood of Man*. If only such a consoling fraternity actually existed! But Larry recognizes the bitter truth, knows it as well as he knows the back alleys and unmarked byways of the traffic knot south of Dover Street, understands that the city is nobody's friend and that daily life is not the labor of love that leads one toward some sublime and exalted pinnacle of self-actualization, but merely a tedious and malignant struggle for survival. At least for him. A handful of anointed souls rise above the humdrum and the fray, but these are good-looking men, talented men, men who are conspicuously not Larry Bloom. The greater part of humanity lead lives of not-so-quiet desperation and die unnoticed. These, at least, are Larry's bitter thoughts at the moment. Yet even he is surprised, if confirmed in his own worst suspicions, when he rounds the corner of Gold Street and spies, smack in the middle of the municipal workers' parking lot, belly-up like a beached porpoise in the sun, a white-faced and wide-eyed human corpse.

Larry sees the body over Van Huizen's shoulder and breaks off his spiel in midsentence. Although he has never seen a dead man before, not even at a funeral, his instincts tell him that the victim is long past hope. There's something finite in the man's heavenly gaze, something rigid in the thick arms reaching for his throat. Larry pushes his way quickly through his entourage. He bends over the body and instinctively checks for a carotid pulse. It is an exercise in futility. The sorry fool before him has died unnoticed, like so many others, and neither his ritzy pocket watch nor double-breasted suit have made his death any more memorable. A rich, portly man has died and must now struggle to pass through the eye of a needle. It is sad. It is inevitable. It is life. And yet somehow, as Larry rolls the cadaver to its side, he feels a whole lot better. Not because he is alive and this other man is dead; he is not that heartless. It is rather that the deceased businessman exudes a certain placidity, even a refined composure, which reminds Larry that death is not a negative, but a neutral. If Larry does not achieve immortality through prose, he will never know what he has missed. He will never suffer.

The Dutch tourists have encircled their leader and his unfortunate companion. A camel-nosed woman announces her credentials as a physician and confirms Larry's diagnosis. The man is unequivocally dead. But what now? The summer heat has cleared the back street of pedestrians, and the guard booth at the parking lot entrance stands unmanned. The future of the dead man is entirely in the hands of Larry's party. And he is their leader. He must take action. As much as he'd like to avoid the wear and tear of a police investigation, especially on such a harrowing afternoon, one look at the man's corpse warns Larry that he cannot abandon the departed to his fate. The beleaguered soul has been betrayed by his own body, ravaged from within. He deserves better than a mass of heat and flies. While Larry calculates whether he is better off transporting the corpse the four blocks to Police Plaza or simply calling the local precinct, Rita Blatt intercedes and dials 9-1-1 on her cellular phone. Neither she nor the Dutch tourists appear terribly fazed by the corpse. Van Huizen begins to tell a story about a time he found a stray arm on the beach, and then Rita Blatt relates her experience visiting the morgue for a feature on abandoned body parts. The Dutch tourists begin snapping photos with the deceased. The scene acquires a comic, almost festive dimension that disgusts Larry. His burghers are acting as though the man has died for their entertainment, as though he were just some prop for their anecdotes, and Larry will not endure it. The crisis is over. It is time to hit the road.

"Let's get going," he announces crossly. "The police are coming. We don't need trouble."

The Dutch murmur their collective assent. They have no desire for trouble. If their leader suggests that they have done their duty, then he knows best. They still have bridges to cross, churches to admire, souvenirs to purchase. They have already experienced enough of police and ambulances for one day. Only Rita Blatt appears unconvinced, but she buckles under Larry's icy glare. He runs his hand over the dead man's forehead and draws shut the deep blue eyes. Then he points his finger northward, toward the bridge, and leads his entourage forward at a rapid clip. This is a tragedy, but unlike the loss of the letter, it is not *his* tragedy. Besides, Larry assures himself, the deceased man will be provided for. His body will be examined, recorded, and appropriately dispatched; a team of driven pathologists will sample his liver and lungs. Gotham takes care of its corpses.

Larry briefly envies the dead man. Then he suffers a burst of perverse insight, one he knows he can never share, in which he conceives of the municipal morgue as New York's greatest irony: What is it, after all, except a lost and found for the dead?

# THE BIOLOGY OF LUCK
# CHAPTER 6
## BY LARRY BLOOM

Starshine's first job in New York, as a nineteen-year-old nonentity fresh off the bus from San Francisco, was working the cash register at a Kosher-style delicatessen on Broome Street. The proprietor's name was Nat Napthali. He was a stunted, droopy creature, a pension-fund manager turned restaurateur, who sincerely believed that with enough up front capital and a wax pencil tucked behind his ear, he could reap a cash cow from overcooked brisket and third-cut pastrami. His goal was to franchise, to "do for the Jews what Pizza Hut had done for the Italians." Napthali's Noshes survived for nine months; Starshine's tenure lasted eleven days. She despised the ingrained stench of sizzling meat that seeped into her pores during the workday, that accompanied her home like an unwanted puppy; she hated Napthali's gambit of intentionally overpaying her at the end of a shift to probe her integrity. But more than anything else, she detested the proprietor's oblique and ongoing critique of her attire. He never said Please wear this, please don't wear that. Instead, he confined himself to periodic barbs of the most pernicious sort, speciously casual observations on the height of hemlines and the merits of pantyhose and the podiatric dangers of wearing sandals, all phrased in the abstract to preclude any response. But when he finally informed her, point-blank in response to an accounting error, that a successful businesswoman showed less thigh and more thoroughness, she pulled up her skirt, gave the dumbstruck old ass a lot more than thigh, and stormed out. The next morning, Starshine adopted her employment mantra, a variation on the counsel to mistrust all enterprises that require new clothes, and she has never since worn shoes to any job interview. She stashes them in her handbag beforehand as a matter of principle. It they won't hire her barefoot, she won't do their bidding.

Starshine glided from counter girl to canvasser without the cushion of a golden parachute, without even the security of unemployment benefits. Wing-tipped loafers merit severance packages; barefoot women get paid under the table. So she stumbled through a series of short-term positions, maxing out her credit cards, nearly making ends meet, one foot on the threshold of gainful occupation and the other in the door of the almshouse. She answered phones for an East Village piercing parlor, rolled bagels in a mom and pop doughnut shop, played hostess at a short-lived restaurant for sadomasochists. One summer, she clerked at Brooklyn's only vegan pet-food store; another, she painted fire hydrant heads for the city's Department of Public Works, red for high pressure, green for low pressure, until her foreman decided to finger-paint the inside of her uniform. She even tried out as a lap dancer for an upscale Tribeca strip club, but never replied to their job offer. In four years, Starshine has briefly dabbled with babysitting, lifeguarding, fact checking, copyediting, dog walking, billboard design, yoga instruction, reproductive counseling, acupuncture promotion, and vintage clothing retail, a veritable pharmacopeia of thirty-six different jobs that don't require footwear, only to conclude that employment of any sort is both arduous to obtain and highly overrated. Her goal has always been fame, not fortune. As a teenager, long before she'd cycled off her extra baby fat and conquered her relentless acne, before she'd learned to color her hair so it looked more natural that it did without dye, her fantasy had been to walk into a room as though strutting onto a stage, forcing all around her to take notice. Fame was the opposite of isolation, of insignificance. Fame meant you mattered. But rising above the fray in a city where overexposed, underqualified young women are as abundant as Norwegian rats and summer mosquitoes, standing out in this mecca for would-be celebrities, where each displaced heartland farm girl aspires to be a fashion model and every undiscovered waitress in a tight sweater fancies herself the next Lana Turner, has proven itself an elusive feat. And Starshine's lack of a specific calling, what she terms her versatility, has made it all the more difficult. For Starshine doesn't covet any particular form of stardom; she doesn't yearn to play Broadway or sing at Carnegie Hall or dance at Lincoln Center. She simply wants to be famous, a household name. The end is imperative; the approach incidental. So in the meantime, having served her apprenticeships and mastered the art of marginal employment, she ekes out her living from month to month on the payroll of the Cambodian Children's Fund.

Starshine's appearance eases the monotonous routine of the building staff on her way into the office: She lets the lobby clerk ogle her cleavage while she signs the register, smiles at the elevator porter until he turns red as a sugar beet. An overalled maintenance worker carrying a ladder pauses in the corridor to undress her with his eyes. She throws him a seductive leer over her shoulder. It is fun; it is harmless. Off the streets, in the quasi-public office building that the Children's Fund shares with the Better Business Bureau and the Veterans Administration, the attention of strangers is flattering. And evanescent. She is protected by the comforts of numbers, by the knowledge that these men are professional gawkers and not personal threats.

The waiting room is empty when Starshine arrives. There's no sign of Jessie, the part-time receptionist. The girl is one of Starshine's favorite living beings, a nearsighted Irish kid out of the Bronx who speaks with a thick New York accent and runs the office like a machine tool shop. She's all spunk, that Jessie, and Starshine loves her to death. But today, just when Starshine wants to pick her brain for romantic advice, get an opinion from someone who has been around the block a few times, a counterbalance to Eucalyptus's morning sermon, it seems that the girl has gone into hiding. Starshine tries the conference room and pokes her head into the supply closet. No luck.

"Anybody home?" she calls out.

"Give me a minute!"

The voice pierces the door of Marsha Riley's office, followed moments later by the rounded form of the fund director herself. Marsha is a widow on the far side of sixty. Her features are sharp, her breasts heavy, her hair colored a synthetic shade of henna. The scallop-shell chain around her neck jingles when she walks. But although Marsha is not pretty, not even for a matron of a certain age, she carries herself with the self-assured elegance of a woman who has outgrown such a minor constraint as homeliness and never looked back. Capitalizing on her husband's small legacy and her extensive connections, she has launched a one-woman crusade for the most innocent victims of the wars of Indochina. And if she can be the archetypal hostess, a poor man's Pamela Harriman who quotes Shakespearean sonnets while smoking cork-tipped cigarettes, she can just as easily bombard you with detailed accounts of the atrocities in Cambodia and Vietnam. Marsha has no compunction when it comes to procuring pasteurized milk for infants or shielding toddlers from land mines. She will talk and put her money where her mouth is. She'll march her way onto the floor of the statehouse or into a cell at Riker's Island. She even made headlines in the late-1980s for pouring a martini into the lap of the Senate Minority Leader. There is no limit to Marsha Riley's love for young people. She has devoted her golden years to playing foster-grandmother to the foundlings of Harlem and Brownsville and to raising funds for the orphans of Southeast Asia. Maybe this is altruism. Maybe it is compensation. For Marsha's love is the peculiar breed of adoration, bordering on awe, unique to maternal women without children. She showers Starshine with all the affection she might show her own daughter, and yet, possibly because her devotion is so universal and non-discriminating, Starshine has never been able to reciprocate.

"What a morning!" declares Marsha. "If it hasn't been one thing, it has been another. Make yourself a cup of tea, dear, and come sit with me a minute. I'm more than ready for a break."

"What's going on?" Starshine asks. "Where's Jessie?"

She pours herself a glass of hot water in the office kitchenette and settles down on one of the vinyl love seats in the waiting room. Marsha sinks into the swivel chair at the reception desk and rests her chin on her crossed arms.

"Jessie's grandmother passed away," says Marsha. "She sounded like a truly amazing woman. She was ninety-seven and still stitched her own dresses. I'm—well, I'm not nearly ninety-seven—and I can hardly sew on a button. I guess ninety-seven's a ripe old age. All the same, I wish the dear lady could have held on another week. The phones have been ringing off the hook all morning. "

"It's pretty quiet right now."

"There's a reason for that, dear. I pulled the central cable out of the jack. It was getting so bad I could barely hear myself think. I didn't have a choice. "

"Why are we so popular all of a sudden?"

"This is why," says Marsha, sliding the op-ed page of the *Daily News* across the reception desk. "The Catholic Archdiocese issued a statement condemning euthanasia at VA hospitals. Read the cardinal's column. The old windbag doesn't hold his punches. He uses the words *pandemic* and *genocide* in one sentence. And I particularly like the passage about more soldiers being murdered in the wards of New York City than in foxholes abroad. But take a look at the bottom of the article. "

"It says call the Veterans Administration to protest. Am I missing something?"

"Nothing the rest of the city hasn't already noticed. That's not the contact info for the Veterans Administration. That's *our* address and phone number. I already called the city desk at the *Daily News* and the editor assured me he confirmed his information with the building switchboard. So I called the switchboard and they said they don't know anything about it. Meanwhile, every Sunday school teacher and Knight of Columbus in the city has a death wish for us. And they're not just calling. There were two priests and a seminary student waiting in the corridor when I showed up this morning. It's never-ending madness."

"I'm glad you're the boss. All I have to do is canvass."

"I don't deserve this grief, dear," says Marsha. "I go to mass every Sunday."

"This too shall pass."

"Not soon enough. The important thing is that I need you to cover the office for a couple of hours this afternoon while I go down to Saint Patrick's and convince them to issue a retraction. Is three to five okay?"

Starshine rapidly calculates the amount of time she will need with Jack and Aunt Agatha. Five o'clock for the Staten Island ferry is pushing it, but she knows she can duck out early. She has done it before. She is about to agree to hold down the fort when a visitor enters the office. The newcomer is a tall, reedy white man who stands bent forward like a broken bulrush. He desperately needs both a shave and a change of clothes. Starshine rolls her eyes at Marsha. Another crazy. They're always headed to the Veterans Bureau to vent their frustrations, but somehow they end up at the Children's Fund upstairs by mistake. Ninety-nine percent of the time these veterans are thoroughly benign. Once, however, a deranged ex-marine bit Starshine on the ankle, resulting in weeks of panic and a battery of medical tests, so she cringes instinctively at the stranger's approach. She keeps one hand near the telephone to call security. Just in case.

"How can we help you?" asks Marsha in a singsong voice. "What can we do for you at the *Cambodian Children's Fund*?"

The visitor steps forward rapidly and slams a stack of carbon copies on the reception desk. "How come you don't answer my letters?" he demands. "I'm fed up with this shit. I know my rights. "

"If you would kindly tell me your name, sir," prompts Marsha.

"My name's King. David King. You know who I am!"

The man's nostrils flare when he speaks; a tick afflicts his left eye. Starshine picks up the telephone receiver and realizes that the lines are dead. She has no idea where to find the central cable.

"Are you sure you're looking for the Cambodian Children's Fund?" asks Marsha.

"How the hell should I know who I'm looking for?" the man shouts back. "All you fuckers give me such a runaround. Go fucking here! Go fucking there! Nobody ever listens to a motherfucking thing I got to say. Meanwhile, I don't get my money. You're all a bunch of gold-shitting Jews and I still don't got my money."

"Please keep your voice down, sir," says Marsha. "I think you've come to the wrong office."

"Don't tell me to keep my fucking voice down! I'll decide when to keep my fucking voice down! You be happy I don't come back and slit your goddam throat. Nobody fucking listens to me!"

The man leans over the reception desk and pounds his fist on his stack of papers. Starshine glances at the door, examines her route of escape. Marsha Riley remains stationary, her heavy arms folded across her chest. Then the man turns to his left, as though trying to scratch his shoulder with his chin, and begins arguing with his own elbow. Starshine picks up the words *Isaiah* and *cupboards*. It suddenly clicks. This is the demented lunatic whom Jessie was fuming about last week, the guy who thinks the messiah is camped out under his kitchen sink and wants to government to perform an exorcism. Or something like that. Starshine didn't take much interest in the story at the time, and she is no more interested now. She pays her taxes. She works for a good cause. She even volunteers twice a month at the Presbyterian Mission. This man is not her problem.

"If you'll kindly follow me, Mr. King," says Marsha, stepping around the reception desk and taking the veteran by the hand. "I'll take you up to the Veterans Bureau. Okay, Mr. King? Maybe they'll be able to help you."

The fund director leads their visitor to the door.

"Three to five, dear," she says to Starshine. "Don't forget."

And then she's gone.

Starshine leans back on the love seat and rests her feet on the magazine stand. She's disappointed in herself and this makes her furious. Why can't she muster more compassion for this unfortunate veteran? Is she really such an evil person that she feels nothing but disgust? It's not his fault that he can't tell a watermelon from a water buffalo. It's not the florist's fault that he's old and lonely. Hannibal Tuck and Jesus Echegaray and Bone, even Bone, are just doing the best they can with what they have. And yet she dislikes them. As much as she wants to take them by the hand and heal their wounds, to play Marsha Riley to all the lost souls in the city, she doesn't have it in her. She's too insecure, too busy, too self-absorbed. But there's more to it than that. Starshine knows the reason she dislikes these men is not that she's a bad person—not even because she isn't so far removed from them herself, because if she hadn't burned off nearly half her body weight and stumbled upon the right skin creams, she could easily have remained unlovable. She dislikes these ugly, confused, desperate creatures for a much deeper, much darker reason. She dislikes them because time is not on her side, because beauty is ephemeral, because, soon enough, she will look like Marsha Riley and then like Aunt Agatha, because it is only a matter of calendar cycles before men no longer turn their heads when she passes.

But no!

She will not think about that.

She is Starshine. She is beautiful. She is happy.

# BROOKLYN BRIDGE

Nearly all of New York's treasured literary luminaries, during some particularly vexing season preceding their apotheoses, have contemplated premature self-censorship in the torrential eddies of the East River. The waterway itself plays an integral role in this rite of passage. The jagged floes of ice that choke the harbor in late fall and early spring foster the appearance of glacial progress, of the soft lap of a gentle stream, while the aquamarine glimmer of the surface at midsummer transforms one of the world's most unforgiving currents into a rural swimming hole. To the bankrupt poet, to the jilted lover, to anyone who yearns to elude the doubt within and the din without, the tidal strait between Manhattan Island and her favorite suburb offers the specious illusion of easy death. Melville prepared for the plunge from the breakwater on the South Street promenade, Whitman at the railing of the outbound ferry, both men redeemed by some Darwinian impulse, maybe some epic vision, which enabled them to change leaden water into lyric wine. Hart Crane rejected the limpid estuary for the brackish swirl of the Caribbean Sea. In each generation, from Washington Irving's to Truman Capote's, countless young men of promise and talent have examined the rippling foam between the nation's literary furnace and her literary playground, questioning whether the reams of manuscript in their Brooklyn lofts will earn them garlands in Manhattan's salons and ballrooms, wavering between the workroom and the water. And the city has done everything in its power to assist these men, to ease their affliction and to steer them toward the most judicious of decisions. It has built them a bridge.

Larry Bloom, the paradigm of the despondent young upstart for whom the structure was commissioned, has traversed the pedestrian causeway on exactly 217 occasions. Every Wednesday for more than two years, at approximately half past noon, he leads a detachment of pleasure seekers, fortified with optimism and bottled water, through the intricate web of suspension cables that supports the majestic span; and every Wednesday at half past one, having conquered several poorly defended corners of Brooklyn Heights, he escorts his merry band back into Manhattan to celebrate its victory. Larry is certainly not the most experienced docent on the circuit. He is probably not classified among the most engaging. He *is*, without a doubt, the only tour leader among the hundreds of underemployed graduate students and retired college librarians and itinerant travel writers piloting foreigners over the channel who can state with absolute precision the number of times he has crossed between boroughs on foot. This anomaly does not reflect some flaw of character, a pernicious compulsion toward the minute and irrelevant. Larry does not double check gas ranges; he feels relatively comfortable in crowds and confined spaces; he does not even recall his mother's date of birth. Yet for Larry, each encounter with the massive pylons and Gothic arches of Colonel Roebling's masterpiece has come to stand for another chapter in his tribute to Starshine. The bridge crossings were his motivation, his benchmark. He determined at the outset of his mission that every passage across Hart Crane's consecrated catwalk, every stroll over Whitman's cherished water, would coincide with the completion of another page in *The Biology of Luck*. For most men, Wednesdays are the hump of the week, a hillock to be surmounted; to Larry, they were milestones in his torpid progress toward passion. He set himself a backbreaking schedule and he stuck to it. Day after day, month after month. Yet now, his letter lost and his romantic prospects dimming, he pities himself for the countless hours wasted in a smoke-filled studio apartment, before an aging word processor, churning out pages of drivel for a woman who could never appreciate them. He focuses his anger upon Starshine. She is the cause of his suffering, his stupidity. She is a selfish, love-spoiled bitch, and he will despise her, hate as strongly as he once loved, because the only alternative would be to heave himself into the water.

Pedestrian traffic on the bridge slows toward early afternoon as the lunchtime flurry subsides into a trickle of middle-aged power walkers and twenty-something couples on bicycles. Larry halts his party at midspan, allowing them a moment to admire the vista, to finish off the film in their disposable cameras, and even these unflappable Dutch are modestly impressed. The skyline rises before them like the furnished minarets of some mythic kingdom. This is the postcard city, the metropolis cleansed of its noxious odors and incessant din, purged of its people, a glass and steel backdrop seemingly constructed for the Kodak moments of foreigners. The Dutch lean over the railing and shade their eyes with their hands. Van Huizen waxes rich on the history of the Empire State Building, peppering his wife and the priest with details of square footage and elevator capacity. Larry does not bother to tell him that he is looking at the Chrysler Building. After 217 crossings, even the mistakes have grown stale. Usually Larry pays tribute to the neglected features of the cityscape, the tin roofs of the fish market, the distinctive black smoke billowing from the Standard Oil Building, the gabled spires of Governor's Island, but this afternoon, without the benchmark of another paragraph to brace him, he retreats to the background and sulks in silence. The Dutch do not need him. Even Rita Blatt does not need him. He is a pathetic creature plagued by limited talent and unrealistic expectations, and he is of absolutely no use to anyone. He cannot hate Starshine. She is the last person he should blame for his shortcomings. She is a gorgeous, generous, thoroughly awe-inspiring young woman who has befriended him out of the kindness of her heart. How can he possibly hate her? He should be grateful. If anyone is the cause of Larry Bloom's suffering, it is Larry Bloom. The matter is truly quite simple: Some people just don't have what it takes. Larry swears that he will never again harbor any ill will toward Starshine, that he will cherish her friendship and respect its parameters for the rest of his life, because she is the lone fountain of beauty and decency in his otherwise arid existence. Then he catches sight of the water.

The river is darker than in Whitman's day. Centuries of barge commerce and unregulated waste disposal have coated the naturally transparent harbor with a tenebrous sheen. Yet the distended reflections of the downtown office towers and the distorted dome of the municipal building instill confidence. The view is so placid, so inviting, like a panorama into which one might step without the slightest discomfort. Larry recalls the impassive face of the dead man, the slack features absolved of all their earthly anxiety, the hollow eyes rid of want and care. What is the use of torturing himself over an improbable book and an impossible girl? Why not spite fate and his own ugliness and end his suffering in the process? Death is not a negative. Death is a neutral. Larry takes one final, lingering look at the Dutch tourists posing for photographs, collecting evidence of their visit for indifferent friends and relatives, contentedly oblivious to the anguish of their ad hoc chieftain. He'd like to think that his death will traumatize them, but he knows that it will not. They have no more interest in his welfare than they do in the fate of the teenage temptress or the protestors beaten at Grant's Tomb or the businessman consigned to the morgue. And why should they? Thousands of people die every day, stumbling over land mines on the outskirts of peasant villages and slashing each other's throats with machetes, while millions more abide in squalid poverty. One Larry Bloom, more or less—and, for that matter, one Walt Whitman, more or less—doesn't make a dime's worth of difference. Life is nasty, brutish, and short. Death is easy. Larry steps to the railing, vaults himself onto the security barricade, and closes his eyes. He is falling, plummeting, nearing death, when he suddenly hears the sound of his name reverberating like a drill inside his skull. A man is calling out Larry's name. A living man. Larry opens his eyes. He is standing 130 feet above the water, on the precipice of death, but he hasn't yet let go of the guard rail.

"Larry Bloom!"

The summons shames Larry into retreat. If the results of suicide are painless, the actual act is highly embarrassing. He rescales the security barricade self-consciously, determined to cover his tracks, only to find himself face-to-face with the piteous Peter Smythe. This is the height of humiliation, a fate worse than death. He now owes a life debt to the one man on the planet who has less to live for than he does.

"Larry Bloom," says Smythe. "I suspected I'd find you here. You're a creature of habit, if you don't mind my saying, and I admire that in a man. If consistency is the hobgoblin of little minds, I say, then I'll take a pea-brained fellow any day. That Larry Bloom, I was saying down at the castle, he's as regular as a bowel movement. You can set your watch by him."

Smythe chuckles heartily. He holds his stubby hands against the girth of his mammoth paunch as though trying to contain his wit. His bushy gray mustache and ginger cap give him the appearance of a pushcart vendor who has sampled one too many apples from his own cart. Smythe is the city's assistant deputy parks commissioner for Historical Cartography. He occupies a dank, cell-like office beneath the battleworks of Castle Clinton where he studies nineteenth-century traffic patterns and the placement of antebellum drainage pipes. Forty years of devoted civil service have bleached his complexion and crippled his vision, so that in his later years, he has grown into a colorless being who might actually have been born Peter Smythe rather than Fyodor Szymsky. Smythe's one claim to Larry's friendship is that three years earlier, on a sultry June afternoon much like this one, he'd introduced the novice tour guide to the city's most attractive woman. Starshine Hart had heard from some ex-boyfriend, a professional treasure hunter, that Captain Kidd's cache of riches had never been recovered. He'd planted in her brain the idea that the missing loot was buried under the Water Street landfill and she'd found her way to Smythe's crypt searching for an easy fortune. Larry, having abandoned his treatise on disasters, was briefly dabbling with the idea of a book on the synthetic geology of Manhattan. The aged cartographer, hoping to impress Starshine with his connections and work his way into her pants, inadvertently brought them together. So Larry pursued treasure and Smythe pursued Starshine. Later, Smythe pursued Starshine's roommate. All parties came up empty handed. Yet Peter Smythe, having used Larry once, culled from this experience a claim for future friendship. He sincerely believes, despite the overt evidence to the contrary, that Larry admires him.

"So congratulate me, Larry Bloom," says Smythe.

"What am I congratulating you for?"

"I'm getting married. You would never have thought it, would you? A bachelor at sixty-eight years and I'm throwing it all away to tie the knot. My friends think I've lost it. What's the point of hitching up at this time of life, they want to know. But I say better late than never. She's way out of my league too. One hot mamma. The way I see it, Larry Bloom, this gal was worth the wait. "

Larry feels the blood pooling in his stomach. He has lost his letter, lost his romance, aborted his suicide—and now the least attractive man he knows, the crass, self-absorbed, grossly obese Peter Smythe is marrying the woman of his dreams. He doesn't know whether to laugh or to cry. His glorious day is rapidly degenerating into some satanic episode of *Candid Camera*. He sees the Dutch priest beside Van Huizen and he wonders whether he isn't better off asking the cleric to marry him to Rita Blatt. On the spot. But then there is the possibility that even she might turn him down, that he'd suffer rejection from a woman for whom he has no romantic interest, whom he actively dislikes, which only reminds him how truly pathetic is his own existence. He'd like nothing more than to roll the hideous cartographer into the water.

"Well, congratulations," says Larry. "I'm happy for you."

"She's really something," replies Smythe. "She's a retired home health aide in Nova Scotia. I met her on the computer. In what they call an Internet chat room. We've been corresponding for nearly a year, but about a month ago, I finally took the train up to meet her and it was love at first touch. So I proposed on the spot. At my age, Larry Bloom, there's no time like the present."

"Well, congratulations again."

"I bet you're green with envy, Larry Bloom, but don't worry. Your time will come. Consistency pays off in the long run."

"I'm sure."

Smythe scratches his ear with his fingers and wipes the wax on his trouser leg. He is just the sort of man who would chase you down on the bridge, interrupt your suicide, and then have nothing worthwhile to share. That is not why Larry dislikes him though. He dislikes the cartographer for the only reason people truly dislike one another, because they are all too similar, because he sees his future in Smythe's isolated labor and Internet romances. He will age into a leaner, less presumptuous Peter Smythe.

"By the way, Larry Bloom," says Smythe. "I almost forgot. This is business, not pleasure. There's a reason I'm here. "

"Which is . . .?"

"I was in the office before you stopped by. You probably didn't notice me. I was *under* the information desk, searching through a crate of mildewed brochures. But I heard you mention that you'd lost a letter, and I figured it had to be a love letter for you to care so much. I've lost many a love letter in my day. The sort of notes that don't mean anything to anybody else but keep you from sleeping late at night, fearing you'll be found out. I've been a bachelor all my life. I know how it is. So when the maintenance guy turned in your letter, I thought I'd do you a good turn and bring it straight to you. I've heard of Stroop & Stone. They used to have an office in the Flatiron Building, as I recall. Later at 500 Fifth Avenue. They move around a lot."

"You have my letter?"

"Here you go, lover boy."

Smythe retrieves the letter from the interior folds of his jacket and hands it to Larry. The envelope bears the scars of both water and coffee, but it is unopened.

"So you're dating a literary gal," says Smythe. "Tell me, Larry Bloom, do they put out?"

Smythe chuckles again, his eyes aglow with schoolyard conspiracy. Larry resists his impulse to hug his savior, to embrace the jiggling ball of flesh and to plant a wet kiss on his drooping forehead. His gratitude is fleeting. The old man's stench of stale sweat and tobacco smoke is engrained. Larry fears that if he does lock his arms around Smythe's chest, his appreciation will instantaneously evaporate and leave only the silt of revulsion in its wake. And from there it would be a short, awkward jig over the railing.

THE BIOLOGY OF LUCK

# CHAPTER 7

## BY LARRY BLOOM

Earning money is one of life's most formidable chores. Asking for money is easy. This is particularly true if you are a well-proportioned blond female between the ages of sixteen and thirty who solicits funds for destitute and disabled children. All you need to do is play to your audience. The older women want to see photographs— not documentation of suffering and torture, certainly not images of one-legged teenage prostitutes and mutilated toddlers—but snapshots of healthy young foreigners, slightly underfed yet never emaciated, who can be restored to full vigor for the price of a cup of coffee. The younger women prefer facts and figures, sound bites for carpool chatter, pamphlets to be left on their coffee tables; they seek tangible evidence of their charitable exploits. This generation gap is conspicuous. It is as though menopause induces a transition from personal insecurity to universal skepticism. Starshine's greatest challenge is deciding whether a woman is too young to soothe or too old to shame. Handling the men is much easier. They may feign interest in figures or photos, but their underlying concern is for breasts and thighs. A generous smile often adds an extra zero to a check; an additional inch of exposed cleavage can clothe five Laotian children. The vast majority of these men do not expect to purchase Starshine's favors. They are husbands, fathers, pillars of the community, the sort of upstanding middle-aged patriarchs who would rather castrate their libidos than compromise their reputations, and even if their three-digit donations could earn them a quickie with the canvasser, they would deny themselves the pleasure. Cheap sex is not their game. What these men desire, and what Starshine dishes out generously, is nothing more than the esteem and gratitude of a beautiful young girl.

These men know nothing of that beautiful young girl, of course, except that her smile touches something primal inside them. And what would they say if they did know? If she added her own girlhood pictures to those of the destitute orphans—of a tearful ten-year-old being warned to smile at her own father's funeral so that her mother wouldn't worry about her? Or candid photographs of her flabby forearms bleeding under the hot tap of the bath on the night of her high school prom? What would they say of her weekends alone tending to her dying mother—of those long afternoons spent lamenting that pretty girls had boyfriends to help them, husbands to help them, attractive male nurses clamoring to offer assistance? Most likely, these men would shrug off her suffering. They don't want to know her, after all. They don't even want to sleep with her. All they want is to think that she'd be willing to sleep with them. It is prostitution without intercourse. And for Starshine, who unabashedly thrives on the attention, provided it is fleeting and stringless, coaxing money from these men is easier than turning a trick. *Almost* always.

Park Slope offers both an element of risk and the potential for a lucrative payoff. This is true of most gentrifying neighborhoods, particularly in the outer boroughs, where newly flush artists and starter couples jostle the long-time locals for space. The indigenous population, usually working class and presuburban, contributes according to its means. Young mothers frequently donate a smile and ten dollars in cash; young fathers hem and haw before producing a twenty. These interactions pose little threat and generate less reward. It is the young artists, an overwhelming proportion of whom are single men under forty, who will either fill Starshine's coffers or fray her nerves. Some write checks on their parents' accounts for hundreds of dollars; others expect her to return their generosity quid pro quo. Once, in Astoria, two thirty-something men whom she mistook for a gay couple locked her in their bathroom and she was forced to flee down the fire escape; the police later scoffed at her charges. One another occasion, a college kid clasped his hands around her ankles and begged her to sleep with him. Not a month goes by without some unpleasant episode, a brush with the city's up-and-coming population of gropers and fondlers and flashers, but Starshine has been canvassing long enough to spot the danger signs and retreat. Sometimes, of course, a perfectly nondescript door hides the gravest of threats.

Starshine has been working Seventh Avenue for nearly an hour when she approaches apartment 4B and pushes Ezekiel Borasch's buzzer. Her take for the day already exceeds $450. If she picks up another fifty, she can depart to meet Jack with a clear conscience. But one glimpse of Borasch, standing arms akimbo in his doorway with a maniacal leer in his eyes and a cigarette drooping between his lips, and Starshine knows she has rung the wrong bell. "Don't look so put out, girl," says the large, unkempt man by way of greeting. "*You* rang *my* bell."

He's wearing only dungarees. No shirt, no shoes. It's enough to make her turn on her heels and run. But that could invite pursuit. So Starshine takes a deep breath and politely states that she has accidentally pressed the wrong buzzer. Her fruit basket slips from her hand as she speaks, dispatching apricots and plums between Borasch's bare feet and into the unknown.

"Oh, shit!" exclaims Starshine.

"Nothing to worry about, girl," says Borasch. "It's just fruit. Life will go on. "

He steps into the apartment and sets about retrieving the lost harvest. Some of the nectarines have rolled a considerable distance, under tables, behind bookcases, and Borasch must crawl around on the carpet to retrieve them. Starshine is surprised to find the flat relatively hygienic. Stacks of notepads and hardcover books clutter the upholstery, and the remains of a desiccated philodendron decay on the radiator, but there are no visible traces of grime and squalor. The room is in much better shape than Jack Bascomb's studio. And Ziggy

Borasch, scrambling around the carpet on all fours, appears much less ominous. She has already inched into the apartment herself and rested the remnants of her basket on the back of his sofa when Borasch steps forward with the salvaged fruit. He holds two nectarines and a plum in one hand, two apricots in the other. He reminds Starshine of a juggler, of an oversized, bare-chested court jester. She can't help smiling as she takes the fruit.

"So what charity do you work for?" Borasch asks unexpectedly. Her question puts her back on her guard.

"You're raising money for some cause or another," Borasch says again. "There's nothing to be ashamed of. You showed up expecting some old lady ready to shell out her life savings to save the whales or preserve old buildings or something, and I scared the living daylights out of you. But there really isn't anything to worry about. This happens all the time. A couple of years ago, a foolish young woman from the Nature Conservancy ran down the stairs and twisted her ankle. I had to phone the police and it put a dent in my workday. So speak up and account for yourself, girl. What charity?"

"The Cambodian Children's Fund," stammers Starshine.

"Never heard of it. I bet you want to know how I figured you out."

Starshine edges back toward the door. Borasch isn't scoping out her breasts or thighs; he's staring her straight in the face. His eyes are sharp as needles. She has encountered men like Ezekiel Borasch once or twice before—her Uncle Luther was one of them—the rare breed of desperate souls who wander through life looking for some elusive formula. Most men are driven by longings for sex and companionship; they want to unload their burdens onto your lap, to drown you in cacti, to follow you home like unwanted puppies. But a select few want to sponge you of your wisdom, to take rather than give, as though a conspiracy of beautiful young women intentionally conceals life's greater meaning. These men are smart. They are also often dangerous.

"You rang my buzzer, not the downstairs bell," says Borasch. "That means you had to be in the building already. Now if your alleged friend had buzzed you in, you would have known her apartment number. The names aren't listed in the lobby, but they are printed on the doors. So I figured you were either begging for money or delivering Chinese food."

'Well, I should be going," says Starshine. "I'm sorry about the fruit."

"Aren't you going to ask me for money?"

Starshine takes another step backward. She braces the fruit basket against her chest.

"Do you want to donate to the Cambodian Children's Fund?"

Borasch runs his hand through his disheveled mane as though deep in thought.

"Not in a million years," he finally says. "Why would I give money to an organization I've never even heard of before?"

His tone is not aggressive. If anything, it is almost curious, but Starshine has had enough of Ezekiel Borasch for one afternoon. She can't provide this man with meaning any more than she can offer sex to the Armenian florist or security to Colby Parker. It's not a matter of *won't*. It's a matter of *can't*. Why don't men understand that? If she capitulated to the needs of every man who wanted something from her, there wouldn't be any Starshine left. She's already being picked to pieces by two men. There isn't any more of her to go around.

'I'm sorry for disturbing you," says Starshine. "I'll be going now."

Borasch stares past her. "Why would I give money to an organization I've never even heard of before?" he asks again—only this time, his voice is distant and philosophical. "Why would anyone give money to anyone else? It's so contrary to the national ethos. So downright un-American."

"I'm going," Starshine says again.

She backs through the doorway, keeping her eyes on Borasch. Better safe than sorry. She's thankful for her caution when the man suddenly breaks free of his trance and charges toward her, past her, through the fire door and into the stairwell, shouting like a lunatic as he goes.

"I've got it!" he cries. "I've got it!"

Nope, mister, you've lost it, Starshine thinks—but this is none of her business. She momentarily debates pulling shut his door, but she wants as little responsibility for this madman as possible. She has seen what a man like Ezekiel Borasch can do to a woman. Her Uncle Luther, at one time a well-respected journalist for the *Herald Tribune*, devoted the last twenty years of his life to studying evil. His pet project was a series of interviews he conducted with widows of war criminals. What made their husbands tick? he wanted to know. How could a man butcher millions of innocent civilians and then read bedtime stories to his children? Her uncle's eyes would fluctuate between sharp and glassy; he often repeated the same rhetorical questions for hours upon end. And he died with absolutely nothing to show for it. But how poor Aunt Agatha suffered! Starshine was still living with her mother at the time, so she missed the worst of the business, but she has heard her aunt's horror stories of serving tea to Lavrenti Beria's daughter-in-law and cooking dinner for Mrs. Heinrich Himmler. Pure torture! So Starshine truly doesn't care what Ezekiel Borasch has got—what pet theory, what clinical psychosis—as long as he doesn't share it with her.

She unlocks her Higgins and coasts up Atlantic Avenue to Court Street and then over the Brooklyn Bridge, the fruit arrangement perched awkwardly in her bicycle's wicker basket. The bicycle causeway doubles as a pedestrian crossing, so she must navigate an obstacle course of middle-aged power walkers and camera-happy tourists. The sightseers have the nasty habit of congregating in packs. They bottleneck the access ramps and clog the straightaways in the best tradition of wayfarers everywhere. They're just making the most of the afternoon, doing as they've been told. Their guides should know better. Starshine makes a point of shouting at the irresponsible tour leaders who refuse to curb their charges; this is among her strongest pet peeves. But this particular group of tourists—either Dutch or German, by their appearance—is conspicuously unchaperoned. It's no wonder they're congesting the footpath. Starshine speculates on the whereabouts of their commander, having recently read in the *Downtown Rag* that an average of three city tour guides die in the line of duty each year, two by suicide and one decapitated by a traffic light, but the bottom line is that she's actually pleased she can't find him. Starshine is feeling fully elated for the first time all day. She has survived breakfast with Colby; she has obtained her fruit basket. Her mood isn't conducive to yelling.

She hooks a right off the bridge onto Centre Street and rides several blocks standing up. Uptown traffic is light in the early afternoon and she is in no hurry. If she is early for her lunch with Jack, he will make her wait. That is his style, his way of marking his territory. Not that much different from what she does with Colby. Maybe that's the grander meaning that men like Uncle Luther and Ezekiel Borasch are seeking. Maybe life involves the pairing of unsuitable people, those who wait and those who keep others waiting, and the key to happiness is finding the one person with whom you share the same internal chronometer. But who really knows? The bottom line is that she can either kill an hour in Jack's apartment, enduring the silence and stench of stale sex while she waits for him, or she can walk her bike through the Lower East Side at a gingerly pace and savor the aroma of fresh leather and homemade kielbasa. Starshine would much prefer to savor.

Chinatown is among Starshine's favorite neighborhoods. At least, in small doses. It is one of the few enclaves in the city where her beauty carries no weight. She can wander up Hester Street and back down Canal Street without so much as one catcall or obscenity. If she crosses into Little Italy to explore the cheese shops and pastry cafés, she will be inundated with suspect praise. Surrounded by pagoda telephone booths and the aroma of smoked mackerel, she feels entirely sheltered. The difference between the two communities is night and day. And it is where these worlds collide, at the intersection of Mulberry and Canal Streets, where her own glorious day takes a turn toward premature darkness.

The wall of televisions in the window of Lin's Electronics has attracted a large throng. The faces reflect a mix of Mediterranean and Asian ancestry, sprinkled with the occasional Waspy intruder, suggesting a broadcast of wide appeal, so Starshine edges her way into the crowd. And then she nearly screams. It is so sudden, so unexpected. And it is so revoltingly public. Although she can't hear the newscaster's words, they are captioned for all the world to read in both Latin script and Chinese ideograms. Poor Colby! Poor, poor Colby! It is truly ghastly! Starshine cringes when they cut to the videotape: first the paramedics loading his father's body into the ambulance, then his mother escorting the Dutch consul to some heritage bruncheon. The headline text below reads:

FURNITURE BARON GARFIELD LLOYD PARKER DEAD AT 79
DISCOVERS WIFE'S INFIDELITY FROM NEWS FOOTAGE
OF GRANT'S TOMB RIOT
MILLIONAIRE COLLAPSES IN PUBLIC PARKING LOT
DUTCH GOVERNMENT TO RECALL ENTIRE DIPLOMATIC CORPS.

Starshine jostles her way through the spectators, pushing, prodding, desperately searching for open air. Her bag falls to the ground and loose change rolls onto the pavement. She doesn't care. She hastily retrieves the bag, resisting the assistance of a muscular man in a business suit, and plows her way down the sidewalk. She is no longer thinking of Colby Parker's parents; she is thinking of Colby and herself. Somehow, she recognizes that this is the breaking point of their relationship, the moment of decision. Starshine mounts her Higgins and attempts to wipe the tears from her eyes. Then she catches sight of the muscular man in hot pursuit.

The man calls after her. He's shouting and waving his arms. She cannot hear what he's saying and she doesn't give a damn. All she knows is that she is a beautiful, desperate woman riding a bicycle through Little Italy, and that she is crying, and that the combination is potentially lethal. It's an open invitation to every well-built stranger on the lookout for a victim to console. Now other men are shouting at her too, offering unwanted assistance. They're on every corner, at every traffic signal. Don't they understand that they're the reason she's crying? That she's tired of being picked at and pulled upon and badgered? That she can't be everybody's Starshine?

An orange slips from the fruit basket and jounces down the asphalt. She does not dare stop, does not dare retrieve the precious fruit.

She has gotten what she always wished for: attention. Yet for the first time in ages, she finds herself wondering, Why won't the world leave her alone?

# BROOKLYN HEIGHTS

Larry's corporeal form may be on Pierrepont Street in Brooklyn Heights, edifying his charges on the difference between Romanesque and Federal-style architecture, but his thoughts have drifted beyond the workday into romance. He sees Starshine lurking behind every portico and smiling form every cornice. The wrought-iron urns of pineapple along Monroe Place remind him of the fruit basket in his novel. The bronze Athenian horsemen lining Grace Court recall Starshine's grace atop her Higgins. Even the stained glass windows of Plymouth Church, where Henry Ward Beecher preached and Abraham Lincoln worshipped, send Larry's imagination spiraling through a latticework of grandeur and intrigue and destiny. The return of his letter is not a coincidence, Larry reflects, but part of a foreordained plan. Ziggy Borasch has taught him well. Whether fortune is biologically determined or metered out in just portions or simply happens, Larry does not know, but he is confident that his abortive suicide and Peter Smythe's timely appearance comprise the foundations of a palace of impending luck. His success at dinner this evening is predetermined. As inevitable as the Dutch girl's rescue, as fated as the businessman's sudden demise. His conviction is the certainty of the delivered victim, the unshakable faith of the reprieved. It will endure until either he begins to take credit for his own successes, or until Lady Luck suffers one of her rapid mood swings and his windfalls mutate into woes.

JACOB M. APPEL

The Dutch do not share Larry's idealism. Their concerns are much more pragmatic, tightly wedded to the exigencies of the moment. They wish to know which of the Middle Eastern oases lining Atlantic Avenue proffers the most bang for their bucks, whether the stuffed grape leaves and honeyed puddings at the Lebanese takeout stand are strictly vegetarian. Willem Van Huizen talks a blue streak through Larry's tour. He enumerates the similarities between the bazaars of Brooklyn and the emporiums of ancient Phoenicia for the benefit of his wife and the hearing-impaired cleric. Some of the younger couples branch off from the group to the lure of Sahadi's pistachios or ice cream parlor sorbet. They pledge to rejoin the company at the foot of the bridge. Larry leads his remaining followers toward the river, following Atlantic and then cutting north into the heart of what was once the city's original commuter suburb. By the time Larry reaches the esplanade with its unfettered view of the Manhattan skyline, prepared to eulogize the literary lions who have strolled the terrace through long-forgotten dusks, pacing, pondering, trying to distinguish the stirring from the sentimental, his audience has contracted to a single follower. Only Rita Blatt wants to hear about Truman Capote's garden parties and Norman Mailer's outbursts of violence. But the journalist is not among Larry's charges. She hasn't paid for the tour, certainly not for a one-on-one guided junket through the history of literature. Larry would like to discuss Starshine. He'd gladly unburden himself to anyone, even Rita Blatt, but he fears the dour woman with her black umbrella may jinx his fortunes. So he opts for the next best alternative. He dismisses the newswoman on the pretext of a business-related phone call. He must ring his boss, he says. He will meet her at the bridge. His real intention, of course, is to pass twenty minutes alone on Atlantic Avenue. He will discuss Starshine's beauty with himself.

Larry traverses Clinton Street and ambles aimlessly in the direction of Boerum Hill. His attention is drawn to the horned beast on the awning of the Unicorn Diner, the windows of the coffee shop where his fictionalized Colby Parker lies in wait on Wednesday mornings, the lamppost where his imagination has chained Starshine's bicycle. Larry wonders whether there is any truth to his narrative, whether he has done justice to this beauty's universe. He does not know. His sketches are secondhand doodlings, the products of brief anecdotes and conversational snippets that he has culled from years of interaction. He has never met Colby Parker. Or Jack Bascomb. Or even Eucalyptus. And yet, as absurd as it seems, he feels that they're as much a part of his life as his Dutch tourists or his own acquaintances. Maybe more so. Starshine's friends are both figments of his fantasies *and* real people. Somehow this gives them an added depth, a fourth dimension, that renders them all the more palpable than the humdrum characters who occupy Larry's day-to-day life. He hopes his creations are plausible. He hopes they are entertaining. But most of all, he hopes that they exhibit insecurities and desires similar enough to the ones he has conjured to drive Starshine into his hands. Or different ones entirely. It does not matter.

Larry pauses before Blooming Grove and prepares himself for his poetic moment. This is the very florist where Starshine's suitor ordered his forty-eight-dozen red roses. Larry vividly recalls the afternoon Starshine phoned him in tears to ask for his wisdom. She bawled for nearly an hour about how she adored this Colby but didn't want his flowers. All she wanted was his love. Larry lacked the courage to tell her that she didn't want either, that her Colby Parker was a fictional ideal culled from fragments of the real Colby Parker. So Starshine learned nothing. But Larry discovered something earth shattering. He discovered that, while listening and soothing, he could reconstruct a relatively coherent portrait of the actual Colby Parker from Starshine's inadvertent distortions. The next morning, he rode the subway out to Brooklyn and bantered for half an hour with the Armenian florist. A sad creature trapped in a world of pseudoscience. That visit occurred two years earlier. It spawned the birth of Larry's manuscript. His second foray into the Armenian's shop, anticipated through months of excruciating labor, strikes Larry as the epitome of the poetic. He will buy Starshine roses in a shop that is both real and of his own creation. He wonders if Whitman ever felt the same proprietary hold over lilacs.

The shopkeeper is engaged with a customer when Larry enters. The old man's beard may be longer, his paunch somewhat fuller, but he is otherwise unchanged. A spitting image of his own facsimile, down to the rolled shirt sleeves and the pencil tucked behind his ear. Only now he appears excited. His leathery skin has suffused to a deep vermillion and he is gesticulating wildly at the handsome young business-type across the counter. Larry pretends to browse the aligned vases of lilies and heliotrope to avoid appearing meddlesome. But he listens to the proprietor's harangue with a certain amount of self-satisfaction. The Armenian is fully living up to his expectations.

"You expect me to help you," cries the florist, "but you don't listen to a word I say. Did I not warn you against the cactus? Cacti are particularly ill-fated specimens. A chrysanthemum, I say. A chrysanthemum or a Hawaiian pineapple. The luckiest vegetation around! But a cactus? You might as well give her a broken mirror. "

"Okay, okay," concedes the customer. "But she said she wanted a cactus. If a woman wants a cactus, you can't bring her a chrysanthemum. You certainly can't offer a pineapple. Isn't there anything else that might work? A happy medium of some sort?"

The Armenian throws up his hands.

"I do what I can," he says. "But happy mediums cost money."

"Money is no object."

"That's right," says the Armenian. "You are a man of much wealth, my friend, but little luck. I will arrange for you a bouquet of butterfly orchids. Strong chromosomal properties, radiant color. Twelve dollars a blossom. But I warn you once again, my friend, that your cause is a difficult one. Extremely difficult. I can read your fortune on your face and it is markedly grim. Two misfortune genes. That bodes the worst of luck. Something dreadful will inevitably befall you. "

"That's my concern, not yours," retorts the customer. "Please just pack up the orchids."

The Armenian retreats into his stockroom and returns

momentarily with an arrangement of bright yellow blossoms. He rolls them in wrapping paper, shaking his head as he labors, and presents the package to his hapless patron.

"I wish you more luck, my friend," he says. "Maybe my fortune will rub off on you. We will hope for the best. But it is a shame that such a wealthy man is cursed with so tragic a fate. It is unconscionable. Two misfortune genes! Your parents should never have been permitted to wed. They are not happily married, are they, if you do not mind my asking?"

"They are quite happy," the customer answers tersely. "Thirty-seven years."

He deposits two hundred-dollar bills on the counter and departs without taking his change.

"Bah!" says the florist, waving the departing customer out his door. "That man knows nothing. I warn him. Three times I warn him. But does he bother to listen? He will dig himself an early grave. "

The Armenian rests his elbows on the countertop and offers Larry a conspiratorial grin. As though to say, "Let us bond over that man's foolishness." As though to say, "I know you are infinitely more reasonable than him." If the florist remembers Larry from his earlier visit, his features betray no recognition.

"How are you today, my friend?" asks the florist.

"Not too bad. I was hoping to get a half-dozen red roses."

The Armenian steps around the counter and rests his rump against an iron plant stand.

"We talk business soon, my friend," he says. "First, I must look at you. Come closer. Don't be afraid."

Larry steps forward. He does not mind humoring the florist.

"Yes!" shouts the Armenian suddenly. "Yes! Yes! Yes! Fleshy nose. Drooping ears. Broad cheeks. It's uncanny."

"What's wrong?" Larry asks nervously.

"Nothing is wrong, my friend. At least for you. Quite the contrary: Everything is right. You have the most fortunate genetic composition. It's as plain as the nose on your face. You're a one in a thousand, my dear friend. Two good-luck genes. You look just like me. "

Larry grimaces at this accusation. He recognizes the similarities between his own soft features and the Armenian, but he certainly doesn't consider this a cause for excitement. The absence of a wedding ring on the florist's hand is not lost on him.

"You are frowning," says the florist. "You do not believe me."

"I'm not very lucky," Larry answers diplomatically.

"Maybe not yet. But soon enough. I will tell you a story. I live up in the Bronx. Across the street from me lived an old woman. A delightful lady, but cursed with ill luck. Year after year, I tell her that she must be on her guard. That she carries two misfortune genes. But she does not believe me. She thinks I'm foolish. She laughs at my warnings. My other neighbors also laugh behind my back. *How can she be unlucky?* They ask. She has lived past ninety. She is in good health. Her grandchildren visit her. . . . But I know the truth! I know!"

"I'm sure."

"Yesterday," says the florist, "Her fate caught up with her. A burglar bludgeoned her to death. How do you like that?"

The Armenian beams like a proud parent. He couldn't appear any more satisfied if he had murdered the woman himself. Larry wonders if the peculiar old man is capable of homicide, if he'd sacrifice an elderly neighbor for the benefit of his pet theory. People have committed worse crimes for lesser reasons. The desire to play God can be overwhelming. This seemingly innocuous old man might easily be a disciple of Leopold and Loeb, the Sweeny Todd of Atlantic Avenue, poisoning his customers with toxic foliage. It is possible, Larry thinks. But highly unlikely.

"A half-dozen roses," says the florist. "Roses are unlucky. Chrysanthemums would be a much better choice. But in your case, my friend, it will not matter. "

"How much will that run me?"

"Bah! Money. We are like brothers, my friend. I never charge a companion in good fortune. And a half-dozen roses is nothing. A trifle. They are—how do you say in this country?—atop the house. "

"Thank you," stammers Larry.

"No, my friend. Thank *you*. "

The Armenian wraps the bouquet. Larry watches the old man work, measuring the cellophane, clipping the stems. He wishes he had something to give the florist in return for his prophesies of good luck, something to reciprocate for the roses. But such a gift is beyond his means. He has immortalized the man in his manuscript, he thinks. That is a worthwhile offering. The very sort of gratuity the Armenian would most appreciate. They have traded fame for fortune, Larry notes with amusement. That is an even exchange. The old man's theories will acquire an international audience while Larry will gain Starshine. And all will be happy.

But he must not think this way, he decides as he thanks the florist. Not yet.

The day is still young. He must still recross the bridge.

THE BIOLOGY OF LUCK

# CHAPTER 8

BY LARRY BLOOM

Jack Bascomb is a dead man.

He served his nation valiantly at Inchon, garnering a purple heart and an officer's commission, but later drank his way out of a field job with the Department of Agriculture and died of alcohol poisoning, penniless and homeless, in the lavatory of a roadside saloon on the outskirts of Sierra Vista, Arizona. His body found its way into the local potter's field at the county's expense, his wallet into the hands of a fugitive. And it is this second Jack Bascomb, Weatherman emeritus and migrant carpenter, who pays tribute to the name on his social security card by living the life of a corpse. The metastasized cancer cannot take credit for Jack's air of morbidity. The disease is impotent; it can only kill him. But there is something much deeper in his composition, maybe a self-destructive impulse, maybe a chromosomal proclivity for misfortune, that cloaks the aging radical in the shroud of a young martyr, of a tragic victim, of a man who no longer exists. His very presence seems anachronistic, symptomatic of an account imbalance in the Book of Life. It is as though he is the last slaughtered revolutionary of the lost generation, part Bobby Kennedy, part James Dean, reprieved like Lazarus to give voice to their collective suffering. He plays the role well. His scraggly mane, a vineyard of black and white tresses, submits to no tonsorial snip; his denim jacket reeks of clove cigarettes and stale sex; cardboard lines the toes of his boots. Yet when Jack Bascomb speaks, lets the contents of his soul roll from his lips in stentorian paragraphs, his voice resonates with the music of a better world. Jack's words are triumphant, even messianic. But they come from somewhere beyond the grave, like the visitation of a bygone prophet, their jubilee for those who will enter the Promised Land though he may not. He carries on his tongue a prophesy of social justice, of wealth redistribution, of each receiving according to his or her needs—and his every word gives voice to a vision that owes debts to Jesus Christ and Karl Marx and Malcolm X and even Timothy Leary, yet at the end of the day, is distinctively his own. While Starshine makes love to Jack, each Wednesday on the pretext of lunch, she purrs and writhes to the cadence of a cadaver.

The neighborhood has gentrified around Jack Bascomb's walk-up. He moved into the sixth-story apartment on Avenue A back in the mid-eighties, at the height of the urban crisis, when the smart money was on continued arson and blight. Decades of neglect had transformed the sidewalks of Alphabet City into a heath of crack vials and syringes, a community garden for the denizens of the Riis Housing Projects and the tent villas in Tompkins Square Park. These were environs for a rusted militant to take pride in, daily corroboration of his forgotten foresight. Nothing pleased Jack more than the popping of gunshots outside his windows in the wee hours of the morning, as soothing as the uncorking of champagne bottles, confirming that little trickles down except ambition. Only now, the after-dark orchestra really does play a bubbly symphony as the brazen gangs of yore have yielded their turf to the offspring of limousine liberals. Jack's un-air-conditioned flat, furnished at tag sales and infested with roaches, used to be the regional standard; the Gestapo antics of a Republican mayor have recast it as a relic. The streets no longer belong to Jack Bascomb. He prefers to cloister himself in his outdated apartment, seated at his home-built folding table, honing his carpenter's skills and composing his memoirs. That's where Starshine finds him, at the appointed hour, self-medicating shamelessly with the door ajar.

"One pill, two pill, red pill, blue pill," he greets her. "Now that's poetry. Simple language, strong rhyme scheme, implied conclusion. Walt Whitman for the post-industrial age. "

The capsules aligned across the tabletop remind Starshine of aircraft taxiing toward takeoff. They include appetite stimulants, protein inhibitors, and painkillers of every variety. Some of the medication has been manufactured in the micromanaged laboratories of the nation's leading pharmaceutical conglomerates; much has been home brewed in the cellars of cranks. The original source doesn't make a dime's worth of difference to Starshine's lover. He acquires the pills from the shady homeopath on the third floor, a defrocked pharmacist, in exchange for woodwork. And they serve their purpose. They cause drowsiness, weight loss, nausea, moodiness, poor digestion, and probably sperm count reduction, simulating virtually all the side effects of radiation therapy without in any way inconveniencing the cancer. This suits Jack perfectly. He will suffer the full effects of treatment without any hope of recovery, so that in his last breath he can curse the American government for denying him chemotherapy. It is all part of his master plan.

Starshine wipes the veneer of dust from a wooden chair and waits while Jack downs his pills with a chaser of bourbon. He winces with each swig, savoring his own pain with all the gusto of an early Christian flagellant. Starshine examines his hairy arms, still muscular despite his illness, admires the serpentine tattoo that runs the course of his bicep. He is a man's man, she thinks, a feral brute tempered only by intelligence. If he were younger, if he were healthy, she might toss her other lover to the wind and follow her fugitive to Amsterdam. He's dashingly handsome in spite of his ragged clothing and unshorn locks. He's the smartest man she has ever met. And he's even a powerhouse between the sheets. In many ways, Jack is leagues ahead of Colby Parker's daily phone calls and hothouse offerings. But there's the other side of Jack, the insecure tirades, the alcoholic binges, the recriminations, the self-accusation, the perennial irritability, and, above all, the inescapable detail that Jack Bacomb was a man born to live alone. And to die alone. This is his preordained destiny, Starshine knows, and not hers.

"All done," says Jack. "I'm high as a kite on placebos. I feel like I could die a dozen times in one day."

"Don't be that way, Jack. It's not funny."

"You didn't expect me to save any pills for you, baby, did you?"

"Not today, Jack. Please. It has been a dreadful morning. You know that other guy I'm seeing, the one you called the Lyndon Johnson of lawn chairs? Well, his father died today, dropped dead in a parking lot."

"Conclusive proof of a generous God."

"Jesus, Jack. I can't deal with this shit. Can't you show an ounce of compassion?"

"For the competition? Not this time around. I already told you, baby, you can screw anybody you please, but I don't want to hear about it. I'm trying to avoid circumstantial jealousy. It's bad for the liver."

"And then this maniac chased me halfway up Mulberry Street. It was just awful."

"Was he cute?"

"Enough," says Starshine, her frustration mounting. "What's gotten into you today?"

Jack pushes his chair away from the table with both hands. He turns to face Starshine and rests his palms just above her knees. "I'm sorry, babe," he says. "I didn't mean to upset you. It's just that I woke up this morning, and I had a vision, one of those rare moments of prescience and clarity that you read about in Augustine or Proust. It was like acid and ambrosia and the finest cognac all rolled into one. It was like a private showing of Woodstock, baby. You can't possibly imagine the totalizing effect it had on me. It was the defining moment of my life."

"Why does that make me so nervous?" asks Starshine. Somehow, she fears that Jack wants to make his vision the defining moment of her own life as well. "I don't know if I can handle a private showing of Woodstock."

"There were flowers everywhere, baby. Poppies, tulips, orchids. You were standing in an endless meadow of the most dazzling flowers, flowers in every direction for as far as the eye could see. And the amazing thing was that there were no price tags, no migrant workers weeding between rows, no toxic chemicals poisoning the soil. It was paradise on earth, the Elysian fields right here in our backyard. I could tell it was someplace close, somehow, but I wasn't sure where. And then suddenly I knew. It just happened. One minute, I had no idea where to find this utopia, and the next, it was as though I'd been handed a road map. And do you know where you were, baby?"

"Where?"

"I'll tell you where, baby. Amsterdam. That's where. You were alone in Amsterdam and I was dead. That's what's going to happen, isn't it? It's not a matter of if, only of when. "

Starshine stands up and braces her arms on the back of her chair. She owes Jack an answer, she has owed him an answer for nearly three months, be she is afraid of the consequences. Jack—unlike Colby Parker—can get along well enough without her. If she rejects his offer, he might emigrate to Amsterdam on his own. He might even do it on the spur of the moment to spite her. She knows he has already made arrangements for the private plane, corralled some ex–Black Panther who operates a charter airline into his death plan. Jack intends to die among socialists and tulips, in a nation with universal health care and state-run industries. She is the only elusive factor in his scheme. Sometimes, she finds herself hoping that he will die before she has to make a commitment, that the cancer bell comes to her rescue, but then she despises herself for her cowardice and her cruelty. She does not want to decide, she thinks, because in some perverse, illogical way, she believes that Jack will not die until she makes up her mind. The longer she stalls, the longer he lives. His death, she knows, will devastate her.

"I don't know, Jack," she says. "I just don't know."

"You *do* know," Jack answers, his voice wavering. "Deep down in the core of your being, baby, you must know. Otherwise, we'd already be picking tulips in wooden shoes. It's sad though, isn't it? I fuck God knows how many women, must be hundreds, and when I finally find the only one I ever should have fucked, the only one I ever really fucked and meant it, I'm out of here like yesterday's news. It kind of makes you wonder. . . ."

"Please, Jack," says Starshine. "I love you. You know that, don't you? It's just circumstance. "

"Maybe I should have done things differently. Maybe I should have cleaned up my act and written cookbooks like Bobby Seale. Can you believe this shit? Bobby-kill-the-pigs-fucking-Seale, the goddamn poster boy for the revolution, he's written a goddam cookbook. *Barbeque'n with Bobby*. It's right there in the window at St. Mark's Books. That's the kind of shit that makes you want to say fuck the revolution and buy a condo in Florida or a fruit plantation or God knows what. It turns my stomach. "

"How about *Humping with Jack*?" suggests Starshine. "After all, you never have gotten around to cooking me lunch. Don't they say you should write about what you know?"

"I like that," Jack answers, grinning. "You want to coauthor?"

Starshine smiles in relief. She knows she's in the clear now, at least for the moment, that Jack's thoughts have drifted from his deathbed to his futon. And somehow, although in hindsight the routine seems as old as a stock chess opening or the lines of a high school play, in the passion of the moment, it never fails to leave her breathless. She will purr, she will gasp, she will dig her nails into the folds of his back and shake the apartment like an earthquake and he will do anything and everything, like no other lover she has ever known, until she falls to earth with drool oozing down her chin and neck. She knows what is coming. So does Jack. He pours himself another glass of bourbon and polishes it off in one shot. Then he is upon her.

But this time is different. Usually there is lightning; today there is thunder. It begins with a soft patter, the gentle rhythm of a spring shower, but it rapidly swells to an angry gale. Starshine focuses on Jack, blocks out everything but the contours of his chest, his arms, the feel of flesh against flesh and sweat lathering her stomach and the violent energy building between them, inside them, then concentrates on her own orgasm, on getting over, on getting through, but her head is spinning, throbbing, with the furious roar of impending destruction. Of artillery, of blasting, of hail pelting tin. The entire universe explodes around her in a deafening eruption of flesh and hair and fluids—and then she is through, over, lost in silence. All she can hear is Jack's hard breathing and the incessant labor of someone behind her head, on the opposite side of the plaster, pounding the wall with what sounds like the sole of a shoe. She is too content to be ashamed.

"Fuck this," growls Jack. He rolls off her and pulls up his trousers. "Goddamn neighbors! I'm going down for a cigarette, babe. I'll be back. "

And this is how it ends, how it always ends. There is no afterglow with Jack Bascomb. For a short interval he is all hers, voracious, craven, but then he recovers like a patient from a bout of fever and he needs his space, his time, his air. Starshine hears the clatter of metal as he retrieves his keys from the table, then the dull thud of the door. The person on the opposite side of the plaster slams the wall one final time, maybe for emphasis, and goes back to his business. Starshine is abandoned to her thoughts. She stares up into the sagging ceiling, into the water wounds, into the chipping paint. She has had her pleasure. Now comes the pain. It is always the same with Jack Bascomb. Somehow sex with Jack drives her back into her adolescence, into her life before Jack Bascomb and Colby Parker and all the others. Into her life before men. Alone in Jack Bascomb's dimly lit apartment among his books and heirlooms, she is once again an ugly duckling, the plain, talentless child who nobody loves. She is once again irrelevant, neglected, a prop in her parents' incessant warfare, an obese teenager deserted by a narcissistic, bankrupt father to care for a dying mother with a soul as fragile as an ostrich shell. Her mind is suddenly flooded with all the hidden insecurities and fears she has struggled so long to bury. She is Starshine before she bought the bicycle, before she discovered her own beauty. She is nothing. And she refuses to be that again.

Starshine runs her hand over the scars on her wrists.

Slowly, decisively, she buttons her blouse.

# THE LOWER EAST SIDE

The pale of settlement beyond the Bowery is the one New York City neighborhood in which Larry has never quite felt at home. The pushcart vendors plying Orchard Street intimidate him; the pickle vats along Roosevelt Park render him tense. Every Wednesday, he introduces a fifth column of outsiders into this last refuge of Old World Jewry, exposing wealthy gentiles and High Holiday suburbanites to the rich texture of immigrant life, but the frequent visits have done nothing to surmount his unease. If anything, they have intensified it. The Dutch admire the dingy sanctuary of the Bialystoker Synagogue and the Tenement Museum's glass-enclosed artifacts with detached respect. They gaze up at the roof of the Ritularium and feign regard for the caftaned Hasids who collect rainwater in cisterns for use in their *mikvah* baths. They shake their heads at the interior windows *between* apartments that turn-of-the-century slum lords constructed to evade the zoning codes. They gorge themselves on pan-fried blintzes and pierogis. But although they defer and praise, they do not relate. Larry alone feels a comradeship with the small-time peddlers and elderly widows who cling to the haunts of their forebears—not just Jews, but Greeks and Poles and Romanians—and it is this undesired fellowship that makes him self-conscious. His maternal grandfather ran a haberdashery from one of these run-down storefronts. His paternal grandfather examined fresh eggs for embryos at a processing plant on Montgomery Street—a man his own father, Mort Bloom, boasts worked 365 days each year and an extra on leap years. Both of his grandmothers stitched gloves at the same Cleveland Place sweatshop. Their shame is Larry's inheritance. Although the Blooms have since escaped the warrens of the Lower East Side, traded in their workmen's aprons for judicial robes and lab coats, the guilt of urban poverty still afflicts the third generation. This heritage is a latent genetic malady, a Tay Sachs disease of the soul, which may smite without warning. These streets explain why Larry's father phones every month to press his son to apply to law school; they drive Larry's quest for literary immortality and his fear of failure. But their legacy runs far deeper than mere psychology. For it is this swarming ghetto, amidst the bedbugs and rats, where four short broad-faced Eastern European peasants tendered the promises and whispered the sweet nothings that ensured their progeny its ugliness.

Larry leads his entourage on a skin-deep tour of the community from Seward Park to the foot of the Williamsburg Bridge, then consigns his charges into the hands of the local merchants. The younger couples will take photographs of themselves crossing Delancey Street and load up on designer brand knockoffs imported from Hong Kong. The older couples will purchase leather goods and accessories for grandchildren, belts and ties and purses, before recessing to a Kosher sandwich at Katz's Delicatessen or a more expensive but legitimate entrée at Ratner's. Although this downtime is not part of the official itinerary, it suits both shepherd and flock. The Dutch are tired of Larry's blather. He is fed up with their boredom. This separation ensures that when they reassemble at four o'clock in front of the old police headquarters and board the coach for midtown, neither party will resort to violence. So it is a happy arrangement. Except that Larry has two hours to kill among the remnants of his heritage and not enough time to wander too far afield. For a brief while, long before Larry's affiliation with Empire Tours, there was one oasis east of the Bowery that could draw him down to this Ashkenazi Sahara: a hole-in-the-wall deli called Napthali's Noshes. The inauthentic ambience and decidedly gentile clientele made the sojourn tolerable, while the well-done brisket and extra-lean pastrami elevated him to gustatory heights. But this Disneyfied eatery went the way of all preserved flesh, so Larry usually passes his Wednesday afternoons hiking up to Tompkins Square Park and back down again. Today, however, P. J. Snipe is waiting for him at the bridge entrance.

Larry greets Snipe and brandishes his bouquet as evidence of his date. The tour supervisor shakes his hand and then waits for the Dutch to disperse. Rita Blatt hangs back at a distance of several yards, but makes no effort to leave him. Snipe inspects her warily like a high priest warding off a leper and then discharges a thick wad of phlegm onto the pavement.

"Did you hear the news, Bloom?" Snipe asks. "We're up shit's creek without a paddle."

"About this morning?"

"Yes, about this morning. It's absolute dog piss."

"I don't see why it's such a big deal," says Larry. "I think these Dutch actually enjoyed it."

"Who cares about these cretins? They've already paid for their tour. But after what happened this morning, we won't be able to lead a group of armed robbers through Fort Knox. You did hear the news, didn't you?"

"I'm not sure," Larry answers with trepidation. "What news?"

"That middle-aged broad with the Dutch consul turns out to be the wife of some big-time manufacturer. The television crews ran a short clip of the riot on the noon newscasts and they caught her on camera. They didn't even know what they had their hands on until the husband saw the coverage and ran out of his office shouting that his wife was porking a Fish Head. He made it as far as Municipal Plaza and dropped dead of a heart attack in the parking lot. Say, you must have passed right by there. You didn't see anything?"

"Not a thing."

"Anyway, Bloom, now Empire Tours is front-page news. And you know what that means. That means we're shoulder deep in dog piss."

"I see your point."

"Don't see my point," growls Snipe. "Eat, breathe, and shit my point, okay? Every two-bit journalist in this city would love an exclusive with the Dutch tourists who helped expose the scandal of the millennium. That's what they're billing it. That and Nethergate. Do you hear what I'm telling you, Bloom? You're a wanted man. You need to keep these cretins as isolated as possible. Make sure they stay far away from trouble and get them back to their hotels in one piece. We've already taken the liberty of rescheduling their flights. They're on a KLM charter out of Kennedy at ten thirty this evening. No need to hold them here overnight and give the media a crack at them. So be on the lookout, Bloom. And whatever you do, don't talk to any reporters."

Larry glances at Rita Blatt. She has retreated into the shade of a sickly poplar. She smiles at him when he looks at her and waves her fingertips.

"What about her?" Larry asks.

"Who the hell is she?"

"The reporter from the *Downtown Rag*. The one doing a feature on historic tours. She showed up at Castle Clinton and said you had okayed it. "

"Dog piss," says Snipe. "Just our screwy luck. But you know what to do, Bloom. Act like a man and ditch her."

"Ditch her?"

"That's right. Lose her. Scram. Gone. Good-bye. Make it look like an accident."

It would be my pleasure, Larry thinks. But easier said than done.

"And Bloom—"

"Yes?"

"I'll see you up in Riverdale at seven o'clock. Here's the destination."

Snipe gives him a business card with the grandmother's address printed on the back. Larry is about to object—he needs to meet Starshine in the West Village at eight thirty—but his boss is too quick on the draw. He numbs Larry's fingers with a ruthless handshake and immediately hails a passing cab, leaving his employee speechless at the curbside. The move is just like Snipe, Larry thinks. Act first, ask later. It makes Larry's blood boil, but it works. The self-serving prick will earn brownie points with his floozy of the week while Larry's dream date dines alone. He wishes he could call Starshine and postpone by an hour, but then she might outright cancel. She keeps a busy social calendar. His only hope is to drive like Big Louise and hope for the best.

Larry lights a cigarette and sets off for Tompkins Square Park. He has walked half a block before he senses Rita Blatt strolling beside him. She has stowed both her notepad and her umbrella inside her heavy canvas bag, so she no longer resembles an uptight journalist. Yet liberated from the protection of her professional disguise, the newswoman appears all the more undesirable. Her so-called shtick is her only redeeming grace. It justifies her appearance in a way that a circus sideshow legitimizes dwarves and bearded ladies. Without it, she appears haggard and spent. Like a plywood puppet, Larry thinks, crowned by a papier-mâché head.

"Where to?" she asks.

"Just walking."

"Then you won't mind walking me up to my flat, Larry, will you? It's not terribly far. Avenue A on the park. I want to phone the office to let them know that I have a story. My angle is going to be romance and tourism—putting the *guy* back in tour *guide*. I have a camera up at my place. You won't mind a photo, will you? And we'll need to put those flowers in some water. "

Larry tenses and instinctively clutches the bouquet to his chest.

"You can knock off the act. Just because I'm into this angst-ridden high-strung journalist shtick doesn't mean I'm not also a woman. I can tell when a guy has a thing for me. Call it a sixth sense. So there's no point in us wandering around the city all afternoon, playing cat and mouse games, and then exchanging phone numbers like characters in some 1950s romantic comedy, when you find me attractive and I don't think you're half-bad yourself. I know I'm very forward, maybe even a wee bit presumptuous, but it saves a lot of unnecessary grief in the long run. So I'll put the flowers in water and you'll get the grand tour of my place and we'll take it from there. But I have to warn you. I'm seeing somebody else, and I'm not ready to give him up. I believe I already mentioned that, but I want to put all of my cards on the table. So, anyway, what are *you* thinking?"

"I don't know," answers Larry.

He lets Rita Blatt lead him up Essex Street and onto Avenue A. She prattles endlessly about the gentrification of the neighborhood, about why she didn't attend journalism school, about her considerable experiences with psychiatric treatment and relationship counseling and New Age "personal enhancement" at the Society for Secular Harmony. Some people leap from one form of self-examination to another; Rita Blatt prefers the synergistic approach. The more varied the therapeutic techniques, the better her prospects for overcoming her insecurities. And she is unquestionably a woman with an insecurity for every occasion. Larry knows that he owes it to Rita Blatt to set her straight about the flowers, to inform her point-blank that he's both psychologically and probably biologically incapable of meeting her expectations, but he lacks either the heart or the courage. Most likely a combination of both. He has limited experience rejecting amorous proposals. The few times he has turned down an advance—the blind receptionist at Empire Tours who resembles a porcupine, a broad-shouldered alcoholic neighbor in her late fifties—the spurned women have turned hostile. Larry understands their rage. One had to swallow a lot of self-respect to proposition an ugly person; finding out that even someone you find unattractive won't date you is a damning blow. So Larry truly sympathizes with these poor creatures. He has been on the other side of the conflict and suffered his own slights at the hands of marginally passable females. The last thing he wishes to do is wound Rita Blatt's already fragile ego. He would also like to avoid a drubbing with an umbrella. So he walks and listens, desperately searching for a plausible escape, until they arrive at Tompkins Square Park.

Rita occupies a sixth-story walk-up at the far end of a constricted passageway. The lighting in the corridor is poor and it does not improve inside the confines of the journalist's dreary flat. Her porcelain lamps cast somber ringlets of light from under thick gray shades. The only window in the main room looks out onto a narrow air shaft. Larry surveys the apartment from the vestibule while Rita rummages her kitchen cabinets for a vase. Her walls are plastered with travel brochures and posters from classic films. Katharine Hepburn smiles over Athens. Marlon Brando and Karl Malden keep watch on either side of Milan. A small wooden table stands in one corner, supporting an old computer and a stack of neatly folded undergarments. A futon mattress abuts the far wall. The greater portion of the cramped room is occupied by cardboard boxes heaped high with manila folders. The sparse decor suggests a stage set from an off-Broadway play—ones of those gritty, working-class plays touting frugal living that Larry's father finds so edifying. This is a home without joy. It reminds Larry of his own apartment.

"Take a load off while I pour us some drinks," Rita calls from the kitchen. "I'm sorry there are no chairs. I used to borrow a couple from a friend, but then she moved to Astoria and took them back. So what's your poison? Cheap red wine or cheap whiskey?"

"Nothing, thanks. I'm on duty."

He sits down on the mattress and rests his feet on the faded linoleum.

"You have to have something," says Rita. "It will loosen you up."

"I'll have a glass of water."

"Water it is," agrees Rita. "Draft or on tap?"

The journalist emerges from the kitchen carrying two paper cups. She cozies up beside Larry on the futon, much too close, and swizzles her wine with her pinkie. He inches away and looks pointedly at his watch.

"We should be getting back," he says.

"We have plenty of time," answers Rita. "Don't be so uptight."

A crash behind the plaster cuts off any further discussion. It is rapidly followed by the distinctive sound of human bodies compressing springs. Katharine Hepburn's smile appears suddenly indecent.

"What's that?" asks Larry for no particular reason.

"Every Wednesday," says Rita. "It only lasts about ten minutes."

The sound intensifies. It is punctuated by masculine grunts and feminine moans.

"It gets to me sometimes," says Rita. "Some people have no respect for other people's personal space. But I imagine I make just as much noise, so I never say anything. My guess is that the crackpot next door has a standing appointment with a call service."

"Whatever," says Larry. "It's still outrageous."

And all the hostility he has been nursing toward Rita Blatt now shifts to the indecent sound behind the plaster. What right do these people have to torment this single, funny-looking woman every week? Their lovemaking seems spiteful and cruel. They must be driving poor Rita mad. Their duet is already driving Larry to the brink after only a few seconds. And he won't tolerate it. He'll fight fire with fire. Larry thinks of the nasty old biddy who used to live below him in Morningside. If he so much as walked to the bathroom after midnight, she would pound on the ceiling with a broomstick. He couldn't fathom her obsession with silence. Why couldn't she have just accepted that some friction is an inevitable part of life and that certain irritations are beyond human control? Now Larry understands. He removes his loafer and hammers the plaster behind the mattress.

"Don't bother," says Rita. "It's not worth it."

"It will send them a message."

"Please, Larry. It's really not worth the effort."

Larry keeps pounding. The slap of leather against plaster fuses with the gasps and groans of human passion, producing a cacophonous fugue of eroticism and outrage. The combination is almost symphonic. It rattles the porcelain lamps and the cardboard boxes. Larry's shoe leaves a cuffed outline on the defoliated wallpaper. Shut up, goddamn it! Larry thinks. It is impossible that they don't hear him. And yet the sound of their debauchery increases, as though fed by his own clamor. He throws all of his weight, all of his anger, into his jack-hammering. Their lust soars like a tidal breaker. The universe's two most savage forces have been unleashed. This is a battle of unyielding wills—desire versus desperation. Although nature will tolerate the illusion that this is a competition between equal combatants, the match has been fixed from the outset. Eons of evolutionary biology favor desire. While Larry's hands are locked in a life-and-death struggle with a stranger's wall, Rita Blatt's find their way to his groin.

"Jesus!" he shouts.

"Fuck this!" retorts his hidden opponent.

Then all is quiet. Larry is suddenly alone in a homely woman's apartment and she has her hands nuzzled in his crotch. He pulls away. Then he slams the wall twice more for effect and slips into his shoes.

"What's wrong?" asks Rita.

"I'm late," Larry lies. "I need to be at the pickup point twenty minutes early."

Larry darts out into the corridor. He is relieved, but also angry. Angry at Rita for misreading his intentions; angry at himself if he has caused her any pain. But the greater part of his rage is reserved for the couple behind the plaster, for the assuredly good-looking creatures who have ruined his afternoon with their mewing and whimpering and spite. It is like hosting a private banquet before the victims of a famine. The sound of passion, much more so than its sight or scent, is the greatest of all torments.

A door further up the passageway opens and suddenly, unexpectedly, Larry stands face-to-face with one of his persecutors. The man is unkempt and his denim jacket exhibits the wear of overuse, but there is no mistaking the masculinity in his rugged features. He's a blue-collar Adonis. A shower and a shave would transform this derelict into an older replica of the matinee idol from the Maiden Lane McDonalds. In contrast, it would take extensive plastic surgery to work the same wonder on Larry. He glares at the man, then holds his head high and strides past him at a brisk pace. He keeps his gaze focused straight in front of him until he steps into the street. The last thing Larry desires is a confrontation. He already regrets his antics with the shoe. Although part of him condemns himself for begrudging this middle-aged Don Juan his happiness, another part sees the hirsute ape as a living monument to injustice. As the enemy.

Larry takes a deep breath to curtail his anger. This man is not his enemy, he decides. He's just some ordinary stiff enjoying a roll in the sack. Maybe with a call girl. Probably with his old lady. And there's no harm in that. The truth of the matter is that Larry should feel for this poor fellow, pity him because he's past his prime and hopelessly grizzled and because his female accomplice is probably just as timeworn as he is. Larry suspects that he would never date the wasted woman behind the plaster. And after tonight, he reassures himself, he won't have any cause to envy the husband.

He clenches his fists.

He is Larry Bloom. He will have Starshine. His luck is imprinted in his genes.

THE BIOLOGY OF LUCK

# CHAPTER 9

BY LARRY BLOOM

Somewhere, anywhere, in a city of nine thousand thoroughfares and eight million people, she has lost her house keys. Starshine chains her Higgins on Fillmore Avenue, thankful that she has mastered the craft of misplaced property, that past visits to the locksmith have taught her to separate her latchkey from her bicycle key. The local locksmith is a feeler. He's a taciturn Afrikaner who leers at this customers through the mirror over his electronic buffing machine and then pets their fingers when handing them the merchandise. He is one of those infuriating men who believe that the more physical contact he has with women, even if only the nuzzling of palms or the brushing of shoulders, the more likely it is that they will open themselves to his advances. Thinking of his guttural accent and sable fingers makes Starshine shudder, but she will have to endure his gaping and fondling unless she recovers her keys. And the possibility seems unlikely. They could be almost anywhere. In Hannibal Tuck's spartan cubicle, on the floor of Jack Bascombs's grubby apartment. Or, most likely, neglected on some busy sidewalk, blending with heaps of household trash and discarded newspapers. An airline label with her address and phone number hangs from her keychain. This identification tag struck her as a clever precaution when she attached it, shortly after a previous visit to the locksmith, but now the merit of the safeguard appears doubtful. Nobody will bother to return a latchkey. It has neither sentimental appeal nor the significant monetary worth that might attract a Good Samaritan—especially one hoping for a cash reward. Only the criminal element will see its value. How could she be so careless? She's practically rolled out a welcome mat for every burglar and rapist in the Tri-State area. She will have to change the locks. That will cost a small fortune. She will have to invite the locksmith into her home. That may cost her sanity. And even then there are no guarantees. A determined felon, having traveled all the way out to Greenpoint, won't be deterred by a new lock. He might even see it as a challenge. Starshine runs through a list of all the personal effects she might have lost: her mother's engagement ring, her heart-shaped locket containing photographs of Aunt Agatha and Uncle Luther, the cowery-and-coral bracelet that Jack Bascomb gave her for their anniversary. The latchkey, she decides, is the only one she can't make do without.

Starshine searches the sidewalk for Bone. The one-armed super usually suns himself through the afternoon, his presence as fixed as that of a lawn ornament, but today his aluminum chair rests folded against a mailbox. The Jesus freak and his sister have also abandoned their customary perch. The stoop is untended. On any other day, this desolation would send Starshine's spirits soaring, but this afternoon, it only feeds her escalating panic. The outside buzzers don't work. She has no way to gain access to the building. She also has no guarantee that Eucalyptus is home, although she can't imagine where else her roommate might be, and the super holds the only spare key to the apartment. Her entire kingdom is crumbling for want of a metal sliver. All is hopeless. Starshine sits down on the concrete steps and rests her face in her hands. She is too drained to think straight, too exasperated to go on. What's the goddamned point of fighting off Colby and Jack and Hannibal Tuck if she can't even get into her own home? So much for freedom, she thinks. So much for a life without men. Then the building door crashes open and Frederico Lazar glowers at Starshine. She catches the door as he storms out into the street.

Lazar is Eucalyptus's sometime lover and supplier of ivory. Although his primary enterprise is the distribution of sheet metal throughout the Third World, he also dabbles in small arms and petrochemicals. The arrogant boor fancies himself a modern-day Theodore Roosevelt. He can talk for hours at a stretch about horse breeding and the game of the Serengeti. Starshine once made the mistake of going on a double date with Eucalyptus, Lazar, and Colby Parker. She assumed the two wealthy men would admire each other. Instead, Lazar lectured Colby on the depravity of the welfare state and the dangers of environmental regulation, concluding by accusing "corporate socialists" and "the pansies of industry" of undermining free enterprise and subverting American individualism. Jack Bascomb would have decked the oaf. Colby merely poured ice water into his lap and walked out. Frederico Lazar is at the bottom of Starshine's list of human beings, leagues below even Bone and her downstairs neighbor, and still Eucalyptus tolerates him. Not that she likes him any more than Starshine does. But he provides her with free tusks and he's allegedly great in bed. Some days, Starshine wants to impale Lazar on one of his own horns. Today, now that he has given her access to her own apartment, she'd willingly kiss him.

She races up the steps. Ragged stuffed animals and decapitated action figurines clutter the stairwell. The hallways are an unconscionable mess. Their disarray is trivial compared to the post-apocalyptic nightmare she finds beyond the open door of her apartment.

"What the hell happened?" Starshine demands.

Splintered wood and shattered ivory covers the floor of the common room. The chairs have been overturned, the refrigerator lies on its side. One of the drapes dangles precariously from a fractured curtain rod. The collage of newsprint, torn from the walls of Eucalyptus's bedroom, lies crumpled in the center of her mattress. Even the kitchen drawers have been emptied of cutlery and stacked on the gas range. The devastation is total. But in the center of the battleground, unshaken like a mighty oak after a squall, sits Eucalyptus. She is etching rigging onto her miniature schooner when Starshine enters.

"What the hell happened?" Starshine asks again.

Eucalyptus looks up indifferently.

"I had a fight with Frederico," she says. "But it's over now."

"I should say it's over," snaps Starshine. "There's nothing left to break."

"He's cheating on me," says Eucalyptus. "He denies it, but I can tell he is."

Starshine set the fruit basket on the table and slumps into a kitchen chair. A Bosc pear slips from under the cellophane and topples to the floor with a dull thud. She brushes off the ivory dust and examines its damaged flesh. It cannot be helped, she thinks, tucking the wounded fruit back into the basket.

"He claimed he's been away all month, that he just returned today, but when I told him that two presidents of General Motors died this week, he said he already knew. Tell me, darling, how a man who has been on business in rural Bangladesh since the first of May could possibly get hold of information like that? The bastard's lying through his teeth. He's a two-timing monster. "

Starshine ignores the holes in her roommates reasoning. "And he's a vandal," she says. "You can do better."

"Oh, this," says Eucalyptus, waving her arm to encompass the destruction. "Frederico didn't do this. I did. I'm really sorry. "

Starshine glares at her roommate. She has already primed herself for an attack against Frederico Lazar, but Eucalyptus's confession leaves her speechless. She does not want to have an argument with her roommate. Certainly not in her current state of mind, not on a day like this, but she can't fathom letting the bitch get away with this. Her own roommate, her best female friend, has destroyed her apartment. It is too fucking much. Maybe she should take her to task. Things couldn't get much worse.

A heavy rap on the door breaks her train of thought.

"Who the hell could that be?" asks Starshine.

"It might be Frederico, darling," says Eucalyptus. "You'd better answer it. "

"And why on earth do I want to see Fredrico? Get the goddamn door."

Eucalyptus reluctantly deposits the schooner in her workbox and walks to the entryway. She peers through the peephole.

"It's the nut from downstairs," she says. "He knocked before too."

"We're not home."

"He probably wants to talk about the bed."

"We're not home," Starshine says again. "He'll go away."

The Dominican knocks several more times.

"He's not giving up," says Eucalyptus. "Are you sure it wouldn't be easier to talk to him?"

"If you open that door," threatens Starshine. "I'll strangle him."

"It's your apartment. You're the boss. "

The knocking eventually stops and Eucalyptus returns to the table. The missing latchkey and the ravaged apartment have already oiled Starshine's tear ducts. The Jesus freak's house call releases the sluice gates. She snatches a miniature ivory harp off the tabletop and hurls it against the radiator. Shards of tusk scatter across the floorboards. Starshine bursts into tears.

"Are you all right, darling?" asks Eucalyptus.

Starshine shakes her head.

"No, I'm not all right," she sobs. "I'm as far from all right as I could possibly be. First, this girl starts throwing her clothes off a window ledge, and then Colby tries to coerce me into visiting Italy, and now Jack tries to guilt me into fleeing to Holland forever. I just can't take it anymore. All I wanted was a little peace and quiet, but I come home to a war zone. And to top it all off, I can't find my goddam latchkey. How the hell can I be all right?"

Eucalyptus retrieves a dustpan from under the sink. She sweeps the scrimshaw fragments into piles that resemble Indian mounds. Several minutes pass before she speaks.

"I forgot to tell you," she finally says. "I have good news for you."

"It would have to be good news," says Starshine. "Nothing worse could happen."

"A man named Snipe called from some tour company. He found your key. "

"My latchkey?"

"The one and only. He said you dropped it in Chinatown. He tried to chase you down, but you ran off. He said to phone him. "

"The man on Mulberry Street," reflects Starshine. "Of course!"

"Oh, and more excitement, darling. Your friend Parker called three times. He didn't sound like a happy camper. "

"His father died."

"Garfield Lloyd Parker died?"

"It's national news," says Starshine. "You'll get a front-page obituary for your wall."

Starshine stands up and stretches her arms over her head. She would like to be upset at her roommate for forgetting about the latchkey, for destroying the apartment, but her anger has already faded. She will not need to change the locks. She will not need to visit the Afrikaner. The kindness of strangers has salvaged her day. If she ever sees a discarded key on the sidewalk, she vows, she will make every effort to return it to its rightful owner. That is the least she can do. But right now she needs time to recover from her harrowing morning. She will not cover the office from three to five. The crazies will get over it; they'll find someone to pester in another office. Marsha Riley will never know the difference. And besides, the fund director would certainly understand. How couldn't she? Anybody who has endured a morning as taxing and traumatic as Starshine's is more than entitled to take the remainder of the day off.

# MIDTOWN

Big Louise lights into the accelerator with all the brimming energy of the dying workday, mustering her accumulated rage and boredom and the weight of her three-Quarter-Pounders lunch for one final onslaught against the forces of inertia. At midmorning, her motoring is brash; at half past four, it is outright hazardous. The faster she speeds, the sooner she leaves. If she catches every green light on Madison Avenue, which she never fails to do, she can be ensconced on her sofa, watching syndicated television with her cat, while the rest of the drivers are still dropping off their coaches at the compound. Her objective irks Larry to no end. He has no gripes with Big Louise in principle, doesn't blame her for wanting to punch her time clock and clear out at the earliest viable opportunity, but his already compressed and thoroughly inadequate survey of midtown history is designed to last twenty-five minutes. Big Louise can make Rockefeller Center from Union Square in ten. So Larry has no choice but to keep pace with his pilot, charging through a century of development at sixty seconds per decade, raising Edwardian mansions and the United Nations in the course of one breath. As they approach the Flatiron Building, he is clearing sheep pastures and laying out the street grid; by the breakneck turn at Greeley Square, he has gentrified shantytowns with Morgans and Astors and Vanderbilts. The Empire State Building warrants two blocks; the public library only a passing mention. Not even Carnegie Hall, to which maestros devote lifetimes of practice, is spared the abridger's scalpel; Larry can get his Dutch burghers in and out again in two short sentences. A guided tour, like virtually all other speaking engagements, has no intrinsic length. Its duration reflects the exigencies of the occasion, the stamina of the orator, and occasionally the patience of the audience. This is the first critical difference between art and life. Architects and masons may labor for generations to build Rome out of brick and mortar, but a fast-talking tour guide can shape Manhattan with words in a matter of minutes. Larry is pointedly aware of the second critical difference between art and life: Rome endures.

When they eclipse the formal gardens of Bryant Park, zipping past the overdressed power diners in their glass pavilion, Larry succumbs to his own worst instincts. He is sun-drenched and sore. His sinuses ache. A thin film of perspiration and urban grit mats down his hair. Meanwhile, his audience, indifferent to his ongoing sacrifice, goes about its business without the slightest hint of acknowledgment. The younger couples chatter and exchange addresses; the older companions snooze or gaze vacantly out the windows. Rita Blatt has found a seat at the far rear of the bus, across from the lavatory, where she holds her nose with one hand while scribbling in a notepad with the other. Willem Van Huizen is unabashedly reading the *New York Times*. This is the tour guide's perdition, the docent's equivalent of delivering a lecture in his birthday suit. Larry takes a deep breath and tosses caution to the wind. Now he really will entertain these lemmings. He starts off slowly, tentatively, casually noting that the sloping contours of the W. R. Grace Building double in winter as a ski jump. His account meets with no objection. Then he declares that the dinner fare at Lutece is concocted entirely from soybean paste. Still no outcry. Larry lets his imagination take over. The Chrysler Building was constructed by religious fundamentalists according to the biblical specifications for the Tower of Babel; Dorothy Parker ran a brothel from the Algonquin Hotel; the cutlery at the Yale Club is fashioned from human bone. He reveals that the Museum of Modern Art burned down during the '68 riots and that all the paintings in the galleries are actually hastily rendered reproductions, that Bergdorf and Goodman changed their names from Sacco and Vanzetti. His charges do not care. He is halfway through his harrowing tale of the indentured elves and impoverished trolls who perished carving the latticework on the facade of Saint Bartholomew's Church when the bells of Saint Patrick's toll the turn of the hour. Although it is already five o'clock, they have only just reached Saint Pat's. They're running late. Larry glances at his watch and then turns to Big Louise, fearing some novel calamity, when he suddenly realizes that he has not been without an audience. Big Louise has intentionally slowed their progress. Her hulking frame is convulsing with laughter. For a moment—tears streaming down her cheeks, teeth flashing between ample lips—her face actually appears pretty.

"That was good," she says. "That was real good."

"I know," answers Larry. "That's why I earn the big money."

He pats Big Louise on the shoulder and leads his ignorant burghers off the coach.

They scale the steps of the world's eleventh largest church, necks craned to admire the ornate spires and French-Gothic pinnacles, then pass through a narrow antechamber into the tranquility of the past. The handcrafted rose windows and marble memorials of Saint Patrick's undo all of Larry's reconstructive efforts, razing skyscrapers, depopulating shantytowns, thrusting his tourists into an age before travel and leisure. This is the sacrosanct witchcraft of the Catholic tradition, its ability to elevate one to the heights of the High Middle Ages. There is no longer any need for history or anecdote. The lambent flicker of ten thousand candles speaks for itself. The cathedral is the ideal place to conclude a day of sightseeing, a sanctuary where a person can momentarily escape from the rough-and-tumble of the city and retreat into one's own thoughts. This is the universal allure of cathedrals everywhere, Larry thinks. They are all the same. Like cab rides. Like funerals. And maybe this consistency should be comforting. But the cathedral is a double-edged sword for the beset and the tormented. The vaulted alcoves and solitary chambers force a person to reflect. They demand self-examination. To Larry, who has little faith in a Supreme Being and less in himself, these weekly visits are a form of medieval torture. He prefers to stand on the steps and sneak a cigarette while his charges explore on their own.

Willem Van Huizen has other plans for Larry's visit. Having lost his friend the deaf cleric to the mystique of the altar, the Dutchman reverts to his earlier target. He positions himself between Larry and the entrance, inching him backward toward the candle-lined tables so there is no escape.

"*Meneer Blowm*," he says. "I want to congratulate you on a simply stupendous tour. As we say in the Netherlands, *heel leuk*. Extremely excellent. Your style reminded me of Pastor Bloem's sermons. Are you certain that you are not related?"

"Anything is possible."

"I am in complete agreement. Anything *is* possible, *Meneer Blowm*. Take a look as this contraption, for example. This is truly a wonder of science."

Van Huizen extracts a small silver vessel from his tote bag; it resembles a flat-topped teapot.

"Isn't it remarkable, *Meneer Blowm*?"

"Unquestionably," answers Larry.

"It's an oil lamp, *Meneer Blowm*. Much like those used in biblical times. Only this particular lamp is specially designed for air travel. It can carry a flame across the oceans. Now isn't that something?"

"It is *something*," says Larry. "Now if you'll kindly—"

"My dear friend, Father O'Shea, entrusted me with this marvel. He's a divine man, our Father O'Shea. Pastor Bloem was telling me as much only last week. Even though Father O'Shea is a Catholic, Paster Bloem holds him in the highest regard."

"And why not?"

"My thoughts exactly. No reason to stickle over the finer points. But as I was saying, Father O'Shea procured this little contraption so I could transport a flame from Saint Patrick's Cathedral back to his parish in Utrecht. He's an American by birth, O'Shea is. An expatriate of the most desirable sort. He feared this might be an inconvenience to Klara and me, but I told him I'd be honored. Isn't that right, Klara?"

"It is such an honor for my husband," echoes Klara. "For both of us."

"Now if I could just figure out where I pour the oil," mutters Van Huizen, "I'd be all set. I'm not one for modern conveniences. Do you think you could lend me your expertise, *Meneer Blowm?*"

A tap on the shoulder extricates Larry from this entreaty. He turns to face a full-figured matron on the far side of sixty boasting a scallop-shell necklace and synthetic henna hair. She offers him the sweetest of smiles. He smiles back politely. For some inexplicable reason, although the two women share no physical resemblance, this strangers reminds Larry of his mother.

"I'm hoping you can help me, young man," she says. "I'm looking for some sort of central office. The guard out front said I should ask inside. "

The woman has mistaken Larry for an employee of the church. This has happened several times before. For some reason, either his guide's name tag or his clipboard or possibly some sixth sense regarding his long-term celibacy, middle-aged women regularly take him for a minor clerical dignitary. Experience has immunized him to this insult. He makes no effort to clarify his identity, but offers the woman detailed directions to the administrative wing of the archdiocese. She thanks him profusely and steps out of Larry's line of vision. He recoils with a start. Is it mirage or cataclysm? Unquestionably cataclysm. While Larry was assisting the aging matriarch, Willem Van Huizen has ignited.

"Roll!" Larry shouts. "Get down and roll!"

But the Dutchman does not roll. He stands relatively motionless, his arms elevated and forked at the elbows like a scarecrow, seemingly examining his own predicament. As though self-immolation were an intellectual exercise. The flames have burned up the back of his tweed jacket and engulfed his shoulders.

"Goddamnit!" Larry shouts again. "Get down and roll!"

The crowd draws back to admire the spectacle from a safe distance. A bespectacled priest dashes down the central aisle securing his skullcap with his hand; he stops short at the second to last pew and expresses his shock in expletives. Klara Van Huizen attempts to rescue her husband, but retreats when confronted with a wall of heat. The Dutchman makes no effort to put out the flames. Instead, he staggers forward like a zombie, his face devoid of expression, then rotates in a semicircle and accidentally kicks the oil lamp against the poor box. The clatter of metal striking wood reverberates through the chamber. And it is this sound, surprisingly like the clangor of bedsprings, that spurs Larry into action.

He charges across the gallery and mounts the Dutchman from the front, sending them both tumbling into a stand of alabaster icons. Then they are rolling across the marble tile, amidst the shattered limbs of Saint Peter and Saint Francis, scattering onlookers with their horizontal tarantella. The shock of the fall jolts Van Huizen to his senses and he digs his nails into Larry's throat. Larry must fight both the Dutchman and the flames simultaneously. The heat is scorching his hands. Van Huizen is cutting off his air supply. He attempts to flip the Dutchman onto his back and fails. All seems lost. And then, Larry's reserve energy entirely depleted, Van Huizen takes over. Now it is the Dutchman who rolls them down the central aisle, dislodging statues and lecterns, trying to punish his assailant and extinguishing the flames in the process. Hate triumphs over love and the fire is dead in an instant. Both wrestlers are still alive. Larry pries Van Huizen's hands from his throat and pushes the Dutchman, maybe too forcefully, into a table of prayer books. He examines his arms for burns. His shirt is charred at the elbows and across the waist, but its contents are unharmed. Then he instinctively checks on the welfare of his magic letter. Although singed across the top of the envelope and somewhat the worse for wear, it too has survived the trial by fire. Another ordeal has come to a tolerable conclusion.

Larry is lying sprawled against the back of a pew, panting, when the paramedics join his tour for their second visit of the day. Only this time they want him, need him, make every effort to deluge him with the clinical attention and pseudo-personal concern they so unjustly denied him on the parapet of Castle Clinton. A muscular black man bombards him with questions. Can he speak? Is he in pain? Does he remember what happened? As though the sacred atmosphere of the cathedral has unleashed the medic's ambition to play Grand Inquisitor. But Larry will have none of the man's belated regard. If these fools in uniform had any understanding of the particulars of the situation, they would understand that he rescued an imbecile. And a dangerous imbecile to boot! That makes Larry an aggravated nuisance, not a hero. He should be cuffed rather than coddled.

Larry stands up and double checks that his magic letter is safely stowed in his breast pocket. Then he brusquely steps past the befuddled paramedics and out onto the steps of the cathedral. A team of aggressive professionals is loading Van Huizen onto an ambulance. The patient is fully conscious and beaming; he is thriving on the attention. His somber wife has her hands on the charred patches of his coat, as though assessing the cost of repairs, impeding the efforts of the EMS team. Fools! Larry curses. Goddamn fools, all of them. But the truth of the matter is that Larry isn't angry with the Van Huizens or even with the medical team, but with himself. Why did he risk his own life and his literary career and his future with Starshine for a presumptuous stranger? Why couldn't he put himself on the line like that for the teenage girl at the waterfront? What sort of man can't manage to rescue a beautiful young girl but somehow saves a blustering dolt? Larry thinks of all the single women he knows in their fifties and sixties, the divorcees, the widows, the spinsters, all desperate for a decent, hardworking man to marry. They will be his someday, he fears, when it no longer matters. That is the bitter ironic connection between his heroics and his romantic prospects. It is all a matter of too little, too late.

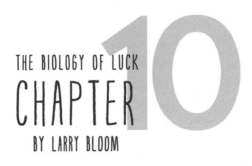

THE BIOLOGY OF LUCK

# CHAPTER 10

BY LARRY BLOOM

The ferry deposits her at Saint George's Station. From there, she must ride the light rail out to Old Town, then catch a bus down to South Beach. The trip takes nearly an hour, but Starshine does not mind the delay. A bout of sea air has done much to soothe her nerves and purge her anger. She relishes another brief recess during which to collect herself, to recover from the jolts of the afternoon, before her impending confrontation with her aunt. Experience has taught her that visits to Aunt Agatha these days are never soothing.

In the old days, it was different. Nobody knew how to repair a shattered heart or mend a shredded ego as proficiently as Agatha. Her home-brewed remedies and perennial altruism faced down a myriad of teenage crises. When Starshine's mother died—shortly after the death of Agatha's own husband—the dear woman moved to San Francisco to save her niece the added trauma of relocation. When no teenage lothario stepped forward to take the girl to the junior prom, the discerning widow scheduled a family vacation in Hawaii to conflict with the dance. She may have been the homely daughter of a Bavarian pipe-fitter with a third-grade education, a mediocrity in the sight of man and God, but to her surrogate daughter, she filled the roles of both heroine and confidante through an otherwise forlorn and turbulent adolescence. But that was before. Before the diabetic blindness and the throat cancer, before age asserted its claim upon her retinas and her larynx, before darkness and silence enveloped the last of her alacrity. All that remains is a withered husk of memories. Now that the old woman's only purpose is to divulge her horde of buried secrets before they accompany her to the grave. Debunking past myth is her principal pleasure. Bosc pears and clandestine cigarettes sustain her on her mission.

Starshine settles into an aisle seat on the commuter train. She rests the fruit basket on her lap and observes the middle-aged nine-to-fivers scurrying through the last lap of their rat race. The men skim ragged newspapers and periodically run their fingers between limp collars and chafed necks; the women examine themselves in pocket mirrors. They take no interest in each other. They do not converse. The trek from ferry to rail to bus is a necessary inconvenience, an unfortunate drain on their pressing schedules. It is far from a pleasure outing. But to Starshine, sheltered from this domain of lackluster routine, these men and women are as exotic (and as menacing) as the big cats at the zoo. She admires their tenacity. She fears their indifference. She wonders what drives them out of bed each morning— onto the ferry, into their offices, through their empty and colorless workdays. She tells herself that this is their business, their choice. Not hers. And at the same time, she longs to warn them, to shake them, to let them know that they are only hours away from their massive coronaries, and that throat cancer and blindness wait right around the corner. Aging isn't a gradual process. It's sudden and relentless. One minute you're visiting your niece in New York City, buying her costly perfumes at Christian Dior, treating her to four-star lunches at Aquavit and the 21 Club, grilling the floor manager at Le Bernardin on his suspicious dearth of female waitstaff, and then some microscopic internal stitch comes undone, or a few cells wake up in a disagreeable mood, and before you know what's happened, you're on your back in a nursing home, rubbing apricots with your earlobes. Or dead in a municipal parking lot. And unless you're famous, unless you're one of the anointed few who are born both photogenic and lucky, you're quickly forgotten. This is Starshine's worst fear. This is Agatha's fate.

She transfers to the bus, rides past the medical center, and then walks the final eight blocks to the glue factory. That is Agatha's pet name for Bayview Manor, something she picked up from a magazine article on horse breeding, although the facility actually offers state-of-the-art care in modestly comfortable surroundings. The home occupies a turn-of-the-twentieth-century mansion. The structure was once the centerpiece of a vast estate, the suburban hacienda of a prosperous bauxite importer, and it has experienced previous incarnations as a coast guard station and a home for incapacitated seamen. The formal English garden and the tennis lawn have long since been cleared for the construction of a cinderblock administrative annex, and the spacious drawing rooms and parlors have been viciously subdivided, but a handful of the ancient sailors remain on the property in accordance with the original deed of sale. The living quarters are copious and sanitary. The food is abundant, if not terribly eclectic. Staten Island Community Hospital is within shouting distance. What more can an old blind woman possibly need? If Bayview isn't the Waldorf-Astoria, it certainly isn't a glue factory.

The day nurse greets Starshine at the registration desk. Miss Bohm is an elfin, puckered creature well past retirement age who could easily pass as an inmate rather than a warden. A jagged scar cuts across the left side of her face, from eye to lip; it brands her one of the last living survivors of the Hindenburg explosion. She is Starshine's opposite—a beautiful young woman thrust into premature ugliness—and maybe for that reason they have struck up a close acquaintanceship.

"Look what the cat dragged in," says Miss Bohm. "And she's brought such a lovely basket. Agatha will be delighted."

"It has been a while, hasn't it?" says Starshine. "I've had a hell of a month."

"A month isn't so long. Your aunt will be overjoyed to see you. She is such a remarkable woman, that aunt of yours. And the stories she tells . . . a regular Gracie Allen. She has us in stitches nearly every morning. But she's also very naughty, my dear. She hides cigarettes inside her wig and smokes them in the middle of the night. You really have to scold her for us. It's bad for her, but it's also dangerous. We can't have our patients smoking in bed."

"How is she?" asks Starshine.

She follows Miss Bohm along the passageway. A shriveled man in a wheelchair bobs his head at her as she passes and she quickly looks away. She can't help viewing the elderly like expensive glassware: any admiration is tempered by a fear of breaking them.

"She's as well as she can be," says Miss Bohm, "Mood swings. Lots of pent up anger. She'll be telling a delightful story and all of a sudden she'll start cussing about being penned up in the glue factory. Her mind wanders. She's like the girl in the nursery rhyme: when she's good, she's very, very good, but when she's bad, she's horrid. And I'm afraid today is one of her bad days. "

"Maybe the fruit will cheer her up. I bought the largest basket I could find."

"That's sweet, dear," says Miss Bohm. "But there isn't really any need. We always tell her that you've brought the largest basket. You are aware that she doesn't eat any of it. Honestly, there's no call for you to be feeding me and Nurse Tithers. But your aunt appreciates the thought."

"I do hope the basket will cheer her up. Last time was just unbearable."

Starshine's previous visit coincided with the farthest advance of Agatha's revisionist crusade. Having decided that her niece was unenlightened with regard to her own sister-in-law's marriage, delinquently so, she bombarded Starshine with a salvo of the woman's secrets and sufferings. Did Starshine know that her father frequented brothels along the San Francisco waterfront? That while her poor mother sewed her own dresses by hand, the bastard she had married lavished hookers with silks and satins? That she had even caught him with one of the whores in their own bedroom? The stories were whetted, painful, and often extremely inconsistent. Brazen streetwalkers instantly transmuted into high-class call girls; the back alleys of San Francisco's Barbary Coast flowed into the boulevards of prewar Munich. Aunt

Agatha further undermined her own credibility by periodically lapsing into anecdotes picked up at the family dinner table, the fragments of the history of genocide that were Uncle Luther's final legacy, so one moment Starshine's father would be carousing at a cathouse and the next he'd be liquidating kulaks. It is impossible to tell where truth lets off and fantasy takes over. But there are two convictions about which Starshine harbors absolutely no doubts. One certainty is that her father's suicide had as much to do with women as with money. Throughout her childhood, he exuded the distinctive hunger of a man on the prowl; it is the only lasting impression he had left on his ten-year-old daughter. The other certainty is that his philandering doesn't matter, that it cannot be undone, that there is no afterlife and no salvation and that the dead should be left to decay in peace. Yet Aunt Agatha values these stories immeasurably, conceives of them as some sort of perverse oral legacy, as her homage to history and justice, and as Aunt Agatha remains among the living, Starshine has no choice but to endure.

Miss Bohm knocks on Agatha's door to announce a visitor and then leaves Starshine to her mission. Starshine finds her aunt propped up on a stack of pillows. The old woman is not wearing her wig and her thin wisps of white hair give her an otherworldly, almost angelic appearance. Agatha stares when her niece enters.

"Who's there?" she demands in a mechanized voice.

"Hi, Aunt Agatha," says Starshine. "I've brought you a basket of fruit."

"I don't want fruit. It rots and it stinks. I want a cigarette."

The old woman sniffs and blinks her vacant eyes.

"What kind of fruit?" she asks.

"Nectarines, oranges, plumbs, apricots."

"Bosc pears?"

"Yes, Bosc pears. I remember what you like."

"How many?" demands Agatha. "How many pears?"

"Five," Starshine lies. There is only one.

"What a waste of money," says Agatha. "I could have made do with one or two."

"Only the best for my favorite aunt."

"Then come here and give your favorite aunt a hug."

Agatha extends her arms like a sleepwalker and Starshine folds into her embrace. The old woman's body smells of industrial soap and disinfectant. She is too clean. Like an object on permanent display in a museum. And it is this aroma, such a contrast to her surrogate mother's lost smell of burning wood and hyacinth, upon which Starshine blames her discomfort. She sits down on the edge of the bed. She will make this a short visit.

"So how have you been since last time I saw you?" asks Starshine.

"I died twice. They melted me into glue. "

"So how have you really been since the last time?" Starshine asks again.

"I don't remember. I can't think back that far."

Starshine places the Bosc pear between her aunt's fingers. The old woman cradles the fruit in both hands and picks at the stem. Then she raises it to her nose and nuzzles the smooth skin against her cheek. A thin smile curves across her face. She is like a little girl with a new toy, a woman after orgasm, a mother caressing a newborn child. This is her happiness.

Agatha lurches forward suddenly and opens her eyes.

"I remember what I wanted to tell you," she exclaims. "I told the nurse to remind me, but she didn't. She's not very efficient. She gets confused and makes all sorts of mistakes with my medication. Yesterday, she tried to trick me into taking two round pills. I told her I take one round pill and one long one. And she had the nerve to argue with me. She's liable to kill someone."

"What is it you remembered?" Starshine prods.

"Code names!"

"Code names?"

"Did I ever tell you how your mother, rest her soul, came to name you Starshine?"

"After the song, right? The song by Strawberry Alarm Clock."

Aunt Agatha frowns gravely. "That's what we told you. That's what your mother, rest her soul, thought at first. But it was pure coincidence that the song came out that year. It was an excuse to give you the name, but not the reason."

"I don't understand."

"It was Luther's idea of a joke. His way of pulling a fast one on all of us. Particularly your father. Luther despised your father. He used to call him a war criminal without a crime. 'My baby sister threw herself away on that monster,' was one of his favorite mantras."

"Names," says Starshine. "Code names."

"That's right. Well, the Office of Strategic Services—that was where your uncle served during the war—used to have code names for big shots. Mostly foreign big shots. Not official names, mind you, just the names they used around the office. I still remember some of them. The men's names were always insulting. Prime Minister Churchill was Old Fuss and Feathers. And . . . let me see . . . Hitler was Napoléon's Penis. . . . That's right. . . . But the woman's names were often rather beautiful. . . ."

Agatha closes her eyes and falls back into momentary reverie.

"Aunt Agatha?"

"What?"

"Code names. You were telling me about my name and code names."

"That's right. I was, wasn't I?"

"You were."

"I remember now. The women all had . . . how shall I put it? . . . names suited to their appearance. I won't tell you what Luther called Mrs. Roosevelt. But you should know who *you* were named after. You were named after Claretta Petacci. She had the code name Starshine. "

Starshine racks her brain. The name does nothing for her.

"Aunt Agatha," she finally asks. "Who was Claretta Petacci?"

"I'll tell you," says Agatha. She grasps Starshine's hand and speaks as though sharing a secret of grave national importance. "It was Luther's idea of a slap in your father's face. Claretta Petacci was Benito Mussolini's favorite prostitute."

"You know that's not true. You made that up."

"It's the God's honest truth. She died hanging from a meat hook!"

"Please, Aunt Agatha," says Starshine. "Don't get all worked up."

"Do you hear me?" Agatha shouts. "A prostitute!"

The outburst has drained the old woman and she slumps suddenly into her pillows. Her breath seems to fade away under her heavy woolen quilt. A soft breeze flutters the curtains, dances through her tufts of gray hair. Agatha's face is expressionless, her frail arms slack at her sides. She is not dead. This is merely a regenerative nap. It is nature's version of the dress rehearsal, an opportunity for the victim to recuperate for her next assault against the past, a warning to friends and family that the curtain call is forthcoming.

Starshine shudders. She wipes a tear from her face and plants it on Agatha's cheek with her index finger. Then she kisses her aunt's forehead and presses her hand. She can feel the brittleness of bone. This is good-bye.

"I love you, Aunt Agatha," says Starshine. "I truly do love you."

And she does love her aunt, cherishes the old woman for all that she has been and for all that she has done, but this must be her final visit. She can no longer endure these pointless stories, the sterile air of Bayview Manor, the pervasive climate of death. She knows that each short stay abrades her own life, somehow scrapes the varnish off all she has worked for, and that her aunt—if the old woman were capable of understanding—would want her to stay far away.

She clenches her fists.

She is Starshine. She will not lose her beauty. She will *not* grow old.

# PART III

## THE HEART OF THE NIGHT

# TIMES SQUARE

Mort Bloom attends a Broadway play once each month.

Mort Bloom is Larry's father, although he often regrets it, a fifty-seven-year-old chemical engineer who accepted an early retirement package from Johnson & Johnson. He is short and beefy. His hands emit a faint scent of shampoo. Mort Bloom is a practical man of little culture and less imagination, an inveterate suburbanite who relishes a five-dollar cigar and the contours of his Barco lounger, and passes his mornings cursing at the stock listings in the *New York Times*. His deepest regret is that he didn't study aeronautical engineering to pursue a career in avionics. His private fantasy is to co-own a minor league baseball franchise. His publicly stated ambition is to purchase a condominium on the outskirts of Phoenix, Arizona, which will reduce his property taxes and enable him to play golf in February. Dry heat and prickly heat compose the gamut of his dinner table conversation. Mort Bloom is, in short, the very last person one would expect to find in a playhouse. And yet, every month for thirty-two years, excepting a brief hiatus for the removal of his gallbladder, Larry's father has boarded the Metro North train in Hastings-on-Hudson to catch a Sunday matinee in the theater district. He eschews glitzy musical and tourist traps; *Oklahoma!* and *South Pacific* are not to his taste. But he has seen much of Strindberg and Mamet, William Inge and Paula Vogel, even the collected works of Berthold Brecht, and although Mort rarely enjoys the experience at the time, more often than not leaving the theater with the nagging suspicion that he has missed something crucial, like the plot, the experience grows on him over the course of the ensuing four weeks, as he summarizes the story line for acquaintances, until he is finally convinced that he has gotten his money's worth. Then he goes back for more. And since his wife never accompanies him on these outings, for although she enjoys theater, she cannot abide public transit, Mort Bloom exposed his only son to twelve plays each year from the time of his bar mitzvah through his departure for college. That, Mort believes, is the primary reason his son is such a good-for-nothing screwup. He may very well be right.

Walking briskly down Forty-Fourth Street, toward Sardi's and the Belasco Theater, Larry experiences the same inchoate longing with which he has grappled since childhood. The neon lights of the Great White Way, nothing more than a glitzy enclave of swank carved between Hell's Kitchen and the Tenderloin District, somehow force him to confront his physical appearance. The dazzling marquees advertising *Cats* and *Phantom of the Opera* remind Larry that he will never walk into a room, much less onto a stage, and dazzle his onlookers. Some men command dinner parties and nightclubs with their distinguished features and lightning charisma. Larry will never be one of these anointed creatures. At the same time, he shares no bond with the homeless vagrants and small-time hustlers who lurk the outskirts of Times Square, the purveyors of designer drugs and teenage pornography, the downtrodden dregs who work the warehouses, whorehouses, sweatshops, and sex shops that keep Broadway's lights shimmering. They are the truly hideous. Larry is merely unattractive, middle class, ordinary. Like his father. Like his grandparents. Like the multitude of New Yorkers who walk from midtown to Seventh Avenue at five thirty each afternoon to board the IRT for home. Although Times Square is a battleground, the international crossroads of those who appear on magazine covers and those who use those magazine covers for insulation, Larry is merely a disinterested spectator to the combat. He holds absolute no stake in the outcome. If there were any feature of the theater district to which Larry could relate, it would not be found among the gaudy dramatic placards or the flashing XXXs of the video rental shops, but a block away from Times Square on Sixth Avenue. It is the National Debt Clock. Ticking. Ticking. Ticking. But accomplishing nothing.

Larry pauses under the awning of the Marriot Marquis to light a cigarette. The avenue is a tunnel of warm air and neither cupping his lighter with his hand nor using the corrugated siding of a nearby newsstand as a wind block accomplish that goal. He has retreated into an alcove of concrete between the Minskoff box office and a trash dumpster when he hears his name. He instinctively strikes a defensive pose, dropping one hand to his wallet and shielding his face with the other. This is not a neighborhood in which he expects to be recognized.

"Larry Bloom! I never thought I'd catch up with you."

Ziggy Borasch accosts Larry and backs him into the dumpster. The philosopher rests his palms on his knees to catch his breath. His entire body is quaking and the veins in his temples have swollen to capacity. Clad only in a pair of dungarees and tennis shoes, sans shirt and socks, his chest hairs a thicket of perspiration, Borasch no longer resembles an absentminded scholar. On the beach, equipped with a metal detector, he might pass for an eccentric. At the intersection of Broadway and Forty-Fourth Street, there is no mistaking him for anything other than a maniac.

"You nearly killed me, Bloom," says Borasch, pounding his chest. "How do you expect me to keep a pace like that?"

"I'm in a hurry," says Larry. "I need to be in Riverdale in two hours."

"You have plenty of time. That gives us at least an hour to celebrate."

"Celebrate?"

"I did it, Bloom. I have the sentence. "

"Are you going to tell me?"

"Not here. Not on a street corner. Let's get a cup of coffee and I'll explain."

"I don't have time right now," says Larry. "I'm going to be late for my date."

Ziggy Borasch deflates like a punctured tire. The maniacal gleam fades from his eyes and they take on a wooden cast that matches his expressionless face. Larry does not possess the ruthlessness, maybe merely the self-interest, to ignore the desperate whims of his single-minded friend. Not even for Starshine. He glances at this watch and then at Borasch's listless eyes. There is no contest. If the philosopher can find a restaurant in Times Square willing to serve him in his scant attire, Larry will yield him the time for a cup of joe.

"So where to?" asks Larry.

Borasch leads Larry up Broadway, against the commuter tide, peering through the windows of crowded restaurants. He devotes equal attention to upscale bistros and self-service food courts, as though deciding which establishment to bestow the luxury of his patronage upon. Nothing meets the needs of the occasion. Some restaurants are dismissed as too crowded. Those boasting vacant tables are inherently suspect. Every place is either too bright or poorly lit or unlikely to brew its own coffee. And Ziggy Borasch absolutely refuses to drink instant coffee. So they march northward, impatient homesteaders and bare-chested frontiersman, drawing stares from tourists and locals alike. Even on Broadway, they are worthy of attention. Larry fears that his companion intends to walk him all the way to Morningside. Or possibly Riverdale. But the philosopher ducks east onto Fifty-First Street and stops decisively before the Equitable Center. Under the distinctive maroon awning of Le Bernardin.

"We can't eat here," says Larry.

"Why not? It's a special occasion. I can afford it. "

"You're not wearing a shirt."

Borasch stares down at his chest as though this is the first he has heard of the matter.

"I'm sure they'll give me a jacket and tie," he says. "They do that in posh restaurants. I'm a paying customer. I have my rights. "

Larry examines his deranged companion. Borasch's ponytail

has come undone and strands of long silver hair dance before his eyes. Then he looks through the windows of New York's finest restaurant, absorbing the distinguished bankers and lawyers savoring appetizers of foie gras and crepes. Larry has gazed through these windows many times before. Usually, he notes that at the diners are nearly all male, all good looking. Today, it strikes him that every last one is wearing a shirt.

"Please Ziggy," says Larry. "It will take too long. Some other time. "

Ten minutes later, they are seated at a wooden table in an Irish pub on Sixty-Third Street. A chalkboard rests behind the bar announcing baseball odds. The walls are decorated with the head shots of obscure actors and association football pennants and an inordinate number of Rheinhgold clocks. Across from their booth, two burly young men in matching New York Yankees paraphernalia are sharing a pitcher of Coca-Cola. The soft drinks are the giveaway, Larry thinks. Undercover cops. He sips his club soda and waits while Ziggy Borasch measures three packets of sugar into his cup of black coffee.

"So?" prompts Larry.

"They must have brewed this shit yesterday," says Borasch. "It tastes like carburetor fluid."

Borasch pushes his coffee cup to the center of the table and appropriates Larry's soda.

"Are you going to tell me the sentence?" Larry asks.

"In a minute, in a minute. I need to calm my nerves."

Borasch's minute lasts a quarter of an hour. Larry is about to risk prompting his mentor a second time when the philosopher looks up from Larry's drink.

"I was in my apartment, working on my opus," he says, "when the most beautiful woman I've ever seen dropped a basket of fruit in my doorway. So I helped her retrieve the fruit, thinking I'm doing her a favor, and then she had the nerve to hit me up for money. For some cockamamie charity. I forget what it was called. And then it struck me, Bloom. Like Martin Luther in the outhouse. Like Franklin and his kite. That pushy kid had more to reveal about American culture, about the state of American capitalism, than all the Emersons and Edisons ever will. Do you see my point?"

"More or less."

"My point is that people work all their lives trying to pay off their bills. College loans and mortgages and God knows what. Our entire society rests on the principle of acquiring capital. Nothing sounds better than the clink of money in the bank. Absolutely nothing. So why in hell do people give their hard-earned dollars to charity? And why do they give each other gifts? Why? Why? Why?"

Borasch pounds the table with his fist. Larry glances apprehensively at the undercover cops, but they are too busy playing thumb football with a quarter to notice the proximate threat.

"I don't know," Larry says in a soft voice. "Why?"

"I'll tell you why," answers Borasch. "And when I tell you why, you'll understand my excitement. You'll see that I'm not as nuts as you suspect, just because I'm willing to demand service at Le Bernardin without a shirt on. I never thought this day would come, Bloom. But promise me one thing. If something should happen to me—let us say I were to walk out of this dive and be plowed down by a bus—swear to me that you'll preserve my work. Swear it!"

"I swear. You have my word. Now will you tell me already? The anticipation is killing me."

"Very well. Are you ready to become the first person to hear the Great American Sentence, Larry Bloom?"

Larry nods. "I'm more than ready."

"Here it is," says Borasch.

He clears his throat and pauses dramatically.

"An American man endowed with sufficient wealth," he declaims, "can purchase anything, but an American woman endowed with sufficient beauty does not need to."

Larry is speechless. Her stares at this mentor in utter awe, his brain racing for words. Ziggy Borasch appears before him in an entirely new light. How could Larry ever, even for one moment, have questioned this man's genius?

"So?" Borasch demands. "So what do you think?"

"I think," Larry answers, emphasizing each word. "I think that I already knew that."

He drops a ten-dollar bill on the table and walks out. He does not look back.

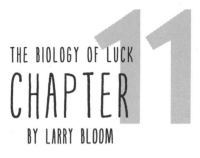

THE BIOLOGY OF LUCK

CHAPTER 11

BY LARRY BLOOM

The bishop of the Society for Secular Harmony praises himself daily at half past six.

His Mystic Eminence, a tubby fifty-seven-year-old Yonkers native, is the eldest of nine children. One of his brothers owns a discount clothing outlet. The other has a cushy desk job with the Westchester County Department of Public Works. Four of his sisters are married to members of the Knights of Columbus and the Yonkers Volunteer Fireman's Association. The fifth choked to death on a chicken bone. The sixth is a Carmelite nun. These are facts that the bishop wants you to know. His Mystic Eminence is a third-generation alcoholic. His father, a motel clerk, beat him frequently with a barber's strop. His grandfather, a sometime longshoreman and hell-for-leather fighting man, beat his father with a plywood board. His mother died of undiagnosed hepatitis. These are also facts the bishop wants you to know. His Mystic Eminence dropped out of Roosevelt High School. He served three months at Rikers for aggravated assault, five years upstate after an arson-for-hire scheme. He lied his way into a dealing job at a posh Atlantic City casino. He mastered the art of card counting, took the bus out to Vegas, and pocketed fifty grand before the house caught on and blacklisted him for life. These are facts of which the bishop gladly informs you. He even wants you to know that he founded the Society for Secular Harmony hoping to turn a quick buck. The tenets of his creed demand absolute honesty: exposure precludes humiliation; secrets breed strife. He further instructs his disciples—the hundreds of lost young men and women who sporadically attend his mutual congratulation sessions—that personal enhancement will be achieved through unabashed narcissism. The only true sin, he preaches, is sin itself.

His Mystic Eminence holds court in a converted Tribeca loft on Reade Street. The international headquarters of the Society for Secular Harmony consists of a cramped reception chamber and a spacious chrome-and-mahogany chapel. The plate-glass windows in the chapel offer worshippers a stellar view of Washington Market Park and the flagship marquee of Cheeses of All Nations. The walls of the waiting area are windowless and painted a tacky shade of canary yellow. Freestanding cork barriers separate the two rooms. When the devotees arrive for secular mass, they must file past the bishop's Lilliputian Japanese wife, who stands at the chapel entrance brandishing a donation basket. Her Mystic Eminence speaks only a few sentences of English, but her tongue reportedly has many other talents. This is also a fact the bishop wants you to know. He is an insecure, self-centered mountebank, a man of few scruples and limited social graces, but he harbors no delusions that he is duping anyone with his lavender robes and scepter of ersatz emeralds. The bishop willingly wears his shortcomings on his sleeve, declaring himself an adulterer and a swindler and a philistine, perfecting a variant of the good life that permits him all transgressions except hypocrisy. He is both medium and message.

The bishop stands behind a silver-plated lectern to praise himself.

"I have cheated on my income taxes," he bellows, "and I am a worthwhile person. I have lusted after my sister-in-law, and I am worthwhile person. I have driven away from the scene of an accident, and I am a worthwhile person."

Starshine reclines on a plush pink cushion while the bishop prays. She is surrounded by two dozen other congregants, teenagers wearing baggy pants, broad-hipped college girls, heavily pierced twenty-somethings, slender women in their early thirties who still carry themselves like overweight undergraduates. All rest on the pillows that serve as pews. All are enraptured. And with the exception of a recovering Hells Angel camouflaged with tattoos, and a grossly obese black man in a bright orange cap, all are white and female. Maybe this homogeneity stems from the nature of the Secularist message, feeding as it does on the appetites of that particular species of urban dweller who has much excess time and little self-esteem. Or possibly the marketing methods of the community: a few well-placed ads in alternative magazines and substantial reliance on the power of the spoken word. But most likely the reason that the Society for Secular Harmony resembles a Bryn Mawr class reunion is that the bishop, despite his bulbous nose and drooping ears, is hot as hell. On the street, of course, you'd walk past him. His physical attributes are few and far between. Yet behind his bully pulpit, engaged in his daily ritual of vainglorious self-denunciation, His Mystic Eminence acquires a magnetism that is part arch-patriot, part arch-revolutionary, part rising caudillo. He is Fidel and Eldridge Cleaver and Reverend Moon all rolled into one. Any of his followers would screw him in a heartbeat.

Starshine—although she'd never admit it to a living soul—lusts after the bishop. To him, she owes the greater portion of her confidence and beauty. During her first session under his tutelage, arranged by a bovine roommate who later became a corrections officer, the bishop counseled Starshine to take pride in her own excess flab. You are fat and you are a worthwhile person, he trumpeted. You are physically repulsive, and you are a worthwhile person. He compelled her to stand emotionally naked before his spellbound congregation and to repeat his pronouncements. Starshine bawled her way through the initiation rite and didn't leave her apartment for the following three weeks. She rummaged her bathroom cabinets for sleeping tablets, but later lobbed the pills out the courtyard window in disgust. She nearly took a carving knife to her wrists for a second time. The stench of vomit emanating from her wastepaper basket grew overpowering. Her roommate threatened to phone the police. Those were the darkest weeks of Starshine's life, the bottom of the abyss, the capstone on twenty years of misery. And then, without warning, the floodgates broke. Starshine woke up one June morning nine years ago, bought a prewar Higgins from a bicycle repair shop in Red Hook, and rode off eighty-five surplus pounds in six months. She fasted all day. She passed her nights in front of the bathroom mirror. Every leaf of boiled cabbage required an entry in her calorie notebook. She sewed herself a new wardrobe, found a slender roommate. Nine months later, she returned to the Society for Secular Harmony to boast of her shortcomings. Only there weren't any. Not really. Foibles, yes. But no true failing. She had become the person she'd always wanted to be. She will never forget her own overwhelming beauty that evening—the evening she first fell in love with the bishop.

His Mystic Eminence has nearly completed his sermon.

"I have defrauded a prostitute," he declaims, "and I am worthwhile person. I have shoplifted a bottle of vermouth, and I am worthwhile person. I have called my wife a yellow whore behind her back, and I am worthwhile person."

The bishop pauses and clears his throat. He is beaming with self-satisfaction.

"Those are my accomplishments of the day," he says. "I am proud of each and every one of them. I am better than all of you. I will worship no gods before myself. I will value no human beings more than myself. I am the most worthy person I know. "

The bishop's pronouncement is met with heated applause. The woman adjacent to Starshine, a dour creature holding an umbrella, slaps her hands together as though murdering mosquitoes. She smiles at Starshine.

"He's just wonderful, isn't he?" she says. "Just wonderful."

The bishop asks if anyone else would like to share her accomplishments of the day. The woman with the umbrella steps up to the lectern and blows awkwardly into the microphone. Her hair is coarse and her face is too narrow. When she speaks, in a nasal, almost bleating tone, she reminds Starshine of Bella Abzug without a hat.

"I've never done this before," the woman announces. "But as they say, there's no time like the present. So let me see. . . . . I'm extremely insecure, and I'm still a worthwhile person. I'm sexually aggressive, as difficult as it may be for you to believe, and I'm still a worthwhile person. . . . I'm presumptuous, and I'm still a worthwhile person. . . . I've libeled a tour guide because he thought he was too good for me, and I'm still a worthwhile person. . . ."

The speaker loses steam after her confession of libel. Starshine tunes out. She hates listening to the pathetic creatures who succeed the bishop, but she knows a premature exit might incur his displeasure. And she really doesn't mind daydreaming on soft pillows. It's a relaxing way to end an otherwise grueling workday. But she'd survived it! She has warded off Colby Parker's Italian adventure and Jack Bascomb's Amsterdam pilgrimage and countless other propositions of a far less delicate nature. She has overcome the bureaucracy at the Dolphin Credit Union. She has made peace with her dying aunt. All of her tasks have been accomplished. Now she can relax. There is still the matter of dinner with poor Larry Bloom, the quandary of the anonymous love note to unravel, but if he doesn't mention it, neither will she. It isn't worth the bother. She isn't insecure and she isn't presumptuous and she hasn't libeled anyone. Life is good.

A light tap on her shoulder startles her from her reverie. The bishop's wife is standing over her like a waitress in a sushi restaurant. Starshine intuitively dislikes Her Mystic Eminence. The woman's unnatural hold on her charismatic husband is unnerving.

"Miss Starshine," the bishop's wife whispers. "You get ring."

Her Mystic Eminence mimes the act of answering a telephone receiver and then tugs at Starshine's hand like a young child. Starshine follows the Japanese woman into the reception chamber. Her stomach tightens with premonition. It feels as though a swarm of butterflies are fox-trotting across her innards. Only her roommate knows where she is and only a true crisis would lead her to summon her from the chapel. Starshine understands this phone call can only mean one thing. Her dear Aunt Agatha is dead. Although she has braced herself for this moment, her preparations have been futile. The tears are already mounting as she picks up the receiver.

"This is Starshine," she says.

"Hey, it's Eucalyptus," her roommate answers. "I'm sorry to call you like this, but under the circumstances, I wasn't sure what else to do."

"They called from the nursing home, didn't they? My aunt died. I can hear it in your voice. "

"Your aunt's fine, as far as I know," says Eucalyptus. "You're the one that's going to die."

"What?"

"You've got a major problem on your hands, darling, and I can't deal with it right now. I'm supposed to meet Frederico in Soho in twenty minutes. We're patching things up. "

The sound of distant shouting emanates from the telephone receiver.

"Jesus Christ! What's going on?"

"Listen, darling. I don't have the time or the energy to explain. But you need to get your ass home as fast as you possible can. Trust me on this one. "

"Please tell me what's going on," Starshine demands again. "You owe me after this afternoon."

A long pause follows, as though Eucalyptus is weighing her loyalty to her roommate and her tusk supplier. "Let me paint you a picture. About an hour ago, Bone showed up with your water bed. And while he was dismantling your old bed to get it through the doorframe, Jack Bascomb stopped by to plead his case for Amsterdam. I was sitting in the kitchen with him when a distraught Colby Parker arrived in tears. He's inherited two hundred million dollars outright, you know—not including his trust fund or what he'll get when his mother dies. Anyway, the two of them were one dirty look away from murdering each other, when . . ."

Another long pause. Starshine hears Colby Parker shouting in the background, senses the vessels pulsing in her temples.

"When *what*?"

"You're not going to believe this. . . . The Jesus freak from downstairs starts pounding on the door. . . . I know you're going to hate me for his, but I gave up and let him in. And do you know what he wanted?"

"My head on a silver platter?"

"Your hand in marriage."

"No!"

"He asked me for advice on how to propose to a sweet young lady like yourself," explained Eucalyptus. "He thinks I'm the one pounding the bedsprings. "

This is all too much. Starshine can hardly think. "So he's the one who slipped he note into our mailbox. Not Larry. "

"Wrong again," says Eucalyptus. "It wasn't either of them."

"How can you be so sure?"

"Because . . ."

Starshine knows the answer even before she hears the words.

"Because it was me, honey. I wrote you that note." A newfound desperation rises in Eucalyptus's voice. "How can I not be in love with you?"

Starshine doesn't answer. She does not know what to say.

"You're not angry, honey, are you?" asks Eucalyptus. "Starshine? Are you there? Please say *something*. . . ."

"I need to go," she answers. "We'll talk later."

Starshine slowly returns the receiver to its cradle.

"Is all good?" asks the bishop's wife.

"Fine," Starshine answers absentmindedly. "Just fine."

But she is not fine. She is as not fine as she has been in many years. She feels betrayed, isolated, friendless. And then she thinks of Larry Bloom. It cannot be a coincidence that she is having dinner with him tonight. Certainly not. If there's anybody who can help her through this predicament, it is Larry. She knows he will not judge her. He will not interrupt. He will not offer unsolicited advice. All he will do is listen, hanging on to her every word, until she talks her way through this madness and is able to see things more clearly.

# THE BRONX

The dead woman did not live in Riverdale.

Her two-story red-brick home stands at the northern terminus of Corlear Avenue, in the Kingsbridge section of the Bronx, at the helm of a row of small single-family dwellings boasting matching fenced gardens and one-car garages. Oak trees line the sidewalk at regular intervals; dogwoods and red maples cast shade from behind hedges. Sprinklers sputter on many a manicured lawn. These streets were once brimming with children, shirtless toddlers of indeterminate gender, but the youngsters have long since worked their way through the state university system on Regents' Scholarships and relocated to ranch-style houses in Rye and Scarsdale. They have left behind aging parents and rusted swing sets. The elderly stroll the neighborhood at early evening like shellshock victims after a conflagration. Ancient couples, the men always taller, promenade to and from their regular corners in silence. Sunken-cheeked widows scowl over rubber-soled walkers. Their enclave of ethnic Catholics and Eastern European Jews will soon succumb to the pressures from the south, the working-poor blacks and Puerto Ricans who have already claimed Morrisania and Tremont and the Grand Concourse as far north as Bedford Park, which might help explain Snipe's dishonesty, his placement of the old woman's residence up the hill in more fashionable Riverdale, but it cannot absolve him of his other prevarication. Snipe's second lie is not a lie of embellishment, but one of omission. He has neglected to inform Larry that his girlfriend's grandmother, although ninety-seven years old, did not perish of natural causes.

Larry waits for his boss on the dead woman's flagstone stoop. He chain smokes and discards the butts in an earthenware pot that probably once housed a geranium but now contains only hardened soil. He traces his fingers over the rusted impression of the name McMull on the mailbox. Across the street, he knows without checking, a similar mailbox will display remnants of the name Kalkhazian. The florist's house is easy to identify. It is the only dwelling without a hedge of azaleas and rhododendrons, the only lawn bereft entirely of foliage. The Armenian's clapboard home stands on a garden of raked earth. This does not surprise Larry. He imagines the man eschews flowers in the same way Larry avoids guided tours. But Larry does fear the prospect of encountering the florist. It is embarrassing enough to be standing on the dead woman's porch, before the wall of yellow police tape announcing the crime scene, so that every passing senior citizen can eye him as the still unapprehended murderer. Larry tries to look official—pacing decisively, glancing irritably at his watch—so that they won't suspect him. So that they won't phone 9-1-1. Although no one has officially informed him that the nonagenarian has been bludgeoned to death, his instincts tell him that the girlfriend's grandmother and the florist's neighbor are one and the same. This explains Snipe's urgency. It also means that there is absolutely no way in hell Larry is assisting him in his "recovery" effort.

The tour director and his girlfriend arrive on foot at twenty minutes to seven. Jessie McMull is a pale Irish girl whose face is dominated by a pair of thick-rimmed glasses. She carries herself like a teenager, not so much walking as skipping, running her hands along the fence posts as she goes. Larry half expects her to cartwheel onto the porch. Instead, she stops directly in front of him and taps the side of the earthenware pot with her shoe.

"You'd better take those butts with ya," she says. "Nobody's gonna know we've been here."

Larry obediently retrieves the cigarette butts and stashes them inside his pocket. He walks down the path and refuses Snipe's hand.

"What's going on here?" Larry demands.

"What do you mean?" Snipe responds innocently.

"You didn't tell me this was a crime scene."

"You didn't ask. No big deal."

"No big deal?" demands Larry. "Your friend's grandmother was murdered, wasn't she?"

"Shhh!" orders Snipe. "As far as you're concerned, she fell in the bathtub and the police patched the place up as part of their routine. That's the party line, okay? That's what Jessie told me and that's what I'm telling you. "

"I'm sorry," pleads Larry. "I can't help you."

"That's dog piss, Bloom. Of course you can help us. Now hurry up and let's get this over with. I'm not the one who's so desperate for time. The sooner you stop being such an imbecile, the sooner we'll be in Co-Op City and you can do whatever you damn please."

Snipe has a point. Larry is going to give in to his boss eventually, as he always does, and clinging to the moral high ground, when he knows that descent into the valley is inevitable, seems fruitless. And even if he refuses to yield, even if he manages to resist Snipe's pressure, resistance will take longer than acquiescence. It always does. Larry can read the writing on the wall. Tomorrow, he can send Snipe his letter of resignation, but for today, he must remain a prisoner of the tour director's depravity.

Larry grudgingly follows his boss up the cracked concrete path. Snipe ducks under the police barrier and helps his girlfriend navigate the cordon of tape. They lead Larry into a narrow, dusty vestibule that harks back to the era when mail was delivered twice a day and gentlemen wore hats in public. Maybe to the era when fresh ice was delivered daily and women wore corsets. The walls, wainscoting below, faded paper above, are decorated with tintype portraits and framed embroidery. A grandfather clock in one corner places the time at twenty minutes past nine; an ogee shelf clock on an end table reads one forty-five. The parlor that opens on the antechamber is overfurnished with upholstered armchairs and knickknack cabinets. The rooms do not reflect any particular style or period. Iron folding chairs service a hand-carved Edwardian table. Color photographs are tucked into the framed daguerreotype above the mantel. The scene suggests a restoration rather than an active residence. For the dead woman's home resembles those of her neighbors, those of thousands of other elderly women, except that the windows at the rear of the parlor have been shattered, and that on the beige carpet, near the base of the piano, traces of a deep brown stain remain visible.

"It's upstairs," says Jessie. "First door on the left."

A second mesh of police tape protects the staircase. Snipe attempts to peel it off in strands, then punches his way through the web.

"Let's get this over with, Bloom," he says.

Larry and Snipe mount the steep steps. The stairs groan under their feet. Larry makes the mistake of leaning his arm on the banister and it actually crumbles beneath him, cashing through the wooden newels and emitting a cloud of plaster dust.

"Goddamnit," says Snipe. "Watch what you're doing."

"I'm watching," mutters Larry. "I'm watching."

They reach the second-story landing and feel their way through the darkness to the designated room. Snipes pushes open the door and they are suddenly blinded by the brightness of the setting sun. When their eyes adjust to the shadeless windows of the dead woman's bedroom, they find themselves in a small chamber that smells like steamed barley. It is the dead woman's musk, her final legacy, clinging to the canopied bed and the rosewood bureaus. The sewing cabinet stands under the far window, between a mildewed hamper and a windup Victrola. They've already hoisted the wooden box onto their shoulders when the one-armed man steps out from behind the door.

"You put that down," he orders. "You put that down and we talk."

Larry lowers his end of the cabinet, forcing his companion to follow.

"Who the hell are you?" demands Snipe.

"You go downstairs," says the one-armed man. "We talk then."

The intruder is not brandishing a weapon. He is a compact, middle-aged creature wearing a Hawaiian shirt and a bolo tie. Even if he were not a cripple, he would be no match for two able-bodied men. Yet something in his tone, maybe its intransigence, maybe its equanimity, brooks no disagreement. Snipe glares at the interloper and grudgingly leads Larry out into the passageway. The one-armed man follows them to the parlor.

"We came downstairs," says Snipe. "Now what the hell are you doing here?"

Jessie steps up behind her boyfriend.

"Who's he?" she asks.

"I have no fucking idea," says Snipe. "He was hiding in the bedroom."

"What are you doing here?" Jessie asks aggressively. "This is private property."

Larry retreats into the background and sits backward on a folding chair. The one-armed man examines the broken banister and grunts.

"That's right, Miss McMull," he says. "This here's private property. You got no cause to be breaking things. "

"Who are you?" Jessie demands again. "I'll call the cops."

The one-armed man chuckles.

"You call the cops, Miss McMull," he says, taunting. "Tell them that you broke into the scene of a murder. They'll like that. "

"What do you want?" Jessie asks. "How do you know my name?"

"Knowing is my business," says the one-armed super. "Let's sit down and be comfortable. We talk. I tell you want I want. Then you go home. "

The one-armed super walks past Snipe and Jessie and seats himself across from Larry at the dining room table. He adjusts his gold-bridged sunglasses and then drums his fingers on the tabletop.

"Sit down," he says. "We talk."

Snipe and his girlfriend exchange whispers before seating themselves.

"Well?" says Snipe. "Talk."

"My name is Bone," says the one-armed super. "Not Mr. Bone. Not Bone something. Just Bone. My friend is Mrs. McMull's granddaughter. She lives in Albany. My friend is a very special friend. She wants the sewing box upstairs. That's all we have to talk about. "

"That still doesn't explain why you were hiding in Grandma's bedroom," snaps Jessie.

"I heard you come in. I thought you were police. I hid. I entered through the kitchen and went up the back stairs. I didn't think it wise to disturb the yellow tape. "

"I see," says Jessie. She turns to Snipe and adds, "Do something."

"There's nothing you can do, Mr. Snipe," says Bone. "I tell you why and then you go home. Do you know how I lost my arm, Mr. Snipe? I tell you how. I was in prison in my homeland. A prison from which no man ever escape. But I escape. They chain me by my arm to a tree branch in the hot sun as part of my punishment. They leave me for days without water. Many times I try to cut through the tree branch, but it is too strong. One day, I cut off my arm with a sharpened clam shell and walk away. Either that, Mr. Snipe, or I caught my arm in a train door. But you will never know. Now go home. "

Larry recognizes Bone from Starshine's description. This has to be the same one-armed man! Is this merely a coincidence, a rebuff to Ziggy Borasch? Or is it an omen? And if it is part of some larger plan, does it improve or injure Larry's prospects? He is too startled to weigh the evidence carefully. He doesn't know. What he does know is that, whether or not there is any truth to the super's story, the man will get what he wants. Bone is the kingpin. Bone is not a man to yield a sewing cabinet without consequences.

"Let's go home," says Larry.

"Dog piss," says Snipe. "I could give a damn about his arm. Let's get the sewing machine, Bloom, and get out of here. He can't stop us. "

"I'm afraid I can," says Bone.

Snipe stands up and backs his way toward the staircase.

"You make this difficult," says Bone. "But I warn you. You are a director of travel operations at Empire Tours, Mr. Snipe. You wear a wedding band. You are unmarried. You say you graduated from law school. You attended. You did not graduate. Shall I go on?"

Snipe stops dead in his tracks. The color drains from his face.

"How the fuck do you know that?"

"Knowing is my business," says Bone. "I know people. I know Mr. Frederico Lazar. He is the man Miss McMull is seeing when she is not with you. I know Starshine Hart. She is the woman with whom Mr. Bloom is to have dinner. I know other things. I know my friend will like her sewing box. "

"That's bullshit," shouts Jessie. "Don't believe him."

"Who the fuck is Frederico Lazar?"

Larry glances at this watch and stands up, his hand in his pocket, the letter from Stroop & Stone braced between his fingers. As long as he has his magic letter, he feels as brave as Bone. He would like to thank the one-armed super, but recognizes that Bone is a man far beyond mere gratitude. Instead, he walks up to Snipe, knowing that he may regret what he is about to do, and slaps the tour leader on the back.

"Dog piss," says Larry. "Isn't it?"

He doesn't stop to listen to Snipe's invective. He is fed up with other people's problems, other people's business. It is already eight o'clock. If he pushes the Plymouth to the limit, he has just enough time to meet Starshine. That is his business. Not sewing machines. Not dead women. He is a new Larry Bloom. He will make his own decisions, look after his own interests, set his own pace. He will not let other people's needs and goals interfere with his life. Except people who matter: And nobody matters more than Starshine. This is Larry's determination as he pulls off Moshulu Parkway and onto the Henry Hudson. It lasts as far as the Kappock Street toll plaza and the gridlock of city-bound traffic.

THE BIOLOGY OF LUCK

# CHAPTER 12

## BY LARRY BLOOM

What better place than Greenwich Village to start a romance, to end a story, to escape?

The urban hamlet radiating from Washington Square is the city's sanctuary, its asylum, the safe haven where generations of weary travelers have found solace after harrowing journeys. Bankers fleeing the cholera epidemics of the eighteenth century, Irish immigrants driven abroad by the potato blight, vagabond artists seeking an oasis from convention—all have been welcomed with open arms. The sidewalk cafes along MacDougal Street uphold no ideological standard. Clothing, loosely defined, is the only dress code in the taverns off Sheridan Square. If you are a trust-fund socialist or a Log Cabin Republican; if you're into understated elegance or bohemian chic; if you know that garlic cures cancer or biology determines luck, if you crusade for the perfect sentence; if you refuse to labor in shoes; if you're a bankrupt poet, a jilted lover, an adventurous tourist; if you're Walt Whitman or Henry James or Jack Kerouac; if you're waving or drowning; if you're squirming under the sword of Damocles; if your future hangs on the narrowest thread of hope; even if you're ugly: the Village will tolerate your idiosyncrasies, sponge your wounds, and nourish your dreams. It may also indulge your fantasies.

Larry races down University Place and past the Memorial Arch at top speed. A day that began on the sleepy streets of Harlem will end in a dash to the finish. The soles of Larry's feet throb after hours of walking; his throat burns from wasted words; his clothes bear the scars of smoked eel and pickled herring. In less than twelve hours, he has saved the life of a pompous buffoon, failed to rescue a beautiful maiden, and abandoned a corpse to the mercies of the news media. An overbearing journalist has kidnapped his bouquet. A one-armed soldier of fortune has threatened to rearrange his kneecaps. He has seriously contemplated suicide. He has frivolously considered murder. It has been the most traumatic day Larry has ever experienced, a whirlwind of dreams extinguished and hopes renewed, but what makes this snippet of June so inconceivable is that the two greatest challenges are still to come. He may yet be an author. He may yet be a lover. All depends on whether Starshine, glorious Starshine, will wait for him.

Larry stops to regain his breath. Dusk has settled over the park and the paths are crowded with strolling couples and evening joggers. The elderly women and chess players who command the benches during the afternoon have yielded their dominion to amateur folk singers and small-time drug pushers. A troupe of acrobats and an African drummer compete for the attention of the passersby. A tender twilight has tamed the city, and all around Larry, like fireflies on a summer evening, young lovers emerge from their dormitories and high-rises and cold-water flats to share the wistful romance of the nightfall. They kiss. They embrace. They dream of other summer evenings, much like this one, when they savored the same verdant air and sensed the same hushed tranquility and caressed the gentle lips of long-lost sweethearts. This is the lovers' truce that envelops the city for a fleeting interval between day and night, after offices have emptied but before bars have filled, when for a few short moments the entire island pairs off in a duet of sentiment and nostalgia. These are the precious minutes when young vows are proffered and old vows are consecrated. This is the interlude that makes the day worth living.

The last of the sun has already dipped behind the rooftops when Larry reaches the corner of Sullivan and Houston. He has selected a cozy, traditional Southern Italian bistro called Il Mandolo, the Almond Tree, in the hope that the soft music and elaborate frescoes will work their magic on Starshine's heartstrings. The restaurant boasts crystal candelabras and decorative jeroboams, but also a smoking section for the high-strung patron. Larry has dined in Il Mandorlo on several previous occasions, all uneventful blind dates, but the lack of passion was as much his own fault as that of his companions. These were not women for whom ships are launched, for whom kingdoms are imperiled, for whom epic literature is composed. They were pleasant strangers who had no more interest in Larry than he did in them. But if the company disappointed, the ambience did not. Larry cannot imagine a more perfect venue for opening his envelope or tendering his devotion. Starshine will have waited. Of that, he is certain. She will be sitting at the reserved table by the window, her face glowing in the candlelight, her flawless beauty openly displayed.

And there she is!

Starshine rises to greet him and plants a light kiss on his cheek. Larry feels the warmth of her body as she gently presses his hand. Her hair exudes a mild fragrance of scented shampoo.

"I'm sorry I'm late," says Larry. "The West Side Highway was a parking lot."

"But you're here," answers Starshine. "That's what matters."

Larry settles into his seat and spreads his napkin over his lap. He polishes off the contents of his water glass, lights a cigarette, watches the curls of white smoke rising through the draft; one of the added perks of Il Mandorlo is the staff's indifference to the city's indoor smoking ban. Larry's hand plays shell games with the silverware. This is the moment he's been planning for two years, the long anticipated audience with the princess, but he finds himself unable to speak. Or even to look her in the face. Paralysis has set in. His vocal cords refuse to vibrate while his mind whirs aimlessly like the gears of a disconnected engine. The truth of the matter is that he has spent so many hours anticipating this showdown, dreading its failure, savoring its success, planning for every possible contingency and consequence, that he's never actually devoted any time to the specifics of what he intends to say. Larry has imagined Starshine's answer countless times, suffered every possible permutation. But he has never, not even once, rehearsed the question. How do you tell a woman that you've written an epic novel recounting her life on the day when she falls in love with you? Will she be frightened? Might she even be insulted? What once seemed like the cleverest of ideas, when hatched in solitude from the vantage point of Larry's smoke-filled apartment, suddenly appears much less promising. The book is a harebrained, presumptuous scheme that can only be a recipe for disaster.

A white-haired, red-faced waiter arrives to announce the dinner specials and to take their beverage order. He is an undersized, skeletal creature decked out in an apron and bow tie. His entire bearing announces his flimsiness. Larry's heart goes out to him as he requests a glass of white wine. The poor man is one of the unchosen, one of the spurned, a kissing cousin to Peter Smythe and the panhandlers of Morningside and the portly women at the Lenox Avenue post office. And to Larry Bloom. They all possess lifetime memberships in the fraternity of ugliness, the voiceless auxiliary to the Brotherhood of Man. This does not mean happiness and romance are forever beyond their reach. It does mean that they must struggle for it, laboring day after day, in a manner that the chosen few, those blessed with outward beauty, will never experience and never understand. Larry Bloom—as tour guide, as author—might not muster the courage to reveal himself to the beautiful woman across the table. But Larry Bloom, self-styled spokesperson for the millions of unattractive and underappreciated men and women across the city, across the nation, suddenly feels capable of facing any challenge. To hell with Colby Parker and Jack Bacomb and all the good-looking, privileged men whom Starshine complains about. They've had their share of happiness. It's time for the Larry Blooms of the world to have their opportunity. This is Larry's deepest wish, his purpose, his calling—and still he hesitates.

He reaches into his pocket and retrieves the letter. Although marred by both fire and water, singed at the edges and stained with coffee, the distinctive quill pen of the agency's letterhead still stands out above the sea of smudged ink. He runs his fingers over the seams of the envelope, as though soaking up luck from an enchanted amulet, worshipping the great gods Stroop & Stone in his hour of need. Then he gazes into Starshine's eyes, so inviting, so forbidding, marshaling his will for a first and final offensive. Now Larry knows his plan of attack. He will have Starshine open the envelope and deliver the verdict. All of his eggs will rest in one basket. The evening will end in a crescendo—of either anguish or bliss. Her answer will be epic and all consuming,

"Starshine," he says. "I have something I need to tell you. Something important. "

She flashes him an elusive smile, more accepting than encouraging. He has seen this expression before, but he has never deciphered its meaning. Is it a mask, a protective barrier, veiling fears and insecurities as profound and as troubling as his own? Or is it merely a courtesy, a mode of interaction, an open admission that there truly are no monsters lurking behind those placid features? He has wondered; he has doubted. Now he will learn for certain.

"I have a lot to say," says Larry. "I'll respect your answer, whatever it is, but all I ask is that you hear me out from start to finish without interrupting. I only have the courage to go through with this once. Is that okay?"

Starshine nods. He feels that she is not looking at him, but through him. That her thoughts lie elsewhere and she has her own burden to unload. Never has she seemed so careworn, so drained. Larry fears he has chosen the wrong evening for their meeting.

"I'll put all my cards on the table," he says. "I'm in love with you."

Starshine does not recoil. She does not reciprocate. She simply nods her head again and smiles pleasantly, honoring his request and withholding her judgment. Her eyes are glassy and opaque. If he didn't know any better, he might conclude that she wasn't even listening.

"I've been in love with you since the first moment I met you," Larry continues. "Do you remember it? We spent all afternoon combing through the maps in Peter Smythe's cellar. You probably don't remember, but I do. Ever since that day, you've been the woman of my dreams, the one person with whom I'd want to spend the rest of my life. I know that sounds insane, Starshine, and maybe it is. But it's also true.

"I'll admit that I don't have much to offer you. I'm certainly not the best-looking guy in the world or the most successful or even the most charismatic. I'm not going to inherit a beach chair fortune. I'll never have the courage to overthrow the government. I'm not even very good in bed. But the bottom line is that I really do love you, and being with you makes me happy—and if you feel the same way about me, then none of those things should matter. Even a poor tour guide is entitled to some happiness."

Larry is suddenly conscious that he is rambling, even pleading. An army of tears has encamped behind his eyes. He wipes his face with a napkin and attempts to regain his composure.

"I've written this book," he says. "It's a novel about you. About your life on the day I tell you how I feel. About today. I think it's a pretty good book, maybe not up to par with Whitman and Melville, but a minor masterpiece in its own right. I've been working on it every night for the past two years and I promised myself that when the manuscript was complete, when I finally had something to offer you, I'd tell you how I felt. Well, I have a letter from a literary agency. A response to my manuscript. I've been waiting to open it all day until I heard your answer, but I thought maybe you'd be willing to open it for me. That's really all I wanted to say. I wanted to tell you that I love you and that I've written a book for you and now I'll shut up, before I make any more of a fool of myself, and I'll let you determine my fate."

Larry stops speaking and fumbles with his napkin ring. He fears he hasn't done justice to the depth of his devotion, fears that he has left so much out, but nothing else he says will make any difference. Yet even as he slides the decisive letter onto the tabletop, his hands trembling, he longs to make one more pitch for her affections. His entire being hangs in the hope of the moment.

Starshine accepts the letter without speaking. Her delicate

hands break the seal of the envelope and she reads to herself for an eternity. Then she looks up. Her expression is inscrutable, almost blank. For several seconds, it is impossible to tell whether she is aghast or aglow. Or merely astonished. She stares at Larry, speechless, like a woman who has been offered Captain Kidd's treasures, like a woman who has been given a puppy she does not want, like a woman who is grappling with a life and death decision at the end of a very long day. Her lips part slowly; she delivers her answer in the softest, sweetest voice Larry has ever heard. It is the answer Larry has expected since his first night at the word processor, since his first crossing of the Brooklyn Bridge, since the first surge of affection and hope in Peter Smythe's subterranean archive that has led to this decisive moment. It is the answer for which ships are launched, kingdoms imperiled, and epic novels written. It is an answer older than Larry, older than Starshine, older than the city, a magical phrase that loses nothing for time or repetition, inspiring each and every one of us to push forward, buoyed by the remotest hopes, through the tumult, through the trauma, through the cloud.

It is the only answer possible:

"Yes and no . . ."

# THE
# BIOLOGY
## OF
# LUCK

### JACOB M. APPEL

# AFTERWORD

A conversation between ERB publisher Jotham Burrello and author Jacob M. Appel.

**Q:** I have read love stories. I have read parallel narratives. I have read books that take place in a single day. I have read books in the present tense. I have not read books where one character has written a novel about another character's day, and then said book is presented as a novel-within-a-novel. What challenges or surprises did this structure present?

**A:** I haven't read a book like that either. That's why I wrote this one. For many years, I studied dramatic writing with the brilliant Tina Howe at Hunter College. Howe's advice to students is to create something onstage, something that you've never seen before. Creating something entirely new is also my goal whenever I write a story or novel. The challenge, of course, is that I didn't have a model to work from. Writing this novel also proved difficult because it is very different, in both structure and tone, from most of my other writings, which often contain magical elements. Not being allowed to have a character spontaneously combust or turn into a penguin without warning proved a considerable constraint on my imagination, and one that took a while to adjust to.

**Q:** When you submitted the manuscript you labeled it the "anti-novel" and "a postmodern love story." Can you break down these two terms in relation to the book?

**A:** I think of this as an "anti-novel" in that it defies as many of the rules of the traditional novel as possible and yet still remains a novel. I was partially inspired in this regard by architect Philip Johnson's iconic "glass house," which breaks as many of the traditional rule of home design as possible, yet remains a house. While the structure is "postmodern" in the spirit of Donald Barthelme or John Barth, that's not what I meant when I wrote of a postmodern love story. Rather, I meant that the love itself is "postmodern"—hyper-aware, ambivalent, fragmented. That's the world of romance that we live in today.

**Q:** For many readers this novel will be their first time experiencing your work. But you are a prolific writer of short stories and essays, plus an accomplished playwright, and work a demanding day job as a psychiatrist. When I sent out blurb requests for the novel, one writer whom I was trying to corral wrote back saying he no longer blurbed books, then added, "that's one hell of a vita" upon reading your accomplishments. For the writers online who blog about you winning so many writing contests, I need to know, do you ever sleep? Are you really a cyborg? Or do you keep a stable of co-writers à la James Patterson?

**A:** Psychiatrists are notoriously bad at analyzing their own behavior. That being said, the primary reason I am so prolific is that I enjoy writing very much. I suppose there's also some fear of literary inadequacy and a desire to be remembered after I shuffle off my mortal coil. But if I wrote all day, every day, for the next fifty years, I don't think I could catch up with Joyce Carol Oates, so my subconscious feelings of inadequacy will remain.

**Q:** Pulitzer Prize winning author Robert Olen Butler described your work as "richly funny and quite smart about relationships." How has your psychiatric training assisted you in depicting such keenly observed characters?

**A:** Everybody asks me that, but the irony is that most of my work is with the severely mentally ill—patients with schizophrenia and similar psychotic disorders. So while my interest in human nature inspired me to pursue a career in psychiatry, my actual clinic training has little bearing on the fictional world I create. If anything, it's observing people in a social setting that has trained my mind in this way.

**Q:** At the time of this interview, I am certain I've read the book more than any other reader. And while I was struck by the humor and voice in my initial reads, subsequent tours reveal a darkness/despair beneath the surface of Larry's and Starshine's lives. I count numerous references to suicide. How did you craft and balance the lightness with the darkness in writing the book?

**A:** Having worked for years in various hospitals and psychiatric facilities, I've come to recognize that life is strikingly unkind and unfair—and anyone who hasn't noticed this yet is either strikingly naive or dreadfully spoiled. Unfortunately, many people see their own lots as unfair, while not recognizing how others suffer. One of the goals of the novel is to make my readers aware of this blindness to the suffering of others through the parallel narratives. Of course, if my message were simply "Life is bleak," people could look out their windows or visit the waiting room at their local prison, rather than reading my book. You have to offer a bit of comedy and joy to lure in the crowds.

**Q:** Larry Bloom traverses NYC one fine June day. In Joyce's *Ulysses* Leopold Bloom does a walkabout of Dublin in a single June day. (The former English majors among us may recall the parallels between *Ulysses* and Homer's *Odyssey*.) This is good company to keep. What similarities did you intend or not intend between these seminal works and *Biology*?

**A:** The only thing I share with Homer and Joyce, I fear, is poor eyesight. (My mother once wrote an entire study on the role of poor vision in *Ulysses*, so maybe that's how I first became aware of the novel.) But I'll concede that I had grand ambitions to parallel the novel after both of its predecessors—although, at the end of the day, the structural parallels often gave way to the need for a compelling read. (*Ulysses*, as you may have noticed, isn't exactly hopping off the shelves in airports.) That being said, I believe a number of the parallels still remain. I can't wait for the day that a reader takes on the challenge of finding these parallels and writes an essay on the subject. I welcome anyone (except my mother) to give it a shot.

**Q:** I am charmed by the minor characters in the book: Colby Parker, Snipe, the Armenian florist, Peter Smythe, Ziggy Borasch, Eucalyptus, the list goes on. Each is individually unique and uniquely New York. What was your inspiration for this motley crew? And can you take us through how you created the backstory for Jack Bascomb or Bone?

**A:** In case you're reading this novel and you believe these characters are based upon you and the people you know, they're not. Really, they're not. I don't wander around the city looking for interesting people to transform into characters. I sit in my apartment and imagine people whom I wish existed. My building's superintendent is nothing like Bone. Yet on numerous occasions, I've dreamed of a super who could get me anything, like an iron at four a.m. on New Year's Eve, or a copy of Greta Garbo's driver's license—and since the managers of my apartment building are unlikely to hire one, I decided to create such a man whole cloth.

**Q:** Walt Whitman appears so often in the novel he could be considered a minor character. Early on Starshine imagines "that she is the corporeal incarnation of a Whitman poem." Later in Battery Park, Larry pays homage to Whitman's statue. You write, "Gazing up into the hero's larger-than-life tribute, the maestro's marble features beaming perpetually over a polished beard, Larry wonders if he has done justice to both master and model." Whitman is one of the strings that bind them. Can you discuss the long shadow Whitman casts over the novel?

**A:** I did not discover Whitman until college. I took a summer class at Columbia with the late, legendary historian James Shenton— probably New York City's most celebrated tour guide—on "New York City in the Era of Whitman and Melville." If secular humanists believed in the notion of saints, Whitman would be the patron saint of New York, of hopeless romance, and of wandering—all of which are at the core of this novel. Anything seems possible after reading a Whitman poem. . . .

**Q:** In an essay entitled "Effective Openings," you wrote: "In writing, as in dating and business, initial reactions matter. You don't get a second chance, as mouthwash commercials often remind us, to make a first impression." You submitted *The Biology of Luck* to Elephant Rock Books during an open submission period. (It was not the first book I read, and in fact, it hibernated in the slush pile for three weeks before I thumbed the ink.) But when I did, the prose bounded off the page—BAM! Minty Fresh! I was sold. Take the opening line of one of the chapters and break it down using your "nine ideas on how to craft a perfect opening line."

**A:** You're asking me to apply what I preach to what I practice, which, as a writer, I find a terrifying prospect; sort of the equivalent of finding out what's in the soup at one's favorite restaurant. But I am grateful my manuscript only hibernated in the slush pile for three weeks. I can't help wondering how many brilliant works of literature are left to hibernate at the offices of major commercial publishers for decades. I have little doubt there is a prominent literary agent somewhere using the unread draft of a masterwork as a doorstop.

**Q:** The genesis of *Biology* is grounded in you being a licensed New York City sightseeing guide. Two questions: How does one become a licensed tour guide? And you've said you wrote the book "to take a shot at creating a convincing and historically grounded paean to the tour guides of NYC." Why do you think tour guides need convincing and historically grounded paeans?

**A:** One becomes a tour guide with great effort. At least back when I earned my license, one had to pass a grueling exam on the history and geography of New York City. I've taken the bar exam and the medical boards, but the NYC tour guide exam is certainly as difficult. And yes, tour guides certainly need a convincing and historically grounded paean. The movies make being a tour guide seem easy and glamorous. In reality, while it's a fascinating experience, it's also hard work.

**Q:** Larry and Starshine tour famous landmarks and neighborhoods throughout the five boroughs, exploring what you have called the underbelly of Gotham. If your long-lost Hoosier cousin Tom and his wife Helen were coming to town, where would you take them sightseeing?

**A:** My favorite sight in New York is a rather obscure memorial known as the "Amiable Child" monument located on Riverside Drive at 133rd Street. It's the most moving and impressive New York City landmark you've never heard of. I've even written an essay in tribute to the monument that was published several years ago in the *Palo Alto Review*. The monument commemorates the life of Saint Claire Pollock, a child who died in the area in 1797. People in the neighborhood still bring flowers to honor the boy. After 9-11, people left candles and flowers, and it became a local shrine to suffering and commemoration. It says something wonderful about humanity that we pay our respects as a community to a child we never knew who died two centuries ago. (And if Tom and Helen are reading this, I want to remind them that they should book a hotel room; I don't run a rooming house.)

**Q:** If you could break bread with any character from literature, which would it be?

**A:** I've always fantasizing of standing up Jordan Baker (from *The Great Gatsby*) for a date, but I suppose that doesn't count. So I'd have to say Elpinore. As you probably don't recall, he's the fellow in Homer's *Odyssey* who gets drunk and falls off a roof to his death. That's all that we really know of him. Ever since I read the Odyssey in high school, I've wanted to learn the back story. I've also had my dreams of eloping with Ántonia Shimerda from Willa Cather's *My Antonia*, but what man hasn't?

**Q:** The end of the book is open to interpretation. I'm curious what you think happened when Larry and Starshine leave the restaurant? Did Stroop & Stone sign Larry? Does he christen Starshine's new water bed?

**A:** Did you really think I'd answer that?

**Q:** I thought I might catch you off guard.

**A:** All I can promise is that if the book is a success, I'll be glad to write a sequel, or even a series, of Larry and Starshine romances to be sold in airports. But that will require a seven-digit advance.

# QUESTIONS FOR DISCUSSION

**1.** When we first meet Larry Bloom, he's striding up Broadway, the *New York Times* under his arm and a pack of cigarettes in his shirt pocket, musing about how there should be a civil rights movement for short, relatively unattractive Jewish men. What sort of first impression did this make on you? And how did your impression of Larry change over the course of the book?

**2.** What do you make of the André Aciman quote Appel uses as an epigraph? Which characters do you think it applies to? And how does it work in relation to Larry Bloom's novel?

**3.** We learn little tidbits of Starshine's personal history throughout the novel, but that history, dramatic as it is, never really gets that much airtime. Did her history surprise you? How did your impression of her evolve as you learned about her past?

**4.** Larry Bloom takes us through a good chunk of New York City, peppering his tour group with historical factoids while also trying to protect them from some disconcerting events. How does Appel's New York City strike you—is he going for authenticity or hyperbole, or something in between?

**5.** Of the three love interests in Starshine's life (reciprocated or not), which do you think is the most appealing? And which makes the most sense for Starshine?

**6.** How important do you think the book-within-a-book structure is to the overall book, and to your enjoyment or frustration as a reader? Can you think of structural comparisons from film, music, or art?

**7.** At the end of chapter one, Larry tucks the letter from Stroop & Stone into his pocket without reading it. Why did Appel make this decision? Can you think of a time when you put off finding out important news like that?

**8.** How would you classify Appel's writing style? Are there other novelists, or periods, that his voice reminds you of?

**9.** Appel has called the book a postmodern love story. In the afterword he explains, "While the structure is 'postmodern' in the spirit of Donald Barthelme or John Barth, that's not what I meant when I wrote of a postmodern love story. Rather, I meant that the love itself is 'postmodern'—hyper-aware, ambivalent, fragmented. That's the world of romance that we live in today." Has he accurately captured the essence of dating in the twenty-first century? What examples from the book, or your experiences, capture hyper-aware, ambivalent, and fragmented attempts at finding a mate?

**10.** *Theme* is a reader's word, and *Biology* is full of many of the big themes we find in good fiction. But one theme that Appel clearly establishes is stated at the end of chapter one. "He is happy, happy in the way he knows he can be if he wills away the inevitable and succors himself with the remotest of hopes. That is the purpose of his book. That is the subject of his book. That is the reason that the city rises from its slumber." How is hope represented in the course of events that transpire on this one June day in New York City?

**11.** All great art owes something to its predecessors. Appel has said he paralleled parts of his novel after Homer's *Odyssey* and Joyce's *Ulysses*. What links did you discovery between these seminal works and *Biology*?

**12.** The most obvious question has to be asked—what is Starshine saying yes to, and what is she saying no to? Can you think of other books, or films, that end like this? Does that opened-ended mode work for you—why or why not?

# ALSO BY ELEPHANT ROCK BOOKS

***Briefly Knocked Unconscious by a Low-Flying Duck:
Stories from 2nd Story***

"This collection will demand, and receive, return
trips from its readers."
–Publishers Weekly, Starred Review

***A Vacation on the Island of Ex-Boyfriends***
**by Stacy Bierlein**

"Stellar collection of heady and affecting stories."
–Booklist

***The Temple of Air***
**by Patricia Ann McNair**

"This is a beautiful book, intense and original."
–Audrey Niffenegger